BENEATH ROCK BOTTOM

IT'S NOT WHAT HE DOES. IT'S HOW SHE HANDLES IT.

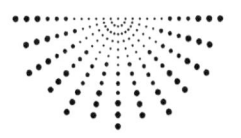

ROCHELLE

*Enjoy!
Rochelle xx*

ROCHELLE BOOKS

Rochelle Books Publishing

Copyright © 2025 by Rochelle

All rights reserved.

No part of this book may be reproduced in any form or by any electronic or mechanical means, including information storage and retrieval systems, without written permission from the author, except for the use of brief quotations in a book review.

Cover design by Rochelle with HL

Paperback edition ISBN 978-1-7341614-4-1

May 2025

❀ Created with Vellum

CONTENTS

Foreword   v

1. Head of Household   1
2. Therapist Crusades   15
3. Summer Rebuild   27
4. WTF   40
5. Count Them Days   58
6. Transformation   70
7. Autumn Fall-down   75
8. Junkyard Parts   89
9. Junkyard Skeleton   97
10. Bottoms Up   113
11. Showdown at High Noon   126
12. Count to Ninety   135
13. Apartment, Relapse, Enough   143
14. Family Weekend   158
15. Poor Pluto   166
16. Trent   171
17. She Can't Keep Her Hands Off Me   186
18. Court   201
19. Twist Ending   214
20. Aloha   221

Acknowledgments   237
About the Author   239

FOREWORD

Dear Reader

Welcome–glad you are here!

Beneath Rock Bottom is a unique psychological thriller of nonfiction. It serves as both a stand alone novel and the sequel to *Shot Glass*. Either could be read first; depends on where you are in life. Names, etc., have been changed for a layer of protection. I am, after all, a Momma Bear.

My heart and soul have poured into this book. My subconscious and truth were mined and polished with craft. These pages are for you!

Warmly,
Rochelle

1
HEAD OF HOUSEHOLD

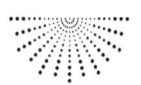

*O*f course I pick the shopping cart with a lame wheel. Navigating Home Goods with such a hindering mass feels ridiculous, but persist I must. My quest is to find a proper digital scale. One that displays any shred of evidence the weight is leaving.

The aisle up ahead holds an insane cluster-fuck of over-stacked, high-priced, bougie throw pillows. One of them, a wintry-satin pillow, is about to pop-off the shelf. Scrolled across the front with silver threads are the tender words, *Bride and Groom*. Aww, that pillow would get a lot more bang-for-its-buck if the other side read, *Defendant and Plaintiff*. I mean, that is what the last judge called us—at my divorce. Well, he called me plaintiff; someone else didn't show. No matter; time to check out. I leave the lame wheel and pillow of broken dreams behind.

For enhanced psychological depth, re-read the first paragraph with the following substitutions:

- shopping cart = husband
- wheel = fill in the blanks
- Home Goods = life
- digital scale = moral compass

- weight = bat-shit craziness

AND SO, we begin…

Olde fairy tales often depict a woman's happiness and success as heavily dependent upon finding her *one true love*. The royal suitor of such a noble pursuit doth clinch her heart in a moment of swooning rescue. Their nuptials ensue. The marriage secures two things: (1) her purpose which is remaining at his side, no matter what. (2) financial stability because she is incapable of generating enough on her own.

But what if those fairy tales went another direction…

Snow White *gets woke* and becomes Snow Storm? For starters, Storm has "a certain set of skills". This damsel can tame an entire forest of wild beasts with her voice; she turns foes into friends. At the end Storm decides she would rather live alone than cook and clean for tiny, incompetent men.

What if…

A self-actualized Rapunzel, trapped asunder in the tallest tower, chops off her own damn braids? She could DIY rope from her hair, sheets, stockings, corset bones, Raven feathers, and save herself. Once that bullshit is over, Rapunzel earns a psychology degree, then builds her own practice. No surprise, Rapunzel, PhD becomes the kingdom's most compassionate therapist for treating abducted, young women.

Finally, what if…

Cinderella's story extends a few more chapters? Prince Charming loses his charm? Behind his persona, come to find out, he is an arrogant, belittling drunk. Cinderella kicks "Charming" to the curb. Now, Ms. Charming is a single mom with three kids, a second job, and a disheartened mare she has to sell for a mortgage payment— It's a lot! None of this could have been known as she slid her bare toes into a well-fitted shoe.

I relate to these women. I have been these women, although my *disheartened mare* was a used camper, and my glass slipper traded up to a hiking boot. I learned the hard way that I cannot save my family, if I cannot save myself.

Sometimes self-worth is handed over like a delicate slipper, lost on a misstep. Other times, self-worth is built through conflict, negotiation, and selflessness. For a stressful five-years my marriage buckled under the devastation of alcohol addiction, narcissism, naïveté, and exhaustion. My training as a therapist in mental, physical and pediatric health fortified my backbone as the mortar to our marriage crumbled. In the beginning our marriage had been worth a fight to keep. By the end, our marriage was worth an even bigger fight to let go.

During the divorce our daughter Jolie, age eleven at the time, had made me a Christmas card. It depicted a plump, red-breasted cardinal on a holly branch. Ink drawn holly leaves and winter berries decorated the border. Inside Jolie wrote: "Thank you for being there and acting like the queen when our castle was crumbling down."

The sale of our former, stately home should have provided the kids and I a large nest egg. However, after paying off two mortgage loans, the leftover funds were barely enough to stay in the town we so loved. Lucky break, the kids and I snagged a bland, one-story, globby-stucco'd, fixer-upper— *Welcome new beginnings!* —fingers crossed behind my back.

Our cottage want-to-be is an off-center house with an off-center door. Beneath the kitchen window mismatched bushes awkwardly line-up like children in a school yard who don't like each other. Despite the off-balance curb appeal, our property has some highlights. A pink dogwood stands centered in the front yard. A mossy, brick pathway winds to the concrete front steps. Lastly, the grandeur of several white pines overlooking our home nestles us modestly into nature.

Friends and family have given me credit for raising three

kids on my own. Single parenting does not mean doing it alone; it means putting in enough effort to equal the missing person, offer another response, provide more unsolicited attention. Occasionally, I had to borrow someone else's husband like when my 14-year-old son refused to go to his town soccer game. Connor was sick of losing every single game they played. One time, Connor's refusal to play erupted at home just before a game. The team—full of his friends since kindergarten—had no substitutes. I offered my fortune-cookie advice: *sometimes you show up for yourself; sometimes you show up for others.* Those sage words got him to the field in uniform, but he would not get out of the car. I flagged down a fellow team-dad; asked him to have a father-son talk with Connor. In seconds he got Connor willingly out of the car and running onto the field.

It was a hard adjustment for my kids to lose their childhood home. They helplessly watched their lifestyle slip away while their father emptied bank accounts, ran off to Canada (a.k.a. abandonment!), and posted pictures of his motorcycle trips while refusing to sign divorce papers. It remains an ongoing big ask for them to understand, dad is an alcoholic who currently needs to live with his parents and pull it together. Overall, I do think my kids are adjusting rather well.

Or Not

"Stop talking! I hate you!" Screams my teenage daughter while slamming her bedroom door shut, my ears burning from the fiery sting of her words.

"Jolie!" I wiggle the locked knob. "Come on."

She does not answer.

"Hey peanut, I know this house is cramped and needs some work. I'm sure a lot of things need some work."

"Forget it," she yells through the door. "You're never home. I don't want to talk to you!"

I steel myself against the wall. In this short hallway I can reach all three of my kid's bedroom doors as well as the shared bathroom behind me. Until the basement renovation finishes, I do not have a bedroom. Even then, one wall will be a curtain. For now, Nicky and I are roommates sharing Connor's old bunkbed. I could have stuck the boys together, but this arrangement allows both teenagers to have their own hormone dungeon. Sulking in this hall of closed doors is not about to turn anything around. I shuffle away to give Jolie her space.

I'm never home. As if she cares. What if, despite being a teenager, she does care? From Jolie's perception both her dad and home washed away like sandcastles. Compound her thirteen-year-old situation by the leap to a Junior/Senior High School. These classes are larger, give less attention, and have older teen influences. As a seventh grader Jolie overheard kids talking about blow jobs her first week of school! My daughter needs her mom, but according to her record keeping, I am not around. Not sure how to fix things; better listening is a start.

Nightfall, a crescent moon with a tilt hovers among the floating tidbit stars. My daughter has yet to emerge from her catacomb of anger; time to pick the lock. Gently turning a skinny screwdriver, the doorknob clicks. "I'm coming in."

Her twin bed flanks the back wall. A floral comforter bunches at the foot of her bed. Jolie's drafting table is full of artwork. Scattered clothes and shoes lay piled on the floor while brushes and markers twist upright in a mason jar. Everything appears normal, except, my daughter is missing. Gauzy curtains billow from the cold air rushing in. Her window is the wrong kind of open.

My gut clenches. We have a runner! Rational thinking computes: remain calm. Jolie is a smart 13-year-old girl. *Is that reassuring?* Hell no! Car keys, purse...I am out the door scouring our mile-by two-mile town. Its crisscross streets form a perfect grid. Initially searching is easy, but there is no sign of her. She is not even at the park where on the 4th of July she entered potato sack races and won a blueberry pie eating contest. The railroad tracks, the woods, the lake…they become too much to cover. I call the police. "We don't need to label her as missing, but please help me find her."

Fifteen minutes later a cop calls me back. "I got her." We meet at the brick schoolhouse. Our cars pull up driver side to driver side. Jolie scowls in the backseat. Her arms are crossed. "Found her walking around town," he says through a rolled down window, "told her you were worried." Jolie turns her head with an angry whip.

"Thank you, officer. I'll drive her home."

The officer turns addressing the cross princess behind the metal grate. "You can get out now. Don't make your mom worry. This is a safe neighborhood, but things can go very wrong in a heartbeat. Nobody wants you to get hurt."

"I get it." Jolie exits the squad car. With a pinch of saltiness to me she blurts, "I'll walk home."

And I say, "Get in the car!"

Jolie huffs herself into the yellow canary Kia. I negotiated with a tough Russian salesman to get a fair price on this bird. The giant of a man smoked in his barebones office. His cigarette pack rested atop piles of poorly stacked papers. Foreign cigarette warnings are brutal. On the label was a naked man's torso with a carved 6-pack, his jeans unbuttoned. Over his crotch a female hand painted with red finger nails gave a *thumbs-down* sign. Our Kia car negotiation was blunt. By the end I got a fair price, and we respected one another.

Police officer-saves-the-day gives me a two-finger salute and drives away. Miss Attitude questions me from the back seat. "Why did you call the cops?"

"Because you're a 13-year-old girl who ran away. Your safety was at risk."

"I was fine."

"You were missing."

Once parked in the driveway, I turn to look at her. "I understand you were hurt and angry. Perhaps this is one of the few options available at your age." My hands cannot let go of the steering wheel. "I was worried. I'm sorry things don't feel right at home. I will pay more attention. That may not feel true, right this second, but I will. Let's work on this together, okay?" Jolie is in no mood to accept promises; however, she does look my way.

Our living room is full of displaced furniture. Packing boxes are pushed against the wall for access to the sofa. "Where did you go?"

"I went to see our old house. Anna met me there. She said it was a beautiful home."

"It was for a decade," I reply. Jolie unzips her jacket. We sit down next to our ten-year old cat, Hamlet, who is by no means skinny. "Believe me Jolie, when I was a kid, I wished we had a pool, or a trampoline, or a huge back yard. Maybe it was easier to never have those things, then to have them taken away; I don't know. But even as a kid, I knew what went on inside a home mattered."

"I miss my old room," she says. "We painted clouds on the ceiling. It had a view of the cherry blossom tree. I just miss it, that's all."

I lean over Hamlet to give her a hug. Every cell in my body yearns to hold her tight. Meanwhile my heart is bruised with sorrow and guilt that I am not measuring up. On the down-low, I fester with latent anger towards her father, because of his blatant inability to hold up his end of parenting.

"Sorry I worried you Mom," Jolie says with a one-armed hug. She is not the first teenager to throw the words, *I hate you*, at a parent. Sometimes those words are not meant to be a fatal hit, just a penetrating wound. Her words, *you're never home*, did cause me to reassess working two jobs as an occupational therapist in addition to home manager. Even though my new, assistant rehab director position is full-time, I am still winding down toddler cases for an Early Intervention service. The plan was to work both jobs until my stamina waned. I am not getting child support. It is difficult to collect from an ex-spouse squatting in another country to avoid paying. Added complications, Josh is neither able to maintain a job, nor his sobriety, which may never change. Alas, I overlooked the impact survival mode had on my family.

The Early Intervention office is given notice to transfer my toddler cases. The moving boxes get unpacked—a relief to us all. I manage the household...show up more at my kid's activities. Tackling the storage pod in our driveway will have to wait. Sorting and integrating a 4,000 sq. ft into a 1,600 sq. ft house will take months. The neighbors will have to kindly endure the rented metal box. Meanwhile, Nicky endlessly kicks a soccer ball at it.

Adjustments

"How's the new job?" Nicky takes his time tying his sneakers. His siblings wonder the living room doing last-minute tasks before school. Connor and Jolie ride the high school bus. Nicolas ambles down the street.

"Thanks for asking Boo," I say tucking extra pens in my scrub pants. "The training sessions are done. Some of it was ridiculous. Twenty of us, nurses, therapists, aides, got paid to wait in line while each of us washed our hands for fifteen-seconds. A manager stood at the sink checking everyone off as competent."

"Wish I got paid to wash my hands," Nicky says lingering by the front door.

Connor stuffs books into his school bag. "We should pay Boo-boy to take a shower. Then he wouldn't smell like such a numb-nut."

"Well, you stink like Black Beard body spray," Nicky retorts. Clearly, Nicky has been the olfactory victim of Connor's 14-year-old hygiene routine.

Jolie, petting Hamlet, concurs. "Light a match near Conner—Kaboom!"

"I wear Black Pearl *kah-logne* scrum-numb."

"Whatever," Nicky says.

"Oh yeah weasle nut—prepare to walk the plank!" With moves of a linebacker Connor rushes to blitz his nine-year old brother. Nicky's spindly body lifts into the air. Connor hoists lil' bro onto his shoulder like a wild parrot.

Nicky squawks, "I can smell your pits!"

The brothers topple onto the sofa with a bounce that sends Hamlet fleeing. Playfully, Connor crashes on top of Nicky's flailing body. It is a roundhouse of pummeling limbs in all directions. Years of playfulness show as their arms sync into a swinging repertoire of slow-motion air punches. This action-packed fight scene reels with dramatic upper-cuts, body jabs, and pulled-back hooks. Each brother dramatically responds to the hard, near-miss blows. Their punched heads twist with exaggeration. They double-over at the gut. Their faces distort with agony. Connor springs to his feet, the confidence of victory set in his eyes. Here it comes, the final blow is a pile-driver to the sternum. Crack!

Nicky clutches his impaled chest, falling limp onto the hard-wood floor with a thud. The groaning child-man rolls across the living room floor until beaching himself on the kitchen tiles. Be still for he is not yet dead, not until the final *death spasm*! Skinny limbs jerk and twitch. Eyeballs of a beautiful blue roll back into his skull. Our beloved rascal succumbs to the Grim Reaper's call. Lying on the floor Nicky utters his final plea to the family he must leave behind. "Re-mem-bah me for-ev-ah!" His young life erased. Tongue popping out. RIP little Nicky.

"Gotta bounce mom. See ya scrum-nuts." Connor flies out

the door. A maroon backpack bounces over his shoulder. When the kids and I went school shopping, I told them, "Pick any color backpack you want, as long as it isn't gray."

Jolie hugs me, good-bye. "I'm proud of you mom. I'm sure you'll help lots of old people."

"Do you want to visit me at work sometime? See your mom in action?"

"Ah, no-o-o." She scoots out the door with a cheesy grin.

Nicky, who quickly resurrected himself, lined up behind his sister. "Hey Boo, you want to see where–"

"Bye Mom!" He scurries down the path to catch his sister.

"Fine—see if I care!" He reaches the sidewalk. "Love you, Nicky!"

"Love you more!"

I watch my scrum-numbs scoot down the street, past weathered trunks of maple trees and drying wisps of curled summer grasses. Their blonde hair and bouncing school bags fade into the backdrop of maple canopies.

The Visit

The renovation of my *basement she-cave* completes. Occasionally at night, Nicky comes downstairs for some special bedtime togetherness. Dressed in pajamas leaning against pillows, he and I either read stories or complete pages from a sentimental Hidden Picture Book; it's the same book Jolie and I worked on for years. The finished pages were dated at the bottom. During this special time of attention Nicky never mentioned any concern nor fear about losing me since his dad's absence over the past eighteen months. Hence, it is of great surprise to find a small note tucked inside my nightstand book. On a torn piece of paper my youngest wrote, "Mommy please don't die. I love you. Thank you for all you do for us. I love you very much~Nicholas."

Writing accesses our deepest of truths, especially when our literal voices fall short. Nicky's note deeply touched my heart as did Jolie's card about our crashing kingdom. Connor expressed his pain more privately. Pain that stemmed from the morning his father pretended to go to work but instead cowardly left the country. Connor hand carved into his birchwood bed frame a tally mark for each night his father did not come home. My son etched one-hundred and seven tallies into his bedrail. Day 108, his dad came to visit; he brought his lurking alcohol addiction with him. So again, he was kicked out. So again, we are on our own, but we do not keep tallies anymore.

My ex-husband has been residing with his mom, Ingrid, in the childhood home of he and his two brothers. I hear Josh is helpful to her, despite being covered in ashes from the bridges he burned and everything he lost. My ex found it healing to be where he did not feel like the bad guy. Ingrid, who lives alone, remains very active in her golden years. She prefers walking over driving, hosts extended family dinners, and for decades has been playing volleyball once a week with the same core group. Ingrid put Josh to work around the house. She does not know how else to handle her son's alcoholism, which she can no longer deny. Her plan is to let Josh figure it out.

Josh calls me one evening. The chronic inebriation seems to be causing cognitive impairment. He shares an idea. Josh wants to create a TV show where he interviews restaurant owners and critiques the food while traveling across the country. He himself is not a bad cook. Josh speaks about this concept with such vigor and detail, as if it has never been done before.

"Josh, I think it's been done before."

"No-o-o," he slurs. "Not like I'd do it. I need to get a crew together. No one here knows how to make that happen. I don't know how to make that happen."

"Landing a network contract is tough. You may want to be at your best for that. Are you doing things to be at your best?"

"I ride my bike everywhere. I mean eh-vree where. I call it Scooty—the bike. Its name is Scoot for short. I thought it was a good name. I think the kids will like it. Mind if I send them pictures of Scoot? I could make, *The Scooty Chronicles* for them. Scooty and I go to some really cool places."

"The kids might like that."

"I miss them. How are they?"

We talk about the kids for a while. He seems childlike, lost, caring and powerless. When he starts to talk about the traveling food show again, I spare myself. I change the topic to modern day events such as a recent speech President Obama gave about gun violence in schools. "His speech was very moving."

"Yes, yes it was. I-I'm glad he contacted me about it."

"Who he? Who contacted you?"

"Obama, he contacted me. I helped him write that speech."

Oh no, he did not just say that. I am totally buying a ticket for this ride. "Uh, Josh are you telling me that you wrote a speech for the president of the United States. The one he just gave on the White House lawn—that speech?"

"I know it sounds, like a lot, like *whoa*. But he asked, and I wanted to help."

"What did he say exactly?"

"Who?"

"The president, when he called you."

"I don't remember exactly. I had sent the president some emails. He called to talk about them; said I had some interesting ideas. Then Obama mentioned this speech coming up, and he thought I could help. I mean, what do you say to that? I told him, 'Sure.'"

"That is uh, a big undertaking."

"It's all right. I still have to get a crew. Maybe I could just use one camera man. Do you think a network would loan me one camera guy to make a pilot for a traveling food show?"

"I don't know. Perhaps Obama could put in a good word in for you."

"Yeah, maybe."

A few days later Josh's sister-n-law, Adrianne, David's wife, calls me from the Europe. Adrianne is a counselor and a very dedicated mother of two sons from a previous marriage. She is freaking out about Josh's grandiose thinking. Living in France, Adrienne and David are limited in their ability to assist Ingrid with Josh. In her French accent Adrianne asks, "Do you know, Josh claims to have written a speech for your President? He is saying this! I don't think Ingrid knows what to do! I think she is waiting for Josh to snap out of it. She does not want to use resources."

"Then I guess Ingrid needs to snap out of it."

"Aren't you alarmed? David and I are. Josh is a psych doctor. He is losing his mind."

Adrianne doesn't get it. The more shocked she gets, the more I realize how much his family didn't know before…the lies they were told…there is no way to unravel it all. Narcissists steal reality. They change the landscape.

"No one believed me when I tried to express my concerns before," I said. "Conversations with Ingrid were and are a dead end. She was told lies involving me about money, fidelity, the kids…. I point out the things that don't make sense, but Ingrid prefers to keep her head in the sand. To answer your question, yes, I know what Josh said about the president's speech. He was talking to me the moment he conjured it up. Look, I couldn't get him into rehab. It scared him. He thought he'd lose everything. Now it seems he's lost touch."

"Hmm, yes. This is not your problem." Adrienne says with concern in her voice. "You need to take care of the kids and yourself. We will do what we can, but he cannot visit us. He has to make better choices. I have asked him to send you some money, but that is a touchy subject. It was the same with my ex-husband."

"Thanks for trying on my behalf. You seem to be the only one."

"He is sick," she says. "He is over some edge."

Indeed, but guess what? I am now the *ex-wife*. I have the option to wash my hands free and clear at least for 15 seconds.

2
THERAPIST CRUSADES

The Atrium sub-acute and long-term care facility staffs over twenty combined physical therapists (PTs) and occupational therapists (OTs). Our mobility gyms have the usual: stationary bikes, parallel bars, weights, and wall pulleys. For activities of daily living (ADLs) the OT room has a full kitchen, bathroom and laundry area. My favorite therapy tools are the fine motor activities. We use them creatively to help our patients gain physical, perceptual and cognitive skills.

Our director, Jacob, has an office at the back of the gym known as the Bat Cave, because Jacob and I like to think of ourselves as the dynamic duo of geriatric care. Right off the bat, Jacob made it clear to me, he's *The Batman*—a brown-eyed, stocky, hairy Italian from Boston who knows his therapy shit.

The closet-sized bat cave forces his desk and chair into a corner. Opposite sits a low bookshelf beneath a window. Outside the glass stands a pine tree we decorate at Christmas time. Upon seeing me, Batman lights up. "Ah, there's my part-nah. I see you did not poke your eyes out from watching corporate videos last week."

"I slept through some." I pull up a wheeled stool. "But I drew eyes on my lids to look awake."

"What a strange coincidence; I did the same thing this morning. I'm talking to you from a nap right now!"

One can hardly tell this Batman is the same height standing up as he is sitting down. His torso and head are of normal size. However, his arms and legs are shortened. This medical condition, called achondroplasia, is caused by a FGFR3 gene mutation. During early fetal development, the cartilage proteins in the limbs fail to convert to bone. The result is a condition commonly referred to as dwarfism. Batman once told me he uses a step stool to climb into bed. I suggested he bounce into the sheets using a mini trampoline. He's considering it.

"Word got out," he shares, "that you and I are the fresh dynamic duo around here. Let's upgrade things while the other directors are open to new ideas."

"Some of us OTs talked about running a cooking group with a weekly theme."

"I like it. Write up a proposal. Get speech involved, too. My idea is to have a weekly graduation ceremony for the patients going home. It would boost morale and…."

Parked just outside Batman's office is Donny McCann, PT assistant. Batman assigned McCann that specific desk to keep an eye on him. Everyone likes McCann the way siblings like an annoying kid brother—with use of tolerance and affectionate insults. McCann eats the *poking fun banter* like candy.

Years ago, McCann was a police officer, a career that tragically ended when he was shot in the head. A suspicious traffic stop turned into a bloody shoot out. His partner, also his twin brother, had to perform life saving measures in the streets until the ambulance arrived. Miraculously, McCann's handsome face was spared disfigurement. His resulting TBI (traumatic brain injury) required months and months of therapy. He would not return to the police force. McCann had admiration and appreciation for this personal therapists...a new career choice grew. His twin brother quit the force and became a nurse.

By the end of McCann's cognitive rehab, two residual effects were prominent. First was a significant loss in his left peripheral vision. This visual disability prevents him from driving. In fact, if Donny Mac doesn't take an extra scan from left to right entering a hallway, he will plow into someone. So not good in a place where everyone uses walkers. His second TBI residual effect was a change in his temperament. According to McCann he is more docile in a very lovable way.

McCann revels in the attention he receives when telling the *I got shot tale*, especially with the ladies. To further impress, he once campaigned for us co-workers to call him Big MacDaddy. Batman, instead, called him MacLoser for a relentless week. They since compromised on the nickname Donny Mac.

Perched on his wheely stool outside the open bat cave, Donny Mac catches threads of our brainstorming cauldron. He interjects, "Pardon me *dynamic duo*," his former cop voice booms in the crowded therapy room, "but you two are more like Bert and Ernie. I'm not saying which one of you is which. Ah-hem," he pauses to spin on his stool glancing around at his peers, "we all know, we're the ones doing the real work around here, especially me. Everybody knows I am the most dedicated worker in this entire department."

I did not see from which direction the pen came, but it is flying clear across the gym like a missile. It hits Donny Mac square-between the shoulders. Another pen soars. Then another, until a full-blown meteor shower of cheap pens is pelting Donny Mac every which way. He curls over his desk shielding the back of his damaged head with a clip board.

Batman hands over my schedule. "You're covering one of Maureen's patients. She called out sick last night."

"Don't you give me her patient." I warn.

"I don't know who you're talking about," he says with a guilty man's sneer.

"The last one picked in the donut box patient."

Batman laughs. "Chris and Amy took an extra two patients each to avoid treating polish grandma. She's all yours."

"Fine. I'll take *Baba Olga*," snatching my sheet,"Those guys are wimps,' and saunter off.

"You're a champ!" Batman placates into the ethers behind me.

The therapists who wimped out of treating Olga give me a mocking thumbs up as I pass.

Bah hum-bug on them. "It's the tough ones who define you," I mutter. Although, as assistant director, I should probably take the hit. It's all right. I treated her before she was passed to Maureen. I have an affection towards her curmudgeonly ways.

Olga

Olga is as grumpy as she is stiff. Olga is a short-stay patient which means she has less than thirty days to get back in shape; otherwise, she will be an assisted living candidate, or more likely, a long-term care candidate leaving her elderly husband home alone. When I attempt to get Olga for her morning session, she isn't ready. We reschedule for after lunch. When I return at the time *she* picked, Olga shoos me away with a boney hand and a hiss because her game show is on. Not until the end of the day, as we are all leaving, do I realize I forgot about Olga. As tempting as it is to document "Patient Refused" I put my purse back in the drawer and call the nurse's station.

"Hey, it's Jessie. Can one of you guys bring Olga down for OT? I think that would be best."

"Sure can. Miss Olga is sitting right here by the nurses station entertaining us— Aren't you darling?"

"Earlier Olga cursed me for interrupting her TV show, not

cursing at me. I think she put a curse on me." (She totally put a curse on me)

"Yez-z, Baba does that. Yesterday Baba forgot she cursed me in the morning; come afternoon time, she cursed me again! Yez, I am talking about you love bug. Guess where you're going?"

An east-wing nurse with satin smooth hair-extensions wheels Miss Olga into the vacated therapy department. Olga fashions an ancient pink sweater clearly from two-sizes ago. In the zone where breasts meet belly the buttons are fit to pop-off and take-out someone's eye. Nurse Jackson parks Olga's wheelchair next to a raised exercise mat. "If I hear you're nice to your therapist, I might bring you some extra pie."

Olga's mouth twists. "I am always nice girl."

"Sure, and I like getting my weave wet." Nurse Jackson taps Miss Olga on the knee.

Olga glances towards me at the weight rack. She scrunches her face. "Oh, it's you."

"Nice to see you too."

"P-fff, I doubt dat." She crosses her arms transforming into an angry wad of bubblegum.

Meandering out the door Nurse Jackson shouts back, "Jessica, let me know how our special friend does in OT–" She turns around rubbing her belly— "because I am exceptionally hungry. I might eat all the apple pie I can find."

"P-fff, you don't need it," snorts Olga. The nurse dismisses her with a flutter of sparkly fingernails.

"Let's get to it," I say and straighten my plum-colored scrubs. I park her wheelchair by a six-foot, free-standing mirror. Olga is assisted to stand for a warm-up activity: hold the mirror's wooden frame with one hand while wiping it clean with the other. This activity increases upper-body range of motion while strengthening postural muscles. Olga's kyphotic spine and torso appear stuck as if perpetually hugging a beach ball. Prolonged standing causes her significant back pain. She has not walked any notable distance in years. Normal gait patterns have a 62% stance phase–improve standing, improve walking.

"You missed a spot," I say spraying the mirror with more water.

"P-fff," escapes her thin lips. Her knobby fingers swirl the cloth with methodical micro-circles. Slowly, the drippings get erased. "Do you know what a ver-shtup-ta-cup is?" she asks in the mirror's reflection.

"Nope," easing her down for a rest, "haven't a clue." Olga's weary neurons lost the memory of us having this exact conversation nearly every past treatment session. "Enlighten me after you stand again, please."

My Polish dumpling's weathered hands re-grip the frame. She stands up. I spray the glass. Grumpy grandma matches my height at 5'3" if we include the bristled hair popping out of her head like a white dandelion on the edge. Olga gazes upon herself at eighty-five-years of age. "Look at dis mop." She touches her frizzy head.

"Look at dis broom." Holding out strands of straw-colored highlights, I flutter my eyelashes.

She sours her lips. "Ver-shtup-ta-cup means, *a head full of nottin'*. Do you get it?" Olga is sly like an innocent fox, except for the chicken feathers.

"Uh-huh," I mumble sitting on a wheely stool beside her. She squats with a plop on her cushioned wheelchair. "You've made progress this week. You can stand longer, get your pants on and off…. Going home should be soon."

"Good, my husband love how I cook. It keep him happy." Olga laughs. "We used to dance polka and what you call *swing*. Dat was long time ago, before we both got fat!" Olga squeezes her jelly belly with brash ownership. Her therapy goal is to be supervision level with stand-pivot transfers, then she will be safe to go home. Supervision level means the ability to perform a stand-pivot-turn from wheelchair-to-toilet, or wheelchair-to-bed with no physical help. Her husband, at ninety-years old, is unable to safely assist her.

One-pound weights are fastened onto Olga's wrists and ankles. She wiggles from her shoulders down to her rump. "My back hasn't felt dis good in a long time." She points a curved finger at me. "I knew you must be good for some-tin."

The rare stillness of the gym feels pleasant and inviting; plenty of room to roll a chair sized, apple-colored, therapy ball back and forth. "Where did everybody go?" Olga asks pushing into the bouncy apple ball with full effort.

"The other therapists went home. Most of the staff has the weekend off." I roll the giant therapy apple back to her.

"How come I don't get day off?"

"Because I'd miss you."

"I got potatoes to peel. Dat is what my mudder would say. Den, she would make me peel dem. P-fff."

There is an ease with having the place to ourselves…no oxygen tanks to work around, no line at the parallel bars where patients take their first steps with the physical therapists. OT's mostly focus on the upper body; however, I specialized in neuro-developmental training. If someone suffered a stroke, I learned about facilitating motor movements for the whole body. Kneeling in front of my little kabob I release the weight cuffs from her wrists. "Would you be interested in trying to walk?" I ask.

"Walk? I can't walk by myself."

"Not by yourself—with me in the parallel bars. I'll show you." I position her wheelchair at one end of the bars and lock the brakes. I duck under the bars and pop-up in front of her. "Watch me. Grab a bar in each hand, like this, then take a step. I'll be in front of you. I think you're ready."

Olga ponders with raised brows. Her pudgy cheeks carved by deep wrinkles melt into her short neck. Her ear lobes almost touch her hiked shoulders which stack above her protruding belly covered in polyester pants that brush the tops of her chunky, scuffed, orthopedic shoes.

"You want dis body to walk? P-fff."

"Come on. Scoot to the edge of your seat." Olga complies. "Widen your feet a little–that's it." My arms secure a firm hold around her doughy middle and petite pelvic girdle. My right shoulder presses against her sternum to provide vertical stability. In response, Olga places her arms around my neck which was not my therapeutic intention. "I'm not lifting you," I tell her. "Push up from the chair." Olga re-grips the armrests.

"Ready?" In unison we rock forward and back to gain momentum. "One, two, three!" Up we go. Wisps of Olga's dandelion hair tickle my mouth. She begins to round over.

"Olga, look at me."

"I am looking at you."

"No, you are not."

"I yam so."

"Really, what do you see?"

"Your sneakers; dey are dirty. You should clean dem."

"I'll tell my maid."

"You have a maid?"

"Sure, my butler and chef can't do it all. I only work here to torture you."

"Pfff."

My knees leverage into her knees. This causes her legs to straighten. My hands articulate her pelvis forward which extends her trunk; her head follows. "Ah, there's your smile. At least, I think it is. Do you know how to smile Miss Olga?"

Her nose wrinkles as if smelling bad milk. "My mudder was a maid. Back in Poland, she wanted me to become teacher. So, I did. I liked it very much. Dirty-five years I was teacher to young children."

"My mom was a teacher, too. She taught sixth grade." Olga's balance is steady; time to walk. "I want you to place your hands on my shoulders. Let go of the bars. One arm at a time is fine."

"I don't thin' I can."

"Take a deep breath. Dance with me."

"What?"

"Dance with me." Automatic cues are a great brain trick. Olga's arms float to beside my neck. Her shoulders retract. We sway side-to-side like a couple of teenagers at a high school dance. Our rocking creates a state of readiness. But first–

"Let's sit and rest, no plopping. Reach back for the chair. Any pain? Good." We rest in silence. Olga's husband and son will visit later today. Her husband comes every-other evening and stays until his wife is tucked into bed around nine o'clock.

Across Olga's forehead determination radiates from her pinched brows. "I am ready," she firmly states. Olga scoots her hips forward; lifts her head without a prompt.

"Use the bars to pull yourself up. I'll hold your hips. The wheelchair will be right behind you." We rock. We count. Together we stand, her arms pressing up from the bars to stay erect. Shifting her weight into her right leg I block her knee with my knee, so she does not buckle. Then using a key turning motion around her left hip socket I facilitate her left femur forward. Her leg responds with a tiny shuffle. I repeat shifting to the left—her butt sticks out. She's sinking!

"Look over my shoulder," I command. "Head-up, body-up."

"Nottin' goes up on dis body anymore." Olga lifts her chin. I readjust her pelvis along with my shoulder to support her trunk. She gets straight.

She takes a couple of meekly steps. Her knees no longer require blocking. Fearing she might fatigue I give her a stamina goal. "Four more steps, then we're done. Give it your best."

"I am," she says.

Olga shuffles forward one, two, three, four— "Fantastic! How does it feel to walk again?"

"Like I got to sit down."

"Okay, okay. I'll get your wheelchair." Worried she might collapse, I continue holding her waist as I kneel down and reach for the wheelchair behind her. Stretching my arm, body, fingers...I cannot quite reach the metal frame. "Keep pushing up on the bars."

"I am pushin'," she scowls.

With an achy lean over Olga's dusty, thick-bottomed shoes, I manage to grasp the wheelchair and pull. It does not move. I wiggle it; nothing. Tug it; nothing. *What*—the brakes are locked! Desperately, I tilt and yank the chair—this combo has worked before, but it's like the chair is stuck in concrete. *Why won't it budge?* Again, I heave the steel wheelchair frame with warrior muscles. This results in a tiny, wheely hiccup. *Well, that's odd.* Then I notice the bolted steel floor rods supporting the parallel bars. Those steel rods are holding back the wheelchair, because the wheelchair is wider than the rods. *Come to think of it, I never did see a wheelchair inside the parallel bars.* Patients always turned around and walked back. My predicament: Olga cannot turn around, and I cannot let go of Olga. *Shit balls!*

"You're gonna have to walk backwards."

"What?"

"Walk backwards!" I shift her bubble-gum body left, so her right leg can slide; it doesn't move. We shift to the right, maybe her left leg will slide; no go. My fear intensifies that her arthritic body will buckle, she hits her head on the way down before landing on the tiles breaking her hip. So I pull Olga against my chest absorbing her gelatinous weight. "Step backwards!" I urge kicking at the toe of her dusty shoe.

"It no want to move."

Switching sides I jack hammer away at her other shoe. Olga's hips begin to bend within my arms. I squeeze her pelvis which brings her hips back to mine. "Olga stand-up!" She mutters something back in Polish as she incrementally gets taller.

Accosting her medical grade shoes has been futile. We are smushed together. I cannot see her expression. I feel blind. *Must think.* Around the room–the weights, arm pulleys, therapy balls–everything appears perfectly serene, a stark contrast to our swirling shipwreck. The department door has a window, but no one is passing. My pulse races. An inner voice bellows, *Do not drop Baba; her bones cannot touch this floor. She will break!* It is time to make the call.

Yo, God. We go way back. This is quite the predicament. How about this: I clear my head; you send a message.

Okay, hit me.

No playing around; bring it on.

All stations are open; chakras, too. Fire away.

Here comes that big solution...heading my....nothing.

Please?

Olga and I are locked in silence. She waits for me. I wait for God. If I scream, no one will hear. We are so screwed. I gave demands, and the Almighty universe sent nothing. Um, perhaps, because *on demand* is not how the mother ship works. A paradigm shift begins. Respectfully, my attitude sets sail. I surrender, and humbly tune into a frequency of reverence. *What would you have me do?*

My eyes close. Time slows way-y down-n. I squat and begin to squeeze doughy, eighty-five-year-old baba. My arms wrap securely around her hips. My hands clutch fistfuls of polyester pants and sweater. I did not know I was going to do this till I did it; rising like a mighty oak out of the earth's surface I pick Olga up clear off the ground. She towers above me while my forehead presses against her chest to anchor her. In this puzzle-arrangement, I carry baba safely back to her locked wheelchair.

With caged unreleased breath, I gently lower Miss Olga towards the seat. Her rolls and folds slide down my body like wax melting on a candlestick. We squish into the wheelchair. I am stuck. Quickly I wriggle my arms to freedom; the release sends me to the floor, panting, as if I just ran a seven-minute mile.

    Olga breaks our silence. "You lifted me right off the ground!" Her eyes seem twice as blue.

    "Sure, whew…did," I wheeze placing a hand over my pathetically heaving chest.

    Olga states, "I am ready to go back to my room."

    "Sure. Thing. Just. Give me. A minute—whew—to catch…." Soon enough I kneel in front of my comrade. Both my ego and swag have reduced to mere stains on the tiled gym floor. My expression cannot fake the need for forgiveness. Indeed, I had fulfilled the prophecy of the ver-schtup-ta-cup.

    Olga, on the other hand, is all a-glow basking in serenity. Expressing the tenderness of a grandmother, Olga envelopes her bubblegum arms around me. She kisses my flushing cheek. I have been pardoned.

    A few days later at the patient graduation ceremony, Olga gracefully performs a stand-pivot-transfer as if doing the waltz box-step. Her husband of sixty-two-years arrives on discharge for his gal wearing a suit and tie. A group of us therapists and nurse Jackson wave good-bye as they drive off into their vintage life–a life they had built together. When they arrive home, Olga will reveal her surprise. The music will play. Olga will stand. And she will dance with her sweetheart once again.

3
SUMMER REBUILD

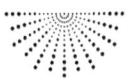

*A*s the weeks pass occasionally I have a conversation with Josh's mother, Ingrid. Her plan has been to let Josh squaller in his own mess. This has some merit. Josh pretty much lost everything. As the money runs down, the drinking weans down. Ingrid's relief is evident about this when she calls to say, "He kind of just quit alcohol altogether. He made jambalaya for his cousins the other night. Everyday he rides his bicycle, Scooty; that's what he named it. He is constantly reading. We do puzzles over coffee. My son has been back to himself making things right."

Indeed, for the next month Josh continues to rebuild his world. Frequently he connects with the kids…tells them stories about the adventures of Scooty. He sends pictures of Scooty hanging out at the lake, Scooty visiting a vintage record store… Scooty is rather busy. Josh keeps in touch with me. He is polite, humble and without bizarre thoughts. We transition into a functioning divorced relationship with simple words of kindness. The heavy burden of a shameful past lessens. A peaceful space is co-created.

As much as I do care about our created peace, I still got bills to pay. My ex-husband with a job equals child support. It behooves Josh and I to invest in each other staying afloat, so everyone stays the course. What's the course? Oh right—finish raising our children. This includes the suck-it teenage years. If I can *woman-up*, Josh can *man-up*.

It is apparent that Josh and the kids (in varying degrees) miss each other. Josh asks if he can visit. This stirs feelings of bitterness. I cannot erase the fact that 2 years ago he pretended to go to work; but instead, went straight to Canada. He emptied our bank accounts. He stuck me high and dry with two mortgages. Cherry on top—Josh refused to sign divorce papers, his attempt to escape paying alimony and child support. Josh made mountain-sized obstacles for me to climb. He expected that avalanche to roll me under, right after he left. Well, I climbed mountain after mountain. Self-reliance, faith and a whole lot of problem-solving got me to the summits. One clear mountain-top view is that the world needs more compassion. This I understand.

Ingrid confirms that Josh has been sober for many weeks, not sure "months" would apply. She questions if his continuing to stay with her is best for his continued improvement. He desires to return and find meaningful employment. After some serious discussions, Josh is welcomed to return with the following goals: find work in the states and help support our family.

Homecoming

Rodger, Josh's old motorcycle riding friend, picks Josh up at the airport. The moment Rodger's truck pulls up, Connor, Jolie and Nicky run to the front door. Josh steps inside. He cannot even close the door before he is covered in hugs.

"Dad!" Connor smashes his face into Josh's chest. His father holds him tight. Then, with teary eyes, Josh leans over to kiss their heads and cup their faces. The kids are bouncy. Josh kneels down. The kids circle around him. He hugs Jolie tight, her long blonde hair sticks out from under his arm. Josh picks Nicky up, then brushes his face against his son's messy matching hair. My ex-husband looks at me, then mouths the words, *thank you.* Josh may have been fine living away from us; however, a part of him broke wide open to hold his children again. Perhaps he recognizes what he lost or where he failed, both were in epic proportions.

My turn is next. The hug is long and sincere. He thanks me for letting him return with dignity. Sobering-up seems to have added more emotional depth to him; his piss and vinegar is missing.

As we chat inside the living room, Josh gazes at each of us with attention not shown before. He seems filled with hope and energy to do right by us. Such efforts are only possible if we give him the chance.

Admittedly, Josh is fun to be around; our usual day-to-day living can get pretty stale. Another person in the mix alleviates the doldrums. Josh is also clean, neat and organized, which makes for an amiable roommate. He quickly takes things off my plate such as cooking some meals, yard work and driving errands. His tone around me is pleasant as he seems to appreciate me. It's about damn time. It probably helps that I am not a dissatisfied wife anymore.

A few folks in town begin to ask, *Why am I taking him back?* Perhaps it appears that way, but I am not. It is a waste of energy to defend myself against those who do not have an empty seat at the dinner table. Josh fixes things around the house (he rebuilt the cement curb out front). The kids enjoy making bread with him during the day and bon-fires at night. The house has gained a rich, acoustic pulse with the sound of his Martin guitar as he humbly sings: The Beatles, Paul Simon and Richard Thompson.

He hugs the kids goodnight; he sleeps in Nicky's bottom bunk. We, his family, are no longer ignored. All of this matters more than town gossip. There is not an ounce of liquor in sight; we keep a stable environment. If Josh thinks we are getting back together—and I don't believe he does—I have zero interest. I enjoy his company, his assistance, and that my kids have both parents.

On a bigger scale, Josh's positive actions and humbleness slowly clear his karma with me. He does not ask for this, I merely feel it happening. Forgiveness does not go on a leash to be pulled back at will. Forgiveness is given freely and asks for nothing in return, like when I forgave him for pulling a gun. He caused me to run from my own home; hide in a neighbor's bush.

Forgiveness and karmic debt are separate line items from child support. So, when Josh receives a solid job offer with a meaningful salary and full benefits, my spirit sings, *hallelujah!* His summer start date is just prior to the kids' return to school date. Josh calls his father to spread the good news. Caleb is thrilled and relieved. He thanks me for giving his son another chance to pull it together and provide for his family. "I've been worried, aye. I kept praying my son would find his way." Josh's father sends a check for $5,000 dollars to use towards a car, suits and to establish a bank account; it was probably most of Caleb's savings.

Connor and Nicky enjoy shopping for cars on-line with their dad. The three of them pick out an old BMW priced at four-grand. Their dad now has the travel freedom to independently shop for outfits like a grown man. Josh models the newly acquired suits as if in a catwalk fashion show. He asks the kids which tie goes best with which suit. His confidence expands. Dr. Josh is ready to be employed!

Horse Before the Cart

Something else had access to the feel-good suits, the money, and the freedom. Who lurks in the shadows with a taste for destruction? The monkey on his back. Guess what? Monkey wants his drink back.

It only took a few days of having money and a car before Monkey took the wheel. I hold back and hold tight because honestly, once the structure and demands of the new job settle in, Josh will reel it in. Besides, pointing out his problem totally sucks-ass. I get labeled a "control freak"; and possibly saddled with carrying out ultimatums. I am not a fan of playing strong-arm games of leverage. There is more peace and better results allowing natural consequences to happen even if it is the longer route. Besides, he is only drinking beer...oh, I guess wine, too. And vodka—it was supposed to stop at wine!

My patience snaps. I confront him in Nicky's bedroom. Joshua slumps on the edge of the bed as if a school boy at the principal's office. Pacing the oakwood floors, I point out what seems bloody obvious. "Alcohol will kick your ass: Every. Single. Time! Josh, there is so much in your favor. Look at what's at stake. Everything!"

Josh lowers his head to shield the wrath.

"It's not fair I have to handle things when you can't. And it doesn't matter how I handle it; you get mad at me for interfering. You never get mad at the alcoholism. Believe me, that is what's taking you down, not me."

Josh softly justifies his actions. "I was just going to have some wine—like everybody else—with dinner." Josh admits he thought a bit of celebratory wine would be fine. In this version of himself, he keeps everything under control. I get it which adds to my frustration at myself because I thought the same thing. Nevertheless, I lean back against the wall. "Josh, if you can't admit its never just a glass, then you'll never grasp how serious this is. Honestly, when was one drink ever enough? Did you ever go into a liquor store and pick out just one can of beer?"

"They don't even sell them that way."

"Uh, yeah they do."

"Doesn't matter. I've learned my lesson. I won't let it get out of control this time."

To live this pattern again sickens me. We just spent the last two months rebuilding Josh with our love, support and being a re-united family. I kneel down beside the man I verbally pummeled and change my tone. "We were married for fifteen years. I know alcohol is a struggle, but we can turn this around. You'll get into a routine with your new job, you'll get some health benefits— It's going to be okay."

"I'm sorry. I know I'm disappointing you."

I sit next to him on the bunk bed. "It's a slip-up. You've been amazing! We'll handle it. You had too much access too soon." We scoot back on the animal jungle quilt. "Your job starts in three days. Let's get rid of the vodka today. Let me hold onto your debit card so you can't impulsively buy more. We'll switch to beer and taper down."

"How about beer and wine? It helps for this to not feel so controlling."

"Fine, whatever. The end goal is no drinks—nada. So, please give me the bottle."

"What bottle?" He asks without any facial expression.

"The seltzer bottle."

Slowly, he reaches under the bed and hands me a seltzer bottle mixed with vodka.

"Your debt card too, please."

He tilts his head. "I will need gas money to get to work."

I mirror his head tilt. "Then I'll make sure the car has gas." Josh shifts his gaze to the floor. I ask him, "Do you want to win this battle, or win the war?"

Josh slides his hand into his pocket and pulls out his wallet. He selects his debt card, then places it in my hand.

"Thank you." I notice the cash. Already feeling like a petty officer, I hold back asking for the few dollars he has left. We are not quite done. "I also need the other bottle."

"What are you talking about?"

"You filled the seltzer bottle from a source. Where's the source?"

"Don't know," he says with aloofness. "I think I used it up."

"Take no offense—" firming my tone, "Where is it?"

"It's gone Jess-i-ca. I don't have it."

"Uh-huh, you want to play games? I'll play. How about you give me five minutes to find the vodka? If I find it in the five, you cannot give me any crap."

Joshua lays flat on the bed. His hands fold over his thinned, stretched t-shirt. The frayed cargo shorts with a pocket hole and worn flip-flops seals the outfit. "Do whatever you want."

"I am trying to help."

Josh closes his eyes. His lips press together ever so tight.

Tick-tock race the clock! The search around Nicky's bedroom begins. There is no bottle behind a curtain, the bookcase or inside the closet. The open travel suitcase in the corner, turns out, is simply piled with clothes. It can't be far; convenience is key. Ah-ha, Nicky's dresser. We loaned him one drawer of real estate. In the top drawer I rummage through men's athletic socks, underwear, a Harley Davidson baseball cap...wrapped up in Josh's red bathing shorts is a half-empty bottle of vodka.

"How ironic—you're swimming in it."

Josh appears unamused. I leave the room to diffuse the situation. Quickly, I hide the vodka in the coat closet inside a tall pair of rain boots. I reset my patience. Tomorrow is another chance for better results.

The next few days Josh's cravings wean by increasing the time between drinks and decreasing the drinks to cheap lite beer. Josh hates the lite-taste, which is part of the strategy. By day three, Josh gets a full night's sleep without a drink. The next morning, he heads to his first day of work without a hitch. High-five!

New Job

Dr. Josh arrives home from his first day. A folded-up tie hangs from his hand as he comes thru the door. Josh states his day was full of HR tasks followed by meetings with different people. He could not explain his specific job expectations—something to do with assessing workman compensation claims. "I'm still trying to figure it all out," he says. He seems a tad loopy as he explains himself. Guess I should have kept the wallet cash. I do not allude to his intoxication. My role is to keep him stable, so he can master his job and keep it. Last time he lost a job, his family had to fly out and rescue him. That was how he came to live with Ingrid.

The next morning: second day of employment. Josh dresses in a dark suit with a coral, rayon tie. We meet in the kitchen. A fresh pot of coffee brews on the counter. Steaming Columbian java fills his travel mug. Rice puffs fill my cereal bowl. I pleasantly mention as he is leaving, "Like the tie. Have a good day."

Hesitating, door knob in hand, Josh asks, "Can I have my debit card back? It's a bit ridiculous I even have to ask."

"I thought you had cash."

"I spent it yesterday on something to eat."

"But you don't eat lunch."

"I didn't want to stick out next to my co-workers by not eating. It is my debit card. We can't do this every morning. I get why you held on to it—thank you. But it's a little nerve racking to drive forty minutes each way and not have access to money or an emergency card."

"I want you to have a solid start. Holding onto your card is like using bumper pads on a bowling lane. It helps the ball get down the lane."

"I can focus *on the lane* without bumper pads."

Whatever, I hand back his debit card.

"Work will be fine," he says softly. "It requires mostly a lot of annoying paperwork. I can handle paperwork." The debit card slides into his jacket pocket.

"Okay." Looking out the kitchen window, I watch his cheap old Beamer drive away. Does he actually make it through another day at work? Well, that depends. Does noon count?

Hours later, during my lunch break, I receive a call from a strange number. The male caller exudes a rather forced calm of articulation. "Hello, Jessica? My name is Dr. Yin. This is a courtesy call. Your husband is here. I am sorry to say this, but he is extremely intoxicated. I am keeping him here in my office. We do not want him driving home. Can you pick him up?"

Son of a bitch! "Uh, thank-you for calling; I am at work. I'd, ah, have to shuffle my schedule around...I see. Text me the address. Is Josh saying anything?"

"No—not really. We are not sure what to do here. My boss is not happy, I'll tell you that. Is this a common occurrence?"

"Look, Dr. Yin, is it? I'm an occupational therapist. I'm going to speak from a personal and professional mindset. First, Josh is my ex-husband, not my husband."

"I see."

"Josh has come back around to his family. He is trying to get himself in order. It would appear he is not ready to handle a full-time job. It was a mistake. He, or we, are still grasping at how to handle his, ah, condition. We honestly thought he was in a good place. We were very wrong."

"Your version makes a lot more sense. His explanations— let's say—had some gaps. My boss is livid. She wants him gone."

"Of course, hiring someone is an investment of time and resource. You are being very accommodating–thank you. Thank your boss as well. I will be there within the hour." And I was.

Josh and I safely arrive home enduring an awkwardly quiet ride. Our deflated man trudges down the hall straight to his cave. This woman on the edge tramps to the dinner table. The pre-ordered pizza already arrived. Many hands are separating slices of stringy melted cheese. Connor plops a piping hot slice of bacon and pineapple onto Nicky's plate. Then Connor puts his face over Nicky's plate and pretends to eat his pizza saying, "Num-num-num-num-num. You get nothing but crust, midget."

Connor is clearly a foot taller than Nicky and half-a-foot taller than Jolie. Penciled measurements of their height vertically climb the kitchen door frame. Nicky bet his brother fifty-bucks that one day he will be the tallest.

Nicky grabs his slice. "At least I will grow. You're stuck with that face for life."

"Good one," says Jolie.

"No, it's not," I say flopping into my chair. "My pumpkin has a handsome face." Connor grins.

Jolie grabs basil leaves from a glass vase. Delicately she tears the green herb. She places the torn bits onto specific spots.

"How was Dad's day at work?" asks Connor. "Did the Beamer get him to work okay?"

"Oh, the car took him where he wanted to go all right." My hand hovers above the steaming pizza box. "Gimme a slice."

"On your hand?"

"Lay it on me, son!" Frustration aching to escape presses against the back of my clenched teeth.

Connor's hazel eyes go wide. "Ooo-kay."

"You want some basil, Momma?" Jolie asks with a sprig in her hand.

"No, I don't want some basil. I'll tell you what I want: for your father to keep a job! Could he just–forget it. Your dad lost his job today."

"No way! Really?" Connor's slice drops from his hand. "He

just started yesterday!" Jolie munches her basil sprig and shakes her head.

"Daddy got fired?" Nicky asks with pizza sauce on his cheeky little face.

I tuck a loose strand of Jolie's hair behind her ear. "Sometime last week, Dad thought he could handle one celebratory drink, that it would not get out of hand this time. It was a lie. Addiction includes lying to yourself. Now he needs a drink all the time. I had to take vacation time to pick him up today."

"Is he going to get in trouble?" Jolie asks.

"We were able to smooth things over with his employer. The repercussions could have been really bad."

"Why would he do that?" Connor's tone is curt. "He wasn't like this before. He's blowing a good opportunity for himself."

"Alcoholism is a progressive disease. Eventually, it advances, and you stop bouncing back. I don't think any of us really understand the type of support and structure your dad needs. We are more like a safety bubble for him. He steps outside the bubble, things fall apart."

"What will he do now?" Jolie asks. Nicky stops eating.

"Beats me." Warm, gooey mozzarella cheese stretches from my mouth to the slice in my hand.

For the rest of the night, we leave Josh alone. He goes to bed without eating or talking to anyone. The next morning, after the kids leave for school, I nudge Josh awake.

"What, am I supposed to do? I need to go to work."

"Then go to work."

"What about you?"

"What about me?"

"I'm not going to act like nothing happened. Don't you think you need help?"

"No, I don't. That job was stupid. They didn't know what to do with me. It wasn't going to work out." He lifts his head. "Don't worry, I'll get another job and give you money."

I hate when he says, "Give you money." You give a homeless person money, a charity money; you pay for services. Nannies get a salary, days off, and paid working vacations. The fact he views favorable-to-him child support as *giving me money* speaks volumes about his self-centered ignorance.

"Money is one issue, Josh. What about–"

"You know something Jess; you are not helping. You are NOT helping at all. You're making it worse."

"What would you like me to do? Please, tell me exactly what I should do."

"Nothing."

"Nothing?"

He sits up to confirm, "Nothing." He rubs his eyes, scratches his head and repeats, "I want you to do nothing."

Here I am, foolishly holding out my plate with a request that he pile some problems on it; he is refusing. He has a point. This is not my problem. It is also NOT my problem that Josh pretends there's NOT a problem. So, I guess, there are no problems. "Fine, Josh. This is me stepping out of the ring." My hands are above my head rubbing clean of responsibility.

"That is your problem, Jessica. You think there is a fight. I am not trying to be a bad guy. I love you. I love the kids. I just cannot have anyone controlling me. You're coming off that way."

The muscles up my spine stiffen. I smooth out my polo shirt and scrub pants. I back away from the bunk beds, then bow at the waist touting like a pissed-off Monty Python character, "I relinquish all perceived authority my liege. Bask in the glow of your choices."

"Thank you. I need some sleep." Josh lays back down; talks toward the ceiling. "I told Nicky I would fix his bike. It's too small for him. I'll get another job. I am waiting to hear a response from some other opportunities."

"Sounds like a plan." Forcing my maturity into overdrive I

close the door quietly, instead of slamming it. Vile visions of kicking him out enter my mind—which entertains my ego, not my humanity. The kids and I cannot ignore the last two months Josh has spent making amends. I mean, does Nicky come home today to a fixed bicycle, or a missing dad? Nicky is nine-years old; there is still a lot of shaping to do. Their father's summer visit has been pleasant, meaningful and without harm. The kids are experiencing life as it affects them. Witnessing how alcoholism continues to strip away at their dad's life explains way more than my words ever could. I will see how this plays out.

4
WTF

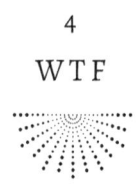

*A*dvanced alcoholism drives fast and without brakes. It is all gas petal. Quite often Josh spends his days home alone. These days began to down-spiral. Shifting in the shadows I catch a glimpse of the Grim Reaper lurking around. This dooms-day creature seeks to rob my Connor, Jolie and Nicky of a father. They will wake-up to find him dead, unless I afford some measure of influence on how things take shape. Whether this is realistic thinking or not, it weighs on me, heavily. I carry these doldrums at work.

The Atrium's therapy gym is a busy view of PTs and OTs instructing their patients through exercise routines, balance challenges, stair climbing and life skills, such as dressing and cooking. Meanwhile, Batman plugs away at his laptop making tomorrow's schedule. Our dark knight's pompadour hair is high and tight as usual adding another few inches to his stature. "There you 'ah, Jess," he takes note of my slump. "How's it going?"

My woes and tush sit and spin on a wheely stool. "Remember how my ex-husband worked so hard to clear his karma?"

"I do. I was rooting fah him. Well, rooting fah you; him by default."

My feet hit the floor to stop the spinning. "How shall I put this? If Josh had a freshly cut log for every good deed he did over the summer, he could build a raft. In theory, he did. He was the captain of his own raft floating down a river of admirable intentions."

"You're a fah bettah woman than me to let your *ex* make amends." Batman confers with a nod.

"Thank you, I think. But that has all gone to shit, because *Captain Morgan* got some money from his pop-pa, and hit the liquor store." I shuffle to the window; gaze at the lone pine tree.

"Such a pissa," Batman says with a roll of the eyes.

Turning to face him, "He's not even having a good time! His raft disintegrated into a bunch of turds floating in a toilet bowl. Josh just keeps pressing the flusher: got fired from his job, he's not safe to drive, the kids are disappointed…yada, yada, flush, flush. As we speak Josh is curled up on Nicky's bunk bed. He already proclaimed everything is under control and I'm over reacting."

"Ah yes," his sarcasm lowers an octave, "everything is fine according to his plan." His stubby fingers wiggle up and down. "I'm sure it's not easy for him. DTs are a wicked pissa! What are you doing about the driving?"

"I hid his car keys."

"Let me guess–inside the freez-a in a bag of…frozen peas. I wicked hate peas." His face contorts with anguish beyond reason. "When I was little, smaller than I am now, my sistah told me peas were the eyes of baby frogs. To this day, if I see peas, I think some poor frog can't find his mud hole."

"That is so gross and really sad." I change to a whisper. "I hid his car keys inside a twelve-pound bag of bird seed. There's a mini-Adirondack feeder outside my kitchen window for the birds."

"Nice," Batman spins around to his desk, then grabs my schedule, "Jess, what you need is a challenging patient."

"Define 'challenging'?" The sheet is already in my hand.

"She's a fragile patient with a ticker on the brink."

"Anything else?"

"She's a no code. Don't send her to the third floor." That's a secret phrase around here; our building only has two stories.

"Got it boss. Bigger problems than mine exist in the world." Off I go to see….

Gertie

Gertie is a 91-year-old resident in the long-term care section. It's not appropriate to call patients cute, but Gertie is totally adorable with her round face and straw brimmed hat. Her body is equally round. Covered by a green, floral muumuu, she looks like a pimento olive stuffed in a wheelchair. Gertie holds out her left arm to give me a hug and–*holy sausage links! What the–?* Gertie's right arm, from wrist to armpit, is three times the normal size of any arm. Lymphatic edema was the side effect from her breast cancer treatment. Gertie could barely wiggle her right hand. Removing lymph nodes from a mastectomy can cause complications, but this is crazy.

"Hi Miss Gertie," I say kneeling beside her wheelchair, "tell me something you need help doing. We'll work on it."

"I can't do nothing honey."

"We'll see about that." I fit her arm for a compression garment. Next, I work on Gertie feeding herself.

ON THE DRIVE home thoughts of Josh legit dying in my house come back to agitate me. On the porch I double check that his keys are still submerged in sunflower seeds. Yup, that's one positive sign. Inside— *Where is everybody?* The counter tops and sofa cushions show no signs of nibbled snacks. No one is a zombie in front of the TV. Josh is not strumming his melodic guitar. The family calendar above the dishwasher reads, *Connor: soccer practice, Jolie: band practice. Where is my Boo?* The refrigerator holds that answer. A yellow note on the stainless door reads, "Mom went to Spencer's. Love you, Nicky." Wonder if his bicycle seat got fixed.

Strewn about the backyard is a Radio-Flyer cruiser and my old triathlon bike. Josh obviously pulled them out from the shed. Inside the shed tool parts are scattered about the plywood floor. Nicky's dirt bike is missing. Appears Josh started accomplishing something today. Odd he left everything in such disarray; it is very unlike him. *Where is the body?*

On the twin bunk bed Josh lies out cold under an animal quilt. A happy lion covers his feet, a rainforest frog grins by his legs, an elephant rests over his chest, and a monkey climbed on his—. I tip-toe around the footboard searching for any liquid toxin. In the top drawer nestled among white socks is a vodka bottle. *Aye, aye Captain, work that plan.*

AROMAS OF CHICKEN marsala arouse Josh for dinner. He peers around a wall of cabinets. "Hey," he says shuffling into the kitchen, a jaundice pallor to the flesh of his cheeks. He stops at the marble counter top separating himself from his family gathered around the glass dining table.

"Thanks for fixing my bike, Dad," Nicky says between munches.

"I did? Right—the seat! I took out all the bikes, greased the chains. I greased yours, Connor, and yours too, Jolie. You have the red bike with the cute little basket," he says with a high-pitched voice. "I even greased mommy's chain."

"Better than yanking it," I mutter.

Josh double blinks and approaches the table. Dinner plates

surround a vase of Gerber daisies, my favorite. "I polished your handle bars too, Jess." His eye sockets look like mushed corn with red pen lines. "I filled your tires with air-r-r."

Connor puts his fork down. "Dad, what else would you fill a tire with?"

"You're right!" Josh announces. "That's a good one, because what else would you use? Hot sauce? Imagine your bicycle tires catching on fire, because you filled them with–hot sauce! Picture this: you're racing down a hill, super-fast. There's no smoke, just massive flames shooting out of the bicycle rims creating a gigantic fireball." Josh opens his arms, then bounces up and down to animate the immense flames that would be… engulfing our children? Josh proclaims to his family, "All because of hot sauce instead of air!"

Jolie and Connor, mouths agape, side glance at one another, then look at me. Eyebrows up I sip my water mixed with less lemon than my current life holds. Witnessing drunk Dad at this point explains way more than my sterile words could. For years, the kids did not recognize when he was under the influence. Neither did I. Heavy drinkers build up such a tolerance: four drinks in does not seem to faze them. No mistaking this disease has taken over their father after many missed chances to stop it.

We refocus on dinner. Fork tines spear chunks of mushroom and chicken mixed with a creamy risotto of feta, garden tomatoes, rosemary and thyme. Josh, standing out of place, tousles Nicky's hair.

Nicky breaks the awkward silence. "Dad, Spencer needs his bike adjusted. Can you make his seat higher?"

"Sure bud. Bring any of your teenage friends around for a bike adjustment."

"Er, we're not teenagers. I'm nine. Spencer is eight."

"Jessica," Josh turns away from the newsflash of his son's age, "did you notice the bikes, I—"

"Yes, I noticed Josh. There's chicken on the stove. You'll need a plate."

"Right. Okay. Thank you." Josh methodically gets his meal and joins us in silence.

Following dinner, we each find a semblance of normalcy. The kids banish themselves into their bedrooms. Josh settles on the sofa with his guitar. Turning the pages of a tattered music book, he sings the pop tune, *I wanna hold your hand*. How can he still be functioning? I'd be vomiting.

The last of the plates fill the dishwasher. Josh finishes a Sting tune disappointed that his voice can't quite hit the, *Every Breath You Take* range. "Maybe I have too much of an Adam's apple," he says in puzzlement scratching his throat. "Or maybe not enough."

"That's why he's Sting, and you're not," I emerge from the kitchen.

"I can live with that."

Crossing into the living room I ask, "Josh, can we talk for minute. I'd like your perspective."

"Sure," he says leaning his Martin against the muted, gray sofa to stretch out his legs.

I ease into a white, overstuffed chair we nicknamed "the cloud". "How are things working for you?"

"Fine."

"You don't need any help?"

"Nope, everything is F-I-N-E."

"You're going to pull the plug on yourself. I can accept that."

"Thanks for the support," he says to the ceiling, "but I do love you." He looks at me. "I still really, really love you."

I reach forward and pat his knee. Any day now, this man will die in my house. I have nothing new to say.

The evening ends with our family watching TV together. Nicky snuggles under Josh's arm. Connor is next to them, his phone within reach. Jolie knits in the opposite corner. Hamlet managed to curl up under the yarn. I sit on the cloud. The TV goes dark. Josh falls asleep on the sofa. The kids disappear to their rooms. I descend to mine in the basement. Our togetherness had value, but these moments are slippery. Ordinary evenings cover our dysfunction like frosting on a tiered cake. The outside looks tempting; but what's inside could be anyone's guess. I sense a train wreck is coming.

OVER THE NEXT couple days things do not improve. I seek advice from my exceptionally level-headed friends Ellen and Mike. Both are long-term, recovered, alcoholics; they have become my personal confidants. Our sons, Nicky and Zeb, are close friends. In the privacy of their library room, Mike and Ellen digest my current situation. They share past alcoholic thinking from a poignant point of view. Ellen pours more jasmine tea into bone china cups. "I understand you were giving Josh another chance to be a father. He was measuring up until that first drink. Mike and I learned the hard way you cannot 'pick up' again. The cost is too much; it's worse with opioids. A one hit relapse can be an instant death sentence."

"Then why take the drink? Why take the hit?"

Ellen sips at the gold rim before responding. "There are a bunch of influences: genetics, social situations, the brain's hard wiring, upbringing, triggers–which are everywhere. Besides, do you make perfect choices all day, every day?"

"Of course not."

"No matter how you look at it, Jessie, here's the bottom line: you can have a drink; I cannot. It is cancer for me. For you, it is not. But talking the talk is not enough. I went to rehab—more than once—read the literature. Eventually, I got a sponsor; she is a life line for me. She calls me out on my shit without judgement."

I say with exasperation, "It's frustrating. Josh is nearing homeless level and doesn't want any help."

Mike thoughtfully interjects, "He's not at his rock bottom yet. The second time I got out of rehab, I went straight to a bar and ordered a beer." Mike throws his curly head back with a laugh. "It was fuck you thinking. It sucks sometimes not having a drink, not going to social events. I'm already depressed, right! Now, I have to cut things out I enjoy. It sucks. But believe me it's worth it. If I didn't get sober, I would not be here talking to you, and I would not have a son. Josh isn't going to remember a lot of things. Blackout periods can last for days. Don't get me wrong, he is absolutely accountable for his actions, but some of it ends up mush in your head."

Hearing the damn truth feels validating. "Josh has lost track of days," I admit.

Mike grabs a butter cookie. "In your twenties that can seem like fun, if no one gets hurt. It's part of the disease. Josh needs rehab; no doubt about it."

"I'm preaching the rehab angle to deaf ears."

"Don't be fooled," Ellen says. "He's taking it in. When you drink, or if you're raised by drinkers, it's very common that your thinking is black and white. You either lied or you didn't; either fucked up or you didn't; either with me or against me. And your temper is quick, 0 to 15 on a scale of 2 to ten. Working a twelve-step program gave me fresh principles."

"Kids should learn about 12-step programs in school," Mike says. "At least, gain some awareness of them."

Ellen reaches for one of the last cookies. "After my final rehab stay, I kept up the support. Then I met Mike. We get each other." Ellen looks at Mike across the antique coffee table.

"Been fourteen years baby," Mike bellows. "We are very blessed," and blows her a kiss.

"So," Ellen asks, "what are you going to do about Josh?"

"Wish he had health benefits," I answer with a sigh.

"No shit," says Mike. "But he doesn't. And that is not your fault."

One Day at a Time

The sacred Tao Te Ching poetically reiterates how mother nature gets all things accomplished in her own time. If my ex-husband is to get sober, it will be on his time, not mine. *Zen as I try, not gonna lie, can't give up hope, child-support would be dope.*

The next day at lunchtime I stop home, unannounced, for a safety check. Entering the house I yell out, "Hello!" I get no answer. On the dining table next to the Gerber daisies a bread bowl rests in the sunlight. A wet tea towel drapes over the top trapping the heat. I peek underneath to find a rising ball of dough glistening with olive oil, no rosemary on top, bummer. Where is the dough baker? He is not passed out on the bunk bed. I sleuth the sock drawer; vodka bottle still there. Inside his suitcase rests an empty Chardonnay. Situation pulse-check is complete. Exiting the bedroom I nearly bump into Josh ambling down the hall, a grocery bag in his arms.

"Looking for something?" he asks.

"Maybe; maybe not. I came home for lunch. Thought you might like the company."

"I'm sure," he says back tracking into the kitchen. He unpacks cans of chick peas, bananas and tied wisps of fresh cilantro.

"How did you get to the grocery store?"

"I rode a bike. I parked my bike. Got us groceries for dinner and rode home." He peels back the tea towel. "Did you see? I am going to make rolls with the kids tonight. You can make one too, if you'd like."

"That was thoughtful," I say neighboring a new triangle of parmesan with some cheddar in the fridge.

"I'm trying Jess. I'm really trying. Every day I wake up and say, *I am not going to think of myself. Today I will do what is needed, and nothing else. I will stay the course."* He passes me vanilla yogurt cups to stack on the top shelf. His promises are stacking, too. I reciprocate his sincerity with a hug. In case he dies–which has to be happening on a cellular level–I prefer Josh recalls I give some hugs, instead of only pointing out the crap.

"Thank you." He squeezes me tight, leans his head on mine. We rock for a moment. Then at arm's length he wiggles his hips asking, "Hey, you wanna have some ex-sex?" His right eyebrow lifts up to complete *the look.*

Palm up, talk to the hand.

Daughter takes a stand

Another day returning home after work reels a re-run of the same episode: Josh works on a yard project, followed by prepping a family dinner, interrupted by his passing out.

In our kitchen of the softest buttercup-hued cabinets, my thirteen-year-old daughter dumps a box of mac and cheese into a pot of boiling water. A pink Gingham apron is tied around her slender waist. Jolie sees me and points with a wooden spoon towards her lights-out father on the sofa.

I sigh. "Did you talk to him today?"

"Yes, and he was drunk Mom. He was telling me not to be fake. 'Don't color your hair. Don't put carpet over hardwood floors. Don't use a rice maker instead of a pot. Don't be fake like your mother.'"

"Ah yes—my evil traits."

"Mrs. Fedario asked why you took him back? You guys are supposed to be divorced."

Ignorant comments from other moms escalate my frustrations. "I did not take your father back. He came here for a summer visit."

"Mom, it's been two months."

"He found a job! Everything else was supposed to fall into place: he would live on his own, you guys would have scheduled visits—other dads seem to handle these basic tasks just fine."

Jolie feverishly stirs the neon orange pasta.

I scurry down the hall shouting back, "Why do I get crucified for trying to share the load with my former spouse like a normal, divorced person?" Under an obsessive spell, I scrounge Josh's bedroom for signs of today's liquor activity. The bonus of living with an addict-narcissist is my own set of obsessive, ruminating behaviors to anchor my reality.

Jolie yells down the hall. Her arm waves the cheesy wooden spoon like an orange exclamation point. "Dad doesn't need to be here for me! What kind of example are you setting for Nicky?"

Oo-o, she is pushing my buttons. I let it rip at the stove. "Prior to this week, we were all having a nice time. Your dad made himself useful. A lot of men don't have the courage to face the people they've wronged and make amends. Mrs. Fedario had a very abusive, alcoholic father. I know, cuz she told me. She became his caretaker because her siblings had blown him off. She hated caring for him because he had no regrets. She also hated that her mother had stayed with him and continued to stay with him. My point is that Mrs. Fedario has missed matched feelings about what a woman should do. So, stop listening to the high and mighty Mrs. Fedario!"

Jolie bangs her neon exclamation point on the side of her bowl, splatting a glob of macaroni.

I am not done. "Regarding Nicky, he deserves to have his nine-year-old Dad needs met, which are different from your 13-year-old needs and Connor's 14-year-old needs. Everyone gets a turn. Guess who goes last?" My hovering index finger flicks at my head. Leaning against the fridge I close my eyes to rest from my martyr monologue. Jolie and I take a moment just to breathe.

Deep inside my heart a whisper rises above the hurt. I turn

my head to look at her. "I just wanted you guys to have two really, really good parents."

Jolie places her neon-filled bowl on the counter. "Mom, when are you going to realize you're enough?"

My fist goes to my stomach. "I didn't— How could I?"

Converse sneakers and mismatched socks step toward me. She repeats. "You're enough."

In one fell swoop I hug my peanut. The words *I'm sorry* spill softly into her golden hair. She smells of cheddar cheese. Her hands press into my back as if she were flattening cookie dough on a sheet pan. We step outside the kitchen to peek at her father. He is asleep in an upright position. A ruffled apron with lavender polka dots is tied around his neck and waist.

"Dad means well."

"I know, Mom. That's what makes it sad."

LATER THAT NIGHT A TOWN FRIEND, who is also a teacher, sends me a text. She is asking if Josh is okay, because she saw him wandering around the grocery store parking lot as if he could not find his car. Eventually, he seemed to recall traveling by bicycle, then rode away.

I thank her for her concern with reassurance that Josh "has been prevented from driving." She picked up what I was putting down.

The following weekend morning, Josh is testy with me about not having access to his car. He confronts me, the *keeper of the keys*. "Where did you put my car keys?"

"They're in my car." I lie to him. "I think it's better the keys stay with me, don't you?"

Josh squares off his shoulders. "I thought you weren't going to interfere. It's legally my car."

"You could not walk a straight line yesterday. In the middle of cooking dinner, you passed out on the sofa wearing polka-dots. It was a little bit cute, but mostly pathetic. The kids just walked by Dad, passed-out on the sofa."

Bravado slid off his deflating shoulders. "Guess I am embarrassing them."

"You have a puddle of empathy here, but it's evaporating. Clearly, you are no longer in the driver's seat of your actions—literally and figuratively."

"Maybe we should talk about getting back together?"

"Holy shit balls! You know what? We're staying on topic. Who do you think you will hit, driving around town? It will be someone we know. Someone I should have protected! Go ahead and drink yourself to death, but you are NOT driving a car. If you think sitting in jail is the same as rehab, think again."

Josh tilts his head. Puts his hands in his jean pockets.

"I have to leave and pick Nicky up. I poured your sock vodka down the drain by the way…oh, wait you already know. Well, I left the wine intact. No more hard stuff; you are on thin ice." I storm out the door.

The Kia and I zip around the corner to oddly get stuck in a traffic jam by the lake. This 4-way stop never backs-up. The line moves quickly along. Off in the lake parking lot are flashes of red and blue lights. Let's see, two police cars and no sign of any accident. This road leads directly to the grocery store from my house. Brimmed-hat officers buzz from car to car at the stop sign. They seem to be questioning each driver before letting them pass. *Holy crap–it's a check point!*

"Hi officer, is everything okay?"

"Yes, ma'am; standard safety-check." His eyes scan the back seat. No-o doubt he is looking for an intoxicated white male in his fifties. "You can go." He taps my car door. Driving away with the spinning cop lights behind me causes my worst fears to compound. If I kick Josh out, where does he go? A shelter? A morgue? Or maybe— Ah-ha! —his mother's house.

"My son cannot come back here. I'm too old for this," Ingrid says without hesitation.

"Your son is turning into a stumbling drunk. The town just created a check point. He's lucky I hid his keys. I am not about to teach my kids how to treat family like trash and kick Josh to the street. But at the same time, Ingrid, I don't want to teach them how to get dumped on either."

"Maybe his father can take him." Ingrid has nothing else to say.

Fine. I will call Caleb.

Unlike Ingrid's coldness, Caleb embodies a state of disappointment and heartbreak. "My boy was doing so well. He had a job. He was clear as a bell."

"Caleb, I'm sorry. The second Josh got money, a car and the belief he was doing well, he took a drink."

"Joshua should have known better." Caleb pauses. "I should've known better than sending him that money."

"A few months of sobriety is no match against decades of a growing addiction," I console.

"You know I went to AA meetings, aye. Some Air Force buddies dragged me. It helped. I know I made mistakes with my boys." He took a moment, perhaps the remorse. "Aye, Joshua is a grown man now. He has to grab hold of his life."

"He can't stay here anymore. Ingrid just took a turn."

"If Joshua stays with me, he's going to meetings, aye. I'll sit next to him the whole time I will."

"If you fly down here, then both of you could drive back in the Beamer. I'll make sure he's well enough to get in the car."

"Shit, he's that bad, aye. I'll have to talk to Jacqueline. I don't know how quick I can get down there."

Caleb has been retired for years and lives with Jacqueline, who is equivalent to a third wife. They live surrounded by her family. In my opinion, she will be fine. Caleb needs to wrap his head around this situation. "Please understand, I leave my job early to supervise your son. His car keys are hidden; he wants them back. I am protecting both Joshua and the neighborhood. You can't take long getting here. Our family is degrading into an 'everyone for themselves' mentality." I do not even mention Josh desiring to sleep with me is an added ego-navigation no one has to deal with except me.

Caleb soon calls me back. His plan is to fly down in five days' time, stay for a short visit with the grandkids, then Josh will be living with him! Canada is more than a day's drive. Caleb cannot handle the distance at his age.

New goal: sober Josh up to drive away and set fire to old goal. Old goal: Josh contributes income and effort towards raising our children. The child support will go up in a cloud smoke leaving me hollow on barren field. It's scary. Nobody wanted this end game, but it is time to blow the whistle.

Informing Josh that Caleb is coming to take him away is not on my short to-do-list; label it post-traumatic stress avoidance from years of dealing with Josh's reactions. Also, fair to say, is that a "polite removal" from the family might be triggering for Josh…on account of the last time I…. News that Caleb will whisk him away is on a need-to-know basis. Joshua will learn at the last possible minute.

TIME TO START the new goal. Shirtless on the back deck, Josh lies on a teak lounge chair salvaged from our formerly upscale Hawaiian life. His tan skin is sweaty from the late day sun. I ask with exasperation, "Did you happen to notice the police check point today?"

He perks up like a gopher out of a hole. "Yaz-z, I saw them. I think they were looking for me! I swerved my bike off the road; dove into some bushes. Look at my arms. Look at my legs." Dried blood scratches run up and down his forearms and calves. A couple band-aides cover his right elbow.

"What the fuck Josh!" I stand blocking the sun for him, agape at his wounds. "Do you know how crazy things are getting?"

"I know."

"Yet, you don't die. Seriously, if I drank what you did, I would be dead; put the fork in, take me off the grill, I'm done. Or, if I dove off a moving bicycle into a thicket of branches, I'd have broken bones. But you are basking in the sun, strumming Hawaiian tunes on a ukulele."

"I still love you."

"Oh for crying out loud," my voice cracks.

"Why doesn't that matter?"

"Cuz it's a line-item Josh. Get wife back: check. That's all you got. It's like handing me a one-dollar bill and calling it a twenty. There isn't another nineteen to back it up."

"I don't even know what that means."

"It means I've changed, and you have not. You can't see much past yourself. Look, it doesn't matter. You are not dying in this house, not on my watch."

"How very kind of you," he says with sprinkled sarcasm.

I wrinkle my nose.

He strums a chord before flipping the Uke over onto his lap. "I am worried about my health, too. I cannot stop." He picks at a finger nail. "I get the shakes. I can't sleep. I lose track of time," he looks up at me, "like all the time. Sometimes I don't even know where I am. I start speaking French."

"Do you want out of the danger zone?"

"Yes, I do. I really do."

"Then the hard stuff goes. We'll wean down the rest. We've done this before."

He sighs. I know he prefers the diversion of talking about us. However, I am done explaining myself to someone who handed me a fake resume at the altar.

Josh, albeit scared, throws his hat in the ring. "I will do it."

"Good; I will hold onto your wallet, so you cannot keep

buying alcohol. I will buy you beer, and I will return your wallet."

Josh tilts his head back; closes his eyes at the sun. "Don't buy the light shit."

"I promise."

THE KIDS and I meet privately to discuss their grandfather's pending arrival. "There is no sense in spooking Dad. He doesn't need to know yet."

"I think that's a good plan," says Jolie.

"When will Dad come back?" asks Nicky

"When he stops drinking," says Connor. "What do we do until Grandpa gets here?".

"First, we hide the bikes."

"Where you going to put them?" Jolie pauses from doodling; sketch books are like another appendage for her.

"In the neighbor's garage; hopefully, Gabriella won't mind."

"When should we hide them," Connor asks.

"Now, while it's dark. Each of you grab your bike from the shed."

The stars are out as I knock on Gabriella's door. Visible through the front window is an impressive ink print of Jerry Garcia with sunglasses and a bearded smile. Hanging over their piano Jerry watches the door.

"Hey Jessie," Gabby says in her Stevie Nicks rasp. She's a town fav at Amateur Song Night. She notices my kids with their bikes on her sidewalk. "What's up, Buttercup?"

"Can we hide our bikes in your garage? It's to stop Josh from going to the liquor store. Time for a detox," my words spoken with exasperation.

Gabby's jaw drops. "He was doing so good! Hell yea, it's fine. We need to move our shit over, but your bikes should fit." She pats my arm. "If you need to talk, let me know. Tom and I think you're a saint. He worries about you."

"Nice to know there's a team on my side. Our divorce was supposed to improve things. Anyway, Josh is leaving with Caleb in five days. He has to be sober enough to drive."

"Shit, five days." Gabriella scratches her eyebrow. "Good luck with that! I'll face my crystals toward your house."

The kids and I power walk to her garage and stash our bicycles.

5
COUNT THEM DAYS

Day 1, Sunday: Pinot noir sips manage the withdrawal symptoms as Josh fluctuates between loopy and agitated. I lure him into healthy distraction with tasks such as… taking a walk to Athena's Coffee Shop, folding laundry, and most exciting the changing of bed sheets. Whatever it is, Josh manages not to embarrass himself. We decide on barbecuing for dinner. Connor and Josh are the grill masters. Jolie, Nicky and I collect flowers from the garden, then create early autumn bouquets for the house.

The first day ends with the family functioning as a team. Tomorrow, while I am at work, Josh will ween to drinking beers as per our agreement. He will not have access to car, bicycle or money.

Day 2, Monday: This entire detox thing distracts me all day at work. But I muddle through. My expectation is that when I arrive home my ex-husband will be notably sober.

Let me say it first, I am an idiot. Based on Josh's condition, there must have been a stash in the yard or somewhere. While

Josh is not passed out drunk, he is not entirely coherent. I neither judge him nor point this out; it is part of the process. As such we coast on through the early evening. However, I crank up the squeeze on Josh's addiction with a vast to my neighbor. I knock on Gabriella's door; throw a nod to the poster-sized Garcia visible through the window.

Gabby opens the door; her leg wedged in the door to block the jumping York-Terriers at her feet. "Hey, Jessie," her shoulder length curls are dyed a metallic blue today.

"Can I hide Josh's wallet over here; there's a few hundred dollars in it. If Josh has money, he will find a way to get alcohol. Caleb can have it once he gets here."

Gabriella takes the leather wallet. "I'll hide it with my weed. How's it going over there?"

"Eh, the alcohol withdrawals will hit Josh harder tomorrow. He has some beers to ride it out."

"Such a shame, Tom and I always enjoyed talking to him. Last summer we hung out during rehearsals for Amateur night. Josh was supposed to play guitar on one of my songs. When he didn't show, Tom and I thought he was on some kind of vacation. We didn't know he had abandoned you guys."

"It wasn't something to advertise. Among other things, I felt embarrassed. It seemed sick and unforgivable."

"Do you think he screwed things up coming back?"

"We all deserve the chance to show up for our kids. He wasn't hiding behind a drink when he got here."

Day 3, Tuesday: Josh sleeps through the night without a drink. The morning routine goes fine. I leave for work with the recovery boat on course.

I come home; Josh and Nicky wave from the sofa, ukuleles pulled tight to their chests. Josh's face is flush. The chords he is attempting to play are distorted. Once again, I wear the idiot cap. There were only beers in the fridge. He is more than three beers in.

"Hey guys," I say mulling around the kitchen. I overhear Nicky utter many an *uh-huh* as his dad proliferates about musicians and music while painstakingly striking one cord at a time. Josh's smile is fake and put on like a sticker bought at a dollar store. With a final strum, he pauses deep in thought or the absence of thought, can't tell.

"Nicky, why don't you join your brother or sister."

"Okay mom." Off my youngest scoots.

Leaning on the counter, fingers tapping I ask, "Josh, how are you so wasted? Did you drink a bottle of wine?"

"No-o-o," as he strums the ukulele.

That is not a reliable answer. I stomp away from the musical noise pollution and search Nicky's room…no bottles. I shove my hand into an abyss of sunflower seeds; car keys are still there. Did Josh see me hiding his evening beers in the canoe? Outside I search the canoe leaning against the side of the house. The beer cans are gone…suppose that's on me. I don't say another word. Ignore and move forth. We all have dinner; we do our own thing.

Nightfall, Nicky and Jolie dive into cereal bowls of Special Ks as we like to call them. Connor grabs his jacket and bangs the closet door shut. I join him in the living room which has become rather cozy with the moving boxes gone.

"Is everything okay kiddo?"

Connor kneels down to tie his skater shoe. He tugs the laces with tight fists. "I told Dad last night he needs to stop drinking."

Yes, one of our kids can challenge their dad! "How did that go?"

"All he said was, 'Yeah, you're right.' I asked Dad to promise he wouldn't drink." He yanks a double knot with annoyance. "Dad wouldn't promise. Not even for his kids. He wouldn't promise."

Kneeling beside him, I hand over his other sneaker. "Sounds like he didn't want to give you his word, if he couldn't keep it. Dad knows you would be more upset, if he didn't keep his promise."

"Why can't he just quit? He wasn't drinking when he got here."

"This is when you have to view it as a disease. He has chemical changes from it. He has a genetic predisposition to alcoholism. He doesn't seem to understand how quickly it takes him down."

"Why doesn't he go to rehab?"

"He considers it but doesn't trust it. Not all rehab places are reputable. Some are just out to make money. He is also embarrassed." Connor ties his other shoe with less tension. "Whatever the reason, it doesn't matter. Dad has no insurance. Rehab costs at least twenty grand. After discharge, you're right back where you started, unless entering outpatient programs which require more money. He's not making choices to address this as a serious problem."

Connor and I stand up. He is a stack of pancakes taller than me. "What doesn't he get that he has a serious problem?"

"He knows, but this is crisis level; it is out of our league. He needs supervision and professional help. As an OT, I deal with treatment decisions like this a lot."

"Do you think he'll ever stop drinking."

"I think he heard your message–you want a dad, not a drunk."

"But do you think he will stop drinking?"

"I-I—"

"Mom, do you?"

"I don't know."

"Take a guess. Will he ever stop?"

"I asked other alcoholics if getting sober was worth it. They swore up and down it was. We are offering that beacon to your dad. I will not waiver on that Connor. If I do, his addiction will manipulate me and mow us over. I'm sorry. I don't have a crystal ball to your question."

"If Dad doesn't want to get better, then I don't want him here." His conviction rings strong and clear.

"How you feel is okay. Grandpa will take care of Dad." His hand becomes warm in mine. "Love you pumpkin."

"Love you too, mom."

"By the way," my tone becomes more official, "you and Dad have the same shoe size. I need all your shoes, except the ones on your feet."

With a garbage bag slung over my shoulder like a Santa in sweat pants and skater shoes, I trek back to Gabriella's house. My glamorous outfit is topped off with one of Connor's striped shirts. He won't wear it anymore, because "strips are stupid". The lumpy bag lands with a thud on her porch. *Yes, Jerry, I'm back; you're not surprised.*

Gabby opens the door. "Hey buttercup—I should just give you a key! " Her laughter probably amuses the wall icon hanging behind her. "What's with the garbage bag?"

I pick up and thrust the bag of thwarted transportation into her arms. "Every pair of shoes that Connor and Josh own are in here. No shoes, no store, no service. His flip-flops are in my car." Gabby puts the bag behind her. "Almost forgot," I say reaching into my pocket. "Here, I know Tom likes whiskey." An airplane-size bottle of JD smacks into her hand.

"I see. Well, Tom won't let it go to waste."

"Oh," reaching into my other pocket, "—this too."

"Why are you handing me a hydrogen peroxide bottle?"

"Smell inside."

Day 4, Wednesday: Batman supports Josh getting exiled from my house, so he lets me take a half-day off work. Two beers were left for Josh to get through the day. Another two are in my car. Tonight, we have a distraction: Connor's high school soccer game.

As I near my front door red maple leaves flitter from a passing breeze. Noting this could be a sign, I take an extra long breath before stepping into the house. *It's going to be fine.* Everything is extra quiet. Josh is not fussing around the kitchen, nor strumming his guitar. His rationed Stella Artois goes in the fridge. Perhaps Josh is sunning himself outback with *a New Yorker* magazine. I got him one from the library; left it as a surprise.

Huh, the magazine remains untouched on the counter. *Is he still in bed, really?*

A barefoot Josh, wearing a faded Hawaii University T-shirt and cargo shorts is out-cold, belly-up on the bunk bed.

"Josh. Josh!" Abruptly I yank at the animal quilt under his body flipping him onto his side.

"What the? Hey—" His acorn squash eyes go wide as quarters. "How-ah, er, was school?" he asks rubbing his face.

"Our kids go to school. I'm Assistant Director of Rehabilitation where sick people make an effort to get better. Does that resonate with you, Freud?"

"No," he blurts rolling over, face down.

My arms cross tight. My merino-wool Allbird runners tap furiously on the oak floor boards.

"What?" His tone abrupt.

"How in the world are you intoxicated? No way you passed out on beer or wine. You should be agitated and functional, not incapacitated."

"I am functional and highly educated."

"I know the difference between passed out and a nap. How did you get the alcohol?"

"I found the breakfast beers you left. You got me Stella, my favorite–thank you. I thought–*she must care about me.*"

"They were for the whole day, not 'breakfast'! You drank something else. I can tell. It's my superpower." My arms drop to a hang. "How is this even possible?"

"I rode my bike to the store."

"No, you did not."

"I did."

"I hid your bicycle Josh."

"You took my bike," he springs up like a jack-in-the-box on the mattress, "my expensive mountain bike? You stole my mountain bike!" He crashes back down, face up. "Whatever; you're going to hate me if I tell you."

"I don't understand. You have no means to get anywhere, and there's no alcohol here." I plop down by his naked feet.

"Don't make me tell you."

"Just say it."

"You'll hate me."

"I won't hate you."

"I walked to the liquor store." He put his forearm over his face.

Slapping his hairy shin, "You did not walk! I hid your shoes. I hid Conner's, too. There was no walking."

Raising his arm off his face, "No wonder I couldn't find my flip flops. Are you crazy? Connor's in on this?" He tugs at his greasy, stiff hair. "The kids must hate me." He closes his eyes, sucks his lips in tight.

While scanning rapidly for clues I reassure him. "Promise I won't hate you." My hand rubs his knee. I am slightly impressed he out smarted me, not that I am going to tell him.

Josh lifts his head; assesses my face. His lower jaw with dense blonde whiskers shifts to one side creating the tiniest crook in the corner of his mouth. "I…found…the vodka you hid. I'm sorry." His head lowers back down to the pillow. The jungle animals are all smiles underneath.

"Vodka? That I hid? I didn't buy any. What are you talking about?"

Josh quick lifts his head to reassess me again. He stares at the ceiling. Silence is the new answer.

"You said, 'I hid it.' Wait—the rain boots in the closet?" I forgot about that bottle of vodka.

"You hid it very well, Jess."

"Oh, shut up!"

"I'm sorry," his blue eyes staring, "I really am sorry."

"Hey-y-y, don't you be sorry. Seriously, this one is my fault."

"This is not your fault."

"Don't take this from me Josh! I hid your car keys. I hid the bikes, your cash, credit cards. I stashed your shoes. But this was a lesson I had yet to learn: if you leave a drop of alcohol in a house with an alcoholic, he will find it!"

"Where the hell are you putting all this stuff?"

A lividness at myself jumps me to my feet. "I should have known you'd find it." I pace around the bunk beds stepping over Nicky's dirty jeans, boxers and— "Ouch!" —a nerf blaster. My voice rises with righteous pain. "I have been consumed with getting you detoxed with a sense of dignity. I have isolated myself from my friends, my family and, give me strength, a dating life. I have cared more about your sobriety than you. But guess what?" pointing right at him, "It is not your fault you're drunk today." I jerk a thumb back at myself. "It's mine! Do you get it? I get it!"

"Jess it's not your fault," he moans from the pillow.

Excuse me. What just happened—he's the rational one? This pisses me off even more! "Know what Josh? This is my fault because I fucked myself. Yup, fuck-k me-e." There—that is the second time I ever said that in my life.

Josh continues to respond with maturity. "What we do now is what's important."

Massaging my temples, I melt onto Nicky's wooden chair

putting myself into a *time-out*. Within a minute I break our moment of composure. "Despite this set back, Josh, you have gotten more sober each day. I'm sorry. That probably has not been easy. Let's just get rid of the remaining vodka and call it even. Where is it?"

"It's gone." He rolls over putting his back to me.

"As I recall it was half-full."

"Actually, it was half-empty."

"You're hilarious. I know it's not all gone. Where's the rest?"

Josh neither moves nor speaks.

"Fine. I'll wait. You'll need another drink in what, five, ten minutes tops. Yup, I'll wait."

The ceiling fan whirs and whirs and whirs above us. "Tell me where it is, and there's a cold Stella in it for you."

The lump rotates his head.

"That's right; a sexy, cold Stella awaits in the fridge. We can toast to tomorrow being your last day."

Josh slides a hand under his pillow. He pulls out the bottle of vodka and places it in my hand with care.

"Muchas gracias," I say tucking the bottle under my arm. "You're going to be okay."

A smidge of smile forms at the corner of his mouth. "I know you're doing a lot for me, an unmentionable amount. I know I am causing you stress. I am sorry." He rises to sit at the edge of the bed. His naked toes and my dark sneakers almost touch on the oak wood floor. "Why did you say, 'we can toast to my last day?'"

Oh shit. My happiness slipped. "Because, I thought it would be your last day of needing a drink."

Josh reaches under the bed; hands me a wrinkled piece of paper. "I wrote this poem for you. It took me a long time, a really, long time. It's in French."

When Josh and I met almost two decades ago, he told me he was fluent in French. Great, our kids will be too, or so I thought. If he had told me the truth, that he had only a rudimentary foundation, I still would have been impressed. But over the years he could only sing the same French nursery rhyme about a blue bird and repeated the same damn phrase about my eyes when I crooned, 'say something in French to me.' More than I hate that he lied is that I swallowed the lie. I swallowed many lies.

Scribbled in blue ink across wrinkled notepaper were five sparse, crooked lines of French gibberish mixed with English. Josh ambles away to retrieve his cold Stella. The legible part of the poem reads: *I love you. That does not seem to matter. Why does that not matter?*

Neatly I fold up the paper and tuck it in a pocket. I cannot lose focus. My ex gave up his vodka too easily. Is there more? On the floor, a plastic bicycle water bottle peeks out from under a towel. I twist off the cap. Sniff — Whoa! I pour the water-vodka into a prolific aloe vera plant in Nicky's room. Forgive me plant.

For the rest of the day, Josh and I muddle through as partners. From the soccer field sidelines, Nicky, Jolie, Josh and I cheer as a family watching Connor and his teammates sprint relentlessly from goal to goal. The ref calls the game. The teams line up, then like train cars on opposite tracks the opposing players high-five each another. Released from the game, the sweaty kids are a swarm of bees making swirling routes to their smiling parents. Connor hugs his dad from the playing field just as his friends do with their dads after every game. Josh holds on to his son the longest, perhaps to convey, *I'm sorry I haven't been here son. Hope one day we can move on.*

DAY 5, Thursday: I take the whole damn day off and cajole a sluggish, no smiles for miles Josh to hike in the woods. "Detoxing feels like an awful version of the flu," he huffs. "I am just trying to get through it." Following our nature hike, Josh wraps up in a blanket, cupping a hot Chai tea. We watch a favorite movie together, *So I Married an Axe Murderer*. We crack up at Mike Meyers as Fat Bastard, a Scottish father who complains to his wife about the size of their son's large head. 'Look at the size of his cranium. It's like a gigantic orange on a stick. It's got its own planetoid system!'

Caleb phones when he is a couple hours away. Bingo! Time to tell Josh he is being evicted. I am kind but there is no mincing of words. We care about him, but he is no longer welcome. The decision is unanimous.

Empty tea cup in hand, Josh processes the news without moving a muscle, until he asks, "Why didn't you call my mom? She would have been better than my dad."

"I called her. She didn't want you back. Said you needed to grow up. Her words, not mine."

Josh curls his lip, stares at the floor. Hearing that your mom doesn't want you is a low place to be. Josh left the room to take a shower, the one he promised to take a couple days ago.

GRANDPA'S ARRIVAL is met with uproarious grandkid hugs. "Oh boy, oh boy, you guys have grown, aye!"

Josh doesn't touch another drop during Caleb's visit. The detox is complete. Grandpa is playful with the grandkids. We take trips to the park. By trade, Caleb is a carpenter and music teacher. One Christmas, he jigsaw-cut wooden, animal string puppets for the kids. Another time, when Connor was three, he took on a massive project. He constructed a bulldozer bed that I designed. It had a full-cab with working levers, rope pull-drawers, and the front scoop was a lower-half toy box, upper-half desk. Josh and Caleb's relationship has long moved on from past transgressions. I admire that their relationship reflects joy and meaning. Before departing, Caleb and Josh put together a wardrobe closet from Ikea for me. Caleb slandered the cheap particle board only once.

Surrounded by a modicum of fanfare, Caleb and Josh pack up the Beamer and drive to the far ends of north. Our relief is immediate. The kids are in a realistic place: secure they have a father, yet not sorry to see him go.

6
TRANSFORMATION

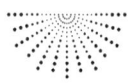

*N*ow that Josh is gone, I can focus on my own wellness with some blunt honesty. A decade ago, I could have easily turned around a surge of added pounds, but hormones are different in your forties; the body is less forgiving. Five to ten pounds per decade—the fee for growing old— is a myth I accepted; my body succumbed. Added weight began to stick like glue when I began devouring a container of ice cream before I even pulled out of the grocery store parking lot. The car door pocket held a stash of plastic spoons for my secret rendezvous with Ben and Jerry. Much clothing has become tight and uncomfortable. My skin is dreary and reddish. My energy— Forget about it! But something else went hand in hand with my physical decline. I felt mediocre as a person, as if my tombstone epitaph would read: *Here lies an exceptional mother and a mediocre woman.* What a shame to shy away from my own greatness. It is one reason we are here.

Attempts to lower my carb intake did not magically shrink my rounding waistline. Drastic attempts to eat less food lead to binge eating later. Peri-menopause has likely been a significant factor. But I thought it was all a lack of discipline on my part. That was my belief until...

Website video algorithms led my health searches to a micro-understanding that sugar and carbs change the gut biome. The pH goes askew (more acidic), the resulting bacteria causes bloating and the craving to eat more of the same. Studies have long revealed the effects of sugar and its cronies (high fructose corn syrup, maltodextrin, red dye 40, etc) on the brain; effects are like cocaine. My take-away to reboot my myself is that stronger willpower and discipline will not work alone to fix the situation. Changing the gut biome is the big ticket. I take pin the updated science as well as admit that my body has an addiction. The bacteria wants what it wants.

Acceptance, even on a small level, brings relief because tackling this requires big gun strategies outside of my usual ideas and thinking patterns. If I do not admit my body has an addiction, then I am a hypocrite. This a private luxury to say I have a sugar addiction without judgements. Whether I jog or not, whether I salad or not, if my gut biome is not different, I am not running the show on the choices I crave.

Beginning weight: 143 pounds. This is not the healthy, fit, feminine version I knew in my early twenties. The only other time I hit that weight was full-term pregnant with Connor. My high school graduation weight was a non-athletic 117 pounds. Since then my weight gain averages out to a pound per year.

IT'S ALL ABOUT INSULIN

My change begins in two ways: (1) Drastic sugar cutback (2) Watching weight loss videos of others; I need their mojo, their proof...to hear the talk and watch the walk so I can enter the transformation game. No more devouring pints of ice cream in the parking lot or in front of the TV 2-3x per week. I cutback to a single pint with lower sugar and no corn syrup 1-2x per week.

This means good-bye marshmallow swirls and caramel centers. I also self-ban parking lot binges; no more private dairy parties.

Meals are planned days in advance. Fewer trips to the grocery store equals less temptation to buy crap food. Salads become interesting playgrounds of healthy ingredients with a side of yogurt. Fat does more than add flavor; it satiates the appetite and buffers insulin stimulation. This kind of balanced lunch helps me to avoid snack stops on the way home from work, such as, a yummy chocolate croissant with a cup of hot chocolate. Instead, on my drive home, I listen to success stories and expert information by Dr. Eric Berg and others about ketosis, how sugar affects insulin and how insulin influences hormones.

A particular video grabs me by author and motivational speaker Gabby Bernstein. She discusses with major tenacity about her positive outcomes stemming from the elimination of sugar. Already a thin, attractive woman, Gabby speaks of better energy, focus, sleep, skin, and mood. She interviews therapist, Jessica Ortner, about the strategy EFT (Emotional Freedom Technique) tapping created by her brother. An intro lesson explains the technique of finger tapping on pressure points while repeating truthful statements about addiction. This builds and is replaced by positive affirmations. EFT taps into the subconscious with a method of find, remove and replace. These affirmations *spark seeds* that grow in this restored energy pattern.

Heck, if a towering tree can grow from seeds, I can at least try. The subconscious is not a bad place to start. Fair to say that might begin with a seed of weirdness. The EFT strategy involves tapping on facial and upper body pressure points in a repeated cycle to decrease addiction cravings. I follow along as the therapist's finger tips tap around the eye orbit, mouth frenulum, chin, below the collar bone, and under the arm pit. Simultaneously, we say phrases such as, *I am addicted. I am so addicted. I know it's not good for me. I feel caught in this addiction. I can't stop. One cookie turns into four. I don't know what to do about this addiction.*

U-turn time; we switch to say the following: *But I'm willing to change. I want to let it go. I know that can be powerful. I believe there is a way. I don't have to be addicted. I don't have to stay stuck in this pattern. I can surrender my will to change. I guess I trust this tapping thing. I can take it one day at a time. I can do my best today. I can do my best today.*

As silly as it seems, I drive to and from work tapping on my face like it's a keyboard. Out loud I voice, "I am addicted to sugar. I cannot stop even though it makes me feel sick...." I also do the quantifying before and after tapping. Using a 1 to 10 scale, I quantify desperate cravings with an 8 or 9; mild cravings at a four, and a fleeting urge as a 2. Believe me after fifteen minutes of tapping, the score does budge 0.5 here; 1.0 there. Day after day the subconscious begins to purge itself. The mind knows what it is hiding. Anything that feels unwell, the mind wants to expel which the affirmations do like a gentle washing machine. The sessions become honest conversations within myself. One choice at a time leads to change. Feeling ready for action I wrap up doing EFT.

BUYING a new digital scale with ounces, instead of my ancient dial scale, was a game changer. Some days, there is an 8-ounce weight loss I would not have otherwise known. Every day I ledger my weight including the ounces. I also make note of every walk, yoga session and exercise effort. Week to week the progress unfolds and the scale befriends me! By the second week 5-6 pounds are gone. My pants are less snug. Eventually, I bounce off 131.2 and stay at 133.8 which is a nine-pound weight loss. Here I remain stuck. I cannot budge the scale beyond a 10-pound loss; I need to focus more on other areas of my life. So, a 133 pounds becomes the new "set weight". With the few eating and activity changes in place I can maintain this weight without keeping notes, tapping or the super-strict eating habits.

My education remains steadfast about ketosis, intermittent fasting, autophagy (a Nobel prize discovery) and the insulin-to-hormone relationship. What I knew growing up was close to wrong and full of information led by corporate marketing agendas, not health. As my focus shifts back to other areas in my life, I continue to stocking knowledge about health because I have a secret. Tucked away is a deep goal: get below 125 pounds. This goal is not just about weight loss. I want the fortitude that gets me to such a far-reach goal. If I can harvest that power, then *what else is possible for me?*

7
AUTUMN FALL-DOWN

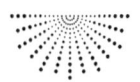

Along the Canadian coastline of polite social graces, lobster traps, and greasy poutine, Josh reconstructs his life. Caleb and Jaqueline own an expansive waterfront property. Their house overlooks a serene river. The wooded banks are lined with private docks and tiny piers. At the wide bend a modest wharf bustles with fisherman unloading their catch of wriggling nets. Scattered across the horizon is a dumped crayon-box of sunny boats. The skinny colored hulls with curving sails zig-zag across the water with careless harmony and joy.

On land Caleb is no nonsense about his son attending AA meetings. Josh must also pull his weight with household chores in exchange for residency. The town has limited clinical job opportunities which is a shame. Josh spent a lifetime achieving professional skills that make a difference to his patients. It is not just an identity; it is his purpose. He tries different laborer opportunities to no avail. Josh pleads to me a case for securing a job near us. He already accomplished a preliminary interview and things looked promising. My response?

"Welcome to try, but you can't stay here."

Josh arranges to stay with Rodger, a contractor friend he stayed with another time he came to visit us long ago. Rodger lives in the other corner of town in a house he built. The A-frame lodge is constructed with ceiling wood beams and floor to ceiling windows that showcase woods so dense that the home remains unnoticeable from the road. Josh rents the bedroom downstairs next to the garage which he had rented before. He shares a bathroom with Rodger's 18-year-old young son, Samuel. This time around, Josh has a mattress off the floor, and he can afford a second-hand desk. Rodger considers himself magnanimous to only charge $500 per month for this small space despite that Josh is unemployed.

The kids still light up as Dad walks through the door; it's been a few months since they last saw him. There is a feeling of hope Josh's sobriety and interest in his family might become the new normal. Josh offers his appreciation to have another chance. "Last time I know I embarrassed all of you. I understand having a healthy distance; staying at Rodger's place is fine. I will get a job and help out financially, as I should." We respond with a charcuterie board of smiles and crossed-fingers. He delivered quite a *bottom's-up soliloquy*. We hope he means it.

An employment recruiter has a couple possibilities on the burner for Josh. During this limbo period, Rodger employs Josh on some renovation job. Josh has been sober for two-to-three months. Josh said Caleb often sat next to him at meetings which he found embarrassing; it made him feel like a kid.

A second round of job interviews leads to an offer. Josh accepts despite a complication: the start date is weeks away. More limbo, further boredom, no job structure…his sobriety will be tested.

Autumn trickles to winter, daylight hours dwindle. The early twilight and coldness put a squeeze on outdoor activities. Rodger has no more project-jobs to offer. Boredom seeps into Josh's life like fresh cut sap on a wounded tree; he can't shake it.

I welcome Josh to be an involved parent anytime, but he is inconsistent with visiting; parenting was never his forte. The kids are not allowed to go over to Rodger's—my rule. However, I come to find out (Mom instincts) Connor snuck over there a couple times.

"I wanted to hang out with Dad and Rodger. They talk about cool stuff. They made me a steak." I get it. Hanging with mom is no substitute for an alpha cave. I remove the option of deceit by allowing short visits for Connor.

While waiting for an employment start date, Josh fills his days with endless walks and the task of splitting wood. He chops wood for Rodger's grand fireplace. He chops wood for our dishwasher-sized fireplace. He chops bonfire wood for the neighbors on the left and the right. A man can only throw an axe for so long…feel useless for so long…live in a house where your roommates drink before…

"Either you tell Rodger, or I will. Rodger said you could stay if you didn't drink." My power play to nip-this-slip is that Josh cares what Rodger thinks.

"It's not your problem," Josh barks with agitation.

"Fix it." I bark back.

Josh admits the drinking slip to Rodger. Rodger in turn admits to me, "I got to be honest Jess, it is hard not to drink in front of him. I'm trying, you know, but I like to drink, right? I keep telling Josh rehab will get your head straight." Rodger speaks from the unfortunate experience of taking his oldest son to rehab. His son turned things around; he had a lot going for him. Then, a single relapse at the old dose took his son's life.

Finally, an employment offer with a start date is official. Josh starts work after New Year's. This time child support may actually happen! I will get to financially rebuild my life, have money to manage house repairs, and afford some family fun. A complication to this near-distant start date is that Rodger and his girlfriend leave for a holiday vacation to Florida. This removes a huge presence of accountability in Josh's home; except for Rodger's youngest son, Samuel. At age eighteen, Samuel will have zero influence.

"No need for worry," Josh claims. He says he is fine despite the snow, the cold, and no friends to call. Although he attends some recovery meetings, he separates himself from the others. "The meetings are run by volunteers. I already know everything."

He visits us 3-4 days a week when he is not wearing himself out chopping wood. Despite Josh being on my mind like a sickness, I mentally ignore touching the reins to his life. But it does not matter what my plan is. Josh's addiction takes its hold and splits Josh into two versions of himself. One version is the calm, helpless, in-denial victim who says, "I know I need to cut down." The other version is stumbling, angry, aloof, sad, and a raw nerve who barks, "You don't know what you're talking about Jess-i-ca." This is all familiar territory. Fortunately, Josh and I have matured past our old patterns of escalation. Instead of arguing, we bark, we listen, consider, and then leave each other to his or her own. But sadly the time has come to inform Josh he cannot come over anymore. A drunk dad is unacceptable in our home. "If you need help Josh, call 911."

Not My Problem

Athena's coffee shop makes a delicious mocha-cappuccino with coconut milk. The shop door jingles as I enter. By the bay window I notice Samual at a bistro table diving into a breakfast bagel. I wave then ask, "How's Josh? It's been days since we last spoke."

"Don't know. I'm staying with my mom. Was there yesterday to get some clothes. From the hall he looked asleep." Samual takes another bite of his egg and cheese.

Back in my, hot cappuccino in hand, I ponder on this information. Across the street is the town's center park. In front of tree-sized holly bushes are a pair of cement-carved chess tables with rod-iron chairs, a thoughtful donation by the local Woman's Club. Viewing nature and sipping my cappuccino has calmed me into a reflective moment. An awareness strikes at my morals. Am I the only person wondering if Josh has a pulse right now? Who does it serve to pretend otherwise?

Rodger's garage door is unlocked. It is a simple walk down the cold hallway to Josh's bedroom. On a bare bones bed lies his body, motionless, under layers of blankets. I tip toe past a bag of sour gummy-patch kids and a half-eaten bag of chips. A near empty vodka bottle stands tall beside the bed. I kneel down to eyeball if the blanket rises and falls. It does; he is breathing. On the desk I leave some bananas I brought, then exit unseen.

Gathered around a Monopoly board game active with colored money and property cards strewn about the floor, the kids bring up their dad. Before I can gently break the news, Connor asks point blank, "Is he drinking again?"

"Yes, I'm sorry."

Jolie rolls the dice. "What is he doing?"

"He's sleeping. I can tell he snacked on some things."

Connor flips up his hands. "He could have stopped so many times." Nicky does not comment.

"I'm not sure what to do kids." They continue their game. None of us have more to say about it. I do not know what the universe wants from me. The marriage is gone. Having a husband is gone. All I owe him is to care; otherwise, I am no better than his addiction.

The following day brings relief as Josh visits us on his own accord. Guess he knew the bananas were from me. He is cleaned up, but his conversational speech is delayed. His brain is not right. He receives no fanfare. The boys focus on their X-box game. Jolie is drawing in one of her many sketch books. Maybe Josh expects me to bridge the gap with them, but I am done with that. He does not inquire about our lives. He departs when he probably needs his next drink.

The sun sets on another couple days with no communication from Josh. I am compelled to check on his existence. Through Rodger's front window I can see Josh. He is sitting on the sofa's edge like a statue, hands on his knees, gazing at the floor in a room of loneliness. As the uninvited voyeur to this struggle, I feel perplexed. Out of respect for his choices, I drive away to go food shopping. And then…

I return to peer in the window, again. Josh is still in the same spot in the same exact position. With the notion to help him, a sense of peace washes over me. This is not to save him—familiar territory my ego has wandered. This act is to lend a hand, so this man can stand back up.

Rodgers's cabin looking house has an open-concept living room, dining room and kitchen design. Josh appears frozen opposite-facing the rough-edged fireplace, not that he is looking at it. Lying on the granite countertop is a rotting package of raw chicken. Josh does not lift his chin to speak until I am standing right in front him. "There's something in my eye. I can't seem to get it out."

"Here, let me see." My coat brushes his jeans as I kneel down. "Both your eyes have fire engine streaks."

"It's this one," he says squinting his left eye.

Gently I hold open his eyelid. "Look side to side for me. Ah, there it is." I pull my sleeve over my finger, and touch the black piece of grit, removing it from his eye. "There you go." I push aside an Aztec sofa pillow and scoot beside him.

Josh blinks. Rubs his irritated eye. "You did it. That is so much better. I've been trying for hours. I couldn't find it in the mirror."

"How much worse do things have to get?"

"I'm thinking about suicide. I can picture it. Nothing makes sense anymore."

"That warrants a hospital, Josh. We have each worked in hospitals. You know they can keep you safe."

"I don't know what to do."

"You could call an ambulance." Josh does not answer. "Over there on the counter a vulture wouldn't touch that chicken. It's worse than roadkill."

"I try to eat, but I get sick. I know it's bad."

"Tomorrow is Christmas Eve Josh. Call an ambulance if you need one."

"They won't be able to get to this house. How can they find it? It's back here in the woods."

"It's behind another house. They'll find it."

"How do I call an ambulance?"

"I'm not playing games Josh."

"My phone is dead. I can't find the charger."

I locate his charger. At the sink I add tap water to the vodka bottle. "Your phone is plugged in by the lamp. You are justified to call an ambulance."

"I will call them if I need to call them," he says across the room with robotic inflection. His only movement is to wipe his eye. He has grown thin. His aura matches the gray poultry I bag up along with the cutting board. On the counter I leave an apple and some cheddar, one of his favorite snacks.

"Good-bye Josh."

Already stone carved and mute, his eyes are locked back toward the floor. My kids are going to lose their father for Christmas.

A LIT-UP CHRISTMAS tree does add magic to a home, especially as we gather around on the tree's base branches to finish gift wrapping. Conner, Jolie and Nicky had each picked out their own household family gifts. Nicky proudly chose a mini-screw driver kit from his school's Santa shop. "Do you think

Dad will like it? I don't think he has one. He can keep it in his car."

"Dad will like it." I toss him a zip lock bag with bows in it.

"Will Dad come with us tomorrow? To Uncle Greg's Christmas Eve party?" Connor asks.

"No, he is not."

"Why not?" Jolie asks.

"When I last saw him, he was not feeling well."

"Is he coming over Christmas morning?" Nicky asks as he slides his dad's gift under the decorated branches.

"Dad's coming over for Christmas, right?" Connor is taping double bows on all his gifts to us.

All of them are looking at me. Only one answer makes sense in their world. I have been living in a different one. "I guess so."

Jolie grabs a wrapped box from under the tree with her name on it. Gives it a vigorous shake. "Can we open a present tonight. Just one gift each?"

"We totally can on Christmas Eve; not the eve before the Eve." I make super big eyes at her and smile.

Connor stands up and discreetly waves me to follow him down the hall. "Mom, I want to show you something." We enter his surfer themed bedroom. He takes out his phone. Connor says, "I saw this documentary video about a kid in his twenties. He was going into rehab. He kept waiting, then he got really scared."

We watch the video made by the girlfriend. The young man is carried out of his house on a stretcher. They are going to a hospital, then a rehab center. The boyfriend's sweet face turns directly towards the camera. "I hope I make it." He and his girlfriend linger in touch as they part ways. The girlfriend tells the camera she did everything she could. They did not have a happy ending; he was too far gone. After one week in the rehab center this kid in his young twenties died. The video was made as part of his desire, then final wish, to help others.

Connor's self-education does not help him solve how to get his dad into rehab. It does not dissolve his agony, confusion or pain as the child of an alcoholic currently in crisis. The education did, however, germinate empathy for what happens to us all when fear and life's problems gets too big to handle alone. My son does not know how close his father is to death; I do. But I am numb, and I am so tired of this bullshitI already know everythingI already know everything— *Snap out of it!* An alarm booms in my head watching my son walks away. Working in a trauma hospital for eight years I read countless charts about moments like these, when victims and families wish they could turn back time...when the car struck the pole, the wave pulled him under, the arm got amputated. If these stories could rewind to the turning point that made the difference...things might turn out all right, or at least better than tragic.

Before me is such a moment. I make the decision. My children WILL NOT lose their father Christmas morning.

Precarious Gifts

Back to Rodgers house, standing over a sparse, twin bed. I nudge his shoulder. "Hey. Would you like to come over tonight for Christmas Eve?"

"Yes, I'd love that." Josh is still wearing the same flannel jacket shirt from days ago. Long facial whiskers show his expanding white-grays.

"Clean yourself up. I will come pick you up after my brother's party. You can stay the night on Nicky's bunk bed."

"You will have me? Thank you."

"You're welcome."

"Is tomorrow really Christmas?"

"It is. Hopefully, the hospital waiting room won't be busy. This makes sense we're going, right?"

"Yes."

"First, we open presents with the kids; then breakfast, then the hospital."

"Presents and coffee," he repeats, then closes his eyes.

UNCLE GREG AND AUNT ANNE, my brother and sister-n-law, always host a winning buffet for Christmas Eve. The lobster ravioli and gnocchi come freshly made from their favorite restaurant. The pastas run out second to the prime rib. My dad whispers to me that he is going in for a second helping. Later, I secretly catch him going back for a third. His longtime girlfriend, CJ, rolls her eyes.

My Dad, CJ, and I find a quiet spot near the warmth of the fireplace. He listens without comment as I explain the rapid descent of Josh's health, and my plan to grab Josh on the way home. "After the kids have Christmas morning with both parents, I will drive him to the hospital."

"Why not pick him up tomorrow morning, instead of tonight?" My concerned father inquires.

"This fosters some dignity. The promise of tonight got him through today. He already texted that he showered. The kids have gifts for him. Jolie made him a card. Don't worry, we're safe."

My Dad leans in. "It's my job to worry about you peanut."

"I know.

He continues. "I am proud of you for giving Josh the chance to measure up. It is probably not easy for him to provide for his family when he doesn't know what his role is anymore."

"He should have that figured out," interjects CJ.

"I know. But he needs to start holding a job," my father insists.

CJ raises her merlot glass in agreement.

I interject. "At least the hospital will keep him with the symptoms he is having. Then we can piece together Josh starting a job and keeping it for a month until his benefits kick in. Then rehab is a viable option, if he still needs it."

"When he still needs it," CJ punctuates. This is not her first rodeo. Her second husband was an alcoholic. Her first husband drowned while trying to save another man out in the ocean. Families on the beach watched in horror as it all unfolded. Another man tried to help them. CJ, along with her 8-year-old-son, watched all three men die. She finishes her last drop of wine. "You need anything, honey, you call us."

"I'll call you tomorrow morning," my father says in a low voice with his arm around me. "Make sure you pick up your phone."

BACK HOME IT is family time around the Christmas tree. Josh pleasantly smells of soap and mouthwash.

"Hey Dad! Mom said we can open a gift tonight," Jolie says as she bops and twirls around the living room. The ruffles of her plaid nightgown dance around her ankles.

Connor crawls on the floor, shaking and listening to various gift boxes. Ornaments of gingerbread cookies and puzzle-pieces glued to grade school photos hang on the pine branches. "I don't want a box with pajamas in it." He pushes aside a rectangular box that contains, I'd bet a million dollars on it, pajamas.

Comfortably sitting on the floor by the tree I suggest to my son, "Maybe Mrs. Claus didn't get you pj's this year."

"You always get us pj's," says Nicky who is currently wearing the footy-pajamas from last Christmas.

"If I had footsie pajamas like yours, I'd wear them," says Josh pulling Nicky onto his lap.

Santa mugs are filled with hot chocolate and stirred by candy canes. No one is disappointed with their Christmas Eve gifts. The kids go to bed late filled with holiday excitement. Each child is oblivious to the serious medical condition of their father. I still have stocking gifts to wrap. This should be a nice task for Josh and me to share as partners; except, he is talking incessantly. Repeatedly, he sits, he stands, his hovering is up my ass. Perhaps he is high on conversation and attention from another human, but it is so annoying. His voice grows louder, he begins to— "Joshua, stop! You're driving me crazy!"

"What?" His body halts, hands in the air.

"All of this," waving my hands up and down his personal space. "You were supposed to be helpful, or tired, or weak and feeble. At least whisper. The kids are asleep."

His head tilts like a loyal dog trying to read the mind of his caretaker. He wants be a good boy.

"You have been of no help wrapping. I need to sleep. My eyes are burning. There's Benadryl in the bathroom if you can't fall asleep."

Josh frowns. His bushy brows go down. Then he asks the hundred-dollar question. "Is there anything else, besides the Benadryl?"

My arms fold as tight as my lips. "There will be no night cap, no breakfast beer and no sympathy. This is your option. If you want to wake up with your children, then tough it out."

His wagging tail drops. His strung-out energy dissipates. I disappear downstairs to my bedroom behind the curtain. Putting up a wall with a door would have cost more. Genuinely, I hope he stays and shares Christmas morning with us. Josh seems to be on the wrong side of his life; the other side is worth the fight. Josh equates getting sober to entering a boxing ring or jail with a death sentence. On the contrary, he has taken too many blows to see he has been in the ring for far too long. My wish is to usher him into a safer place, a professional place. Somewhere he can build his autonomy and self-worth. Somewhere not so close to the flame.

Christmas morning came fast. Little feet creak the floor boards upstairs as they scamper from room to room. I can hear the boys piling on Jolie to wake her up. Ah, they are opening the stockings without! I dash upstairs in my red and green striped jammies. I want to watch their faces. Crinkled holiday paper is tossed and strewn about the living room. The boys discover rubber band shooters, soccer hackie sacks, and protein bars. There is a tiny glass penguin for Nicky's animal collection. Jolie likes her nail polish and lip gloss. In the TV room past the kitchen Josh slumbers on the sofa.

I grab a couple mugs and a Chai tea box. "Good morning Papa Bear. Would you like some coffee?"

"Hmm, good-morning. That would be lovely." He cracks a thin grin.

"Then you'll have to make it." I tussle his thick hair. "I suck at making coffee."

"I know."

"If you prefer Chai, I can make two cups."

"No, I'll get up. I could barely sleep last night. This does not feel good. DTs are scary. It feels like your own body is screaming itself to death in a weird, physical agony."

"I'm sorry it's so difficult. The hospital will help."

"They can't make it any worse."

"Dad!" Nicky runs over.

"Hey, Dad! Merry Christmas!" Connor fires a rubber band with a cute, sly grin. It bounces off my shoulder. "Thanks for the stocking gifts, Mom. Is breakfast soon?"

"Yes."

Jolie slumps onto the kitchen counter. She closes her eyes and moans, "I need coffee."

Josh asks, "When did you start drinking coffee?"

"She doesn't," I say taking no offensive to Jolie's joke.

"That's right," Josh says checking out Connor's rubber-band shooter. "No soda, no sweetened drinks, no coffee. Your mom will have us all living to be a hundred!" Josh's face is pale and worn. He pulls a blanket tightly around himself. We all finish unwrapping. Josh watches us from his cocoon peep-hole as we tear into our gifts with an orderly, turn-taking fashion until our excitement wanes to hunger. Devoured stacks of buttermilk blueberry pancakes fill our bellies. Josh nibbles on dry toast.

As promised my father calls to check in. He is pleased to hear the overnight Christmas mission got accomplished safely. Dad and CJ offer to watch the kids at my dad's house while I take Josh to the hospital. Pop-pop has all the holiday classics on VHS tape. Yup, Dad still uses a VCR.

"Thank you. I'll drop the grandkids off in a bit."

"I'm looking forward to having them over," my father says in his upbeat tone. "If you need anything, give a call."

The emergency room is not crowded. Josh and I enter together. I drive home alone. There is light snowfall on the road ahead. The flakes melt into droplets on the hood and windshield. I watch them pile up until out of necessity the wipers brush everything clear. A relief stirs in my core. It is Christmas Day. Everything is okay. Everyone I love is okay. It is a pretty big gift receive even from Santa.

8
JUNKYARD PARTS

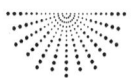

We make it out of our winter storms with my ex-husband employed; however, he is lofting into warmer days with fragile sobriety. Residency at Rodgers provides him bare bones stability; it will have to do. The new clinical job has progressed without a hitch. Does this mean Momma Bear finally receives child support? Nope, it does not. Soon, I will report his job to the state. I thought, if Josh builds a nest egg of financial security for himself first, he will maintain feeling stable. Proper footing precedes taking care of others. There are times Josh readily assists by paying for groceries, soccer shoes or a trip to the snack bar. In the meantime, support monies accrue as back-pay. Maybe, one day in a galaxy far, far away, I will see some of that.

"Hey kids," my announcement comes over the scraping of dinner plates into the sink, "Pop-pop and Grandma-CJ are taking us to Dippy's for ice cream."

"Woo-hoo!" Shout Jolie and Nicky from the TV room.

Connor, my young teen with a popping social life, will not be joining us. He and *his crew* are out swimming and grilling. There are five of them that have been friends since kindergarten. This year each of their voices started to change. My friend Natasha did not fully recognize Lucas's new voice the first time she heard it. For a moment she thought a strange man had come into her house. More drastic for me was the time Connor and I squeezed past each other in the hallway. He had just come out of the shower, so he was shirtless. He was taller, broader, muscular…flashing before me was shoulder, chest, chest, shoulder— When did this *man* get here? Why is he calling me *Mom* in a deep voice?

Oddly, the grandparents are running late this evening. Josh stops over for a brief visit. He watches a little Japanese Anime with Nicky and Jolie. Our fatso furball Hamlet is meowing at the kitchen window. I crank it open so Hamlet can jump outside. As I do, my dad's Acura drives by, at least, I thought it was his car. He did not stop. I wonder if it is because Josh's car is parked out front? The other night at the baseball field Dad made his disapproval, or rather his disdain, toward my ex-husband known. When Dad and CJ arrived at the bottom of the second inning, CJ sat next to Josh and I to watch Nicky play. Dad sat further down the same bleacher; we waved. Under the bright lights of the little league field Dad's message, that he did not approve of how Josh treated his only daughter, rang clear.

Our team's 8- and 9-year-olds left the field with their baseball caps down from the loss. Dad and CJ offered to take Nicky and I out for ice cream. I declined. Nicky enthusiastically went with his grandparents.

Perhaps my father kept driving past our house to avoid his ex-son-in-law. Maybe, it was not his car. After a few unreturned phone calls, Nicky, Jolie and I go over to my father's house. The jet-black Acura is not in his drive way.

"Maybe they are at CJ's house," Jolie suggests as she knits in the backseat. Knitting is not a typical 13-year-old activity except in our town. Last year's *after school knitting class* produced a dozen or so pre-teen knitters. The happy result was all the parents got scarves for Christmas.

CJ's house phone is going to voice mail. After twenty years, they still do not live together. My voice message states that I hope Dad is not ignoring us as part of some emotional angst. We are still waiting to go, but will happily take a raincheck.

As a man of his word, it is totally unlike my dad to not show up. At age 66, his life revolves around four worlds: his partner CJ; Greg and I; our combined six grandkids; and a local theater company in which Dad has been the club president for a dozen years. Acting for him began in high school. He is a pretty good actor, an even better director. CJ is always by his side handling the props. When I was a kid, I used to love running lines with my dad. Usually it was musicals like Oklahoma, South Pacific or Man of La Mancha. The first play I managed to stay awake until the end was Oliver Twist. He played the bad guy. Staying awake meant I got to watch Dad get shot and fall backwards off a bridge. He took Greg and I backstage to see the three-mattresses piled up to catch his fall.

Dad and CJ never show to take us out for ice cream.

LATE THAT EVENING, wrapped in a cashmere blanket, I curl up on the sofa to watch the evening news alone. The only source of light is from the television. With a warm cup of chamomile tea, I listen to a monotone anchorman discuss how the Ebola virus outbreak is worsening in West Africa...low oil prices are damaging the economy...Russia's aggression toward Ukraine looms larger, but sanctions might hold Moscow at bay. The anchorman announces it is time for the local news. At this precise moment, a disturbing sensation hits me. It feels like a tiny hedgehog crawled under my skin and ran up my spine. The prickly critter scratches down my arms and chest—then poof—it's gone. The sensation is replaced with an odd sense of peace. A thought slipped much like a tooth left under a pillow for the tooth fairy: *turn off the tv; keep him for one more day.* Robotically I comply and go to bed not fully realizing the depth of sorrow being held at bay.

николай Next Morning

Next Morning

In a barely lucid state, I hear a knock at the front door. Not wanting to leave my warm, cozy bed I burrow further under the covers. Murmurs of Connor talking with my brother echo above. Greg has never come here this early, especially before work. The door of the basement creaks open.

"Mom," Connor shouts down, "uncle Greg is here."

Blue-jeans and a dreary sweatshirt slip over my numb psyche with ease. My wavy, straw-broom hair condenses into a ponytail. Calmly ignoring all fear I sense what is to come: deliverance of information, the kind I read in hospital charts. My clinical mind is my safe space. Working in an intensive care unit for over 8 years I read countless trauma charts. Under the tab labeled "Physician's Reports" a patient's entire tragedy is reduced to a few sentences: 66 y.o. male driver in MVA (motor vehicle accident) arrived by ambulance. Sustained multiple fractures, possible head trauma and heart attack.

Climbing the stairs, I stoically tell myself, *all I need to do is get through the sentences.*

"Hey," I whisper glancing around the kitchen. Connor has left to get ready for school; his siblings have not yet risen.

Greg leans against the white farmhouse sink. He is awkwardly silent. He attempts to speak, but his lips tighten. A stream of tears fall down his face. He does not even try to stop them. "Jessie—" Emotions cut him off. He wraps his arms around my shoulders. He hugs me tight, very, very tight. My arms do not respond. I await *the sentences.*

"At 5:30 this morning the police called." Greg's voice is at a rasp. "They had news about Dad." My brother steps back. I have not seen him cry since he was little.

"Greg, I know something happened." I want to make it easier for him. "Dad didn't show up last night. Which hospital is he at?"

"I don't know Jessie. They were in a car accident...."

MY FATHER and his gal of twenty years, a grandmother to our children, had taken an old-fashioned Sunday afternoon drive down by the peach orchards and farm fields. The two-lane roads gently roll along horse and cow pastures, past peach cider stands and irrigation systems shooting water across acres of farm fields. An enormous tree dominated the intersection where Dad and CJ made a traffic stop. That Oak tree, perhaps, obstructed his view as a history of accidents at that corner would later reveal. Emerging from the stop sign, my father must not have seen the F-150 truck hitched to a ninety-foot camper. This also meant the F-150 truck driver did not see my father in time to avoid impact. Still, there must have been a moment when they all knew.

His Acura flew across the road. It rolled several times from the collision with the F-150 truck pulling a ninety-foot camper, an unstoppable mass in a short amount of time. Multiple emergency vehicles from multiple townships arrived at the scene. It made the evening news. The driver of the F-150 truck hitched to a ninety-foot camper had no injuries requiring hospitalization.

My brother and I visit the junk yard. We need to see the car.

"It's way in the back," says the whiskered old guy behind the counter. He takes the time to look us in the eye.

We pass row after row of busted cars. The crunch of our footsteps over gravel is the only eerie sound in this rusted graveyard of neglected cars. In front of a towering, wooden fence we see Dad's Acura. Immediately shock takes its hold. The horrific sight forces comprehension: there was no survival. The once sporty, black waxed hood has been completely torn and mangled. The windshield was forcibly shattered. The roof simply crumpled like paper. The driver's side crushed onto itself like the hood. Dad's car has become a violent tombstone.

As somber devastated children peering into the destruction before us, we circle the metal wreckage in silence. The front seats, surprisingly, and dashboard are intact except for the ruptured airbags dangling in explosive disarray. CJ's door remains uncrushed. One of her shoes is on the floor. I open the door and grab her black loafer off the car mat. When I do, I see her purse is there just under the seat.

When I had turned off the news, and when I heard Greg's murmured voice, I knew tragedy had struck. What I did not expect. What shook my heart was that death took them both. Death took my father and death took our sweet CJ. They each held a piece of each another, but we are forever denied even a slither's visit, because death stole that, too. It vehemently ripped them from our lives. That is just the way it is.

Our families are in agreement to have their funerals together. There is a layer of peace that Dad and his southern belle left this earthly plane together. It is a miraculous gift of closure that open caskets are an option for them both. Many guests at the funeral are members of their theater company. Dad was infamous for his opening curtain speeches, because—and I say this without pride—there was always a slap-stick, Dad joke.

Ladies and gentlemen, before you arrived, did you hear the distressing news? A ship full of red sailors collided with a ship full of blue sailors. But don't you worry. Don't you fret. Search parties were ordered to scour the seas all night long to find the maroon-ed men. Ba-dum—ching! Curtain call.

DURING THE FUNERAL, my mom tells the story of how they met back in high school at a basketball game on Valentine's Day. She, a junior cheerleader, was on the court cheering away with her pompoms and saddle shoes. Tucked in the stands my father, a freshman at Drexel, had returned to watch his high school alma mater get an ass whoopin'. Turns out, he could not take his eyes off a particular cheerleader with the prettiest smile. His smooth move was to offer Mom a ride home. On their first official date Dad took Mom to a soda shop for ice cream.

My eulogy speech is last. I speak of Dad singing to my brother and I as he played the coolest of instruments: the electric accordion. This monstrous, bellowing contraption must have weighed fifty pounds. Dad played it with finesse. *The Age of Aquarius* was my favorite request, since he and I are both aquarians. We also share a common playfulness. I tell a childhood story of this one time when Dad had globed toothpaste on the underside of my bedroom doorknob.

Out the bathroom window he yelled, "Jessica, get in here and clean your room!"

I announce to the funeral parlor full of guests, "I knew my room was clean. But I listen to my father and go inside. I get to my bedroom door, turn the knob. Thick, squishy toothpaste oozes between my fingers and sticks to my palm. Dad, hiding behind me in the hall closet to watch my disgust, starts to snicker and giggle like he was twelve. I spin around. He runs down the stairs and out the door, again, like he was twelve. The fact I have any modicum of maturity is a genetic astonishment."

He was my father, my gym partner, my talk-over-oatmeal friend. Dad could be playful, and he could be serious. He was our beloved Pop-pop. And she was our beloved CJ, our loved grandmother. There is no doubt how much we all meant to one another. We had nothing left unsaid. Nicky's baseball team collected money. They gave us a Dippy's Ice Cream gift card. Spiritually, I know it is okay to let my father go. But I don't want to…neither of them.

9
JUNKYARD SKELETON

*I*n our front yard delicate petals of a pink dogwood open into pairs of arched ballerina slippers. Tiered branches of these floating *on pointe* blossoms showcase against a backdrop of freshly painted sage on the house. The benefit of owning a short-in-stature home is that I could paint over the lumpy stucco myself. The earth-tone color palate and craftsman cottage redo blend the house into the surrounding skyscraper pines. Under the dogwood shade, cardinals and sparrows splash in a fluted, patinated birdbath. Beside this popular bird-spa, floribunda rosebushes erupt like magenta fireworks. These roses were purchased with the sympathy card money from my staff. The first rosebush was to symbolize my father; he often brought me flowers. Most memorable were sixteen long-stem roses for my 16th birthday. Rosebush two is for CJ, our southern grandma. The third rosebush honors the life they shared and all that grew from it.

As the weeks passed from the accident, the norm had been that every few days the kids and I saw Josh. Recently, the visits turned random. Todays visit was too short, like the amount of time between needed drinks short. *It* has returned. Exasperated, I seek council with my friend Mike.

"*It* never left." Mike says and laughs at my ignorance. "Addiction waits in the shadows for you. Josh stopped going to meetings. I have enough to do with my own sobriety. I'm not tracking him down." Mike does not advise what I should do. His lifestyle already demonstrates his conviction in skilled recovery and an abstinence from drinking. His life would not contain a wife nor son otherwise.

Holding onto the belief of a therapeutic process toward sobriety, I casually mention to Josh, "A person cannot get fired for seeking treatment."

"Thanks, Jessica. I am fine."

There it is—good talk. Living within the ex-spouse boundaries I let him be…that is…until Josh arrives early for breakfast on a Tuesday and our son is alarmed. Connor pulls me out to the porch. Across the street a weeping cherry tree has yet to go bare. Like Josh, it cannot let go of what it holds dear.

"Mom, why isn't Dad at work? He shouldn't be here offering to make us breakfast."

"I hate to guess the obvious my son."

Connor remains perplexed. "Dad's going to lose his job. Why would he want to go through that again?" Second time around Connor is raising the bar. Before a *half-ass dad* was better than *no dad*. Now "half-ass dad" doesn't cut it.

I pick up what my son puts down. "I will talk to him. You and Jolie should get going so you don't miss the bus." We pause at the door. "Is your baseball game home or away?"

"It's home. I might be pitching."

"All right! The other team better watch out."

"Dope. I'm throwing rockets." Connor flexes his fifteen-year-old guns. He is almost as tall as his father.

Josh leans against the sink washing out the Al-clad fry pan we've had since our wedding. Joining him with a dish towel in hand, I carefully wipe the surface. "Aren't you supposed to be at work?"

"I took the day off," he shakes water drippings from his hands, "I took the next few days off. I think I'm coming down with something."

To observe his functioning level slip away is tough. "Well, I'm glad you're protecting your job."

"I know you're concerned. I admit, it is still difficult being around Rodger. He drinks every evening. He has every right too. I'm only drinking beer and wine; vodka makes me sick. In a couple days I should be able to get through work without a drink. Then I will be back on track."

"Are you going to any meetings?"

"Tonight, Carl and Eddie are picking me up. If you want, I can have them pick me up here. You should meet these guys. I might ask one of them to be my sponsor."

"I would love to meet them."

Josh gives me a one-arm hug around my shoulders. "Do you want me to walk Nicky to school?"

"Let's both walk him. You're welcome to come over for dinner before they arrive." Unbeknownst to Josh, Nicky's school still has in place my order as sole-custodial parent that Josh cannot visit, nor pick any of them up from school, unless I am present.

"That sounds lovely," he says.

Over the course of dinner, the five of us talk about everyone's day. Connor gives the play-by-play of his two strike outs. When it is her turn, Jolie bursts with excitement that she and a couple of other art students were asked to paint a wall mural in the library hallway. Nicky's turn; he yearns for better scooter wheel, ones with faster bearings like Connor's modified scooter. Josh talks about face-timing with his brothers and dad. Apparently, Grandpa is losing his hearing from all the years of working on air force planes. And my turn...gets overlooked.

A Toyota pick-up parks out front. Glad the AA comrades are true. Carl and Eddie come inside for handshakes with the family. Carl has a weird vibe, like he has an overpriced, underperforming car to sell. Carl is in his mid-forties, a decade younger than Josh, and lives with his mom. A severe case of early hair loss spread to Carl's eye brows which I assume he had at one point. Eddie, on the other hand, looks like multiple rough lives got squeezed into one lifetime. His thick wrinkled complexion puts him around late sixties to early eighties. Eddie reminds me of Keith Richard's, the Rolling Stone guitarist rarely seen without a cigarette wedged between his lips.

All three men wave good-bye and sandwich themselves into the cab of Carl's silver pick-up. Within me a sense of hope and trust, about the size of butterfly wings, flutters inside my chest. The butterfly represents Josh's precarious good-willed intentions.

First Domino Falls

Josh hits a curb or something with his old beamer. It is at least a $600 repair. By itself, that could be handled. However, Josh tries to blame Rodger's son for the accident claiming Samuel must have borrowed the car, got in an accident, and didn't fess up. After all, Josh woke-up to a damaged car. This pisses Rodger off, because Rodger knows a black-out drunk period when he sees it. They get into a verbal fight. Rodger kicks Josh out of the house. I call Rodger. It does not go well. Rodger has had enough bullshit. He lays into me even though I am not the intended target.

Josh is invited to stay with us until his car gets fixed, then he has to get a place of his own. First night with us I drive Josh to an AA meeting. We fight on the way, because he is embarrassed to attend while under the influence. I do not give a shit and look for apartments on my phone while I wait in the parking lot.

That is when it hits me. An apartment is not the answer. We are back to needing rehab. And for this, he needs to keep his job for benefits to cover it.

The loss of housing and a friend did smack some reality into my ex-husband. For the next three mornings, functional and sober, Josh drives me to work so he can borrow my car to get to his job; I do not want him to get fired. My efforts are merely a layer glue while Josh struggles to hold his pieces together.

In the past, Josh shared it is difficult to cut back to just beer. Quickly the beer piles up and becomes embarrassing. Continued visits to the liquor store becomes embarrassing. Vodka is convenient, has less smell and provides the illusion, *I can make it last.* It is easier to hide one bottle. I find his current bottle in his work bag, a third of it gone. To this, I say nothing. He is in the throes of it. Something has to change. I need to sit with things; not blow up and disservice myself or him.

The following morning, I propose a deal from which I will not waver. Today is the last day he may use the car, my new car I got a few months back. I point out to him that obviously we —"we" are a team tackling a common enemy—are in crisis mode. Expecting him to stop on his own is not possible, or he would. The plan is reviewed.

"Josh, give notice to your job today that you need to take a medical leave. Do NOT abandon your job. Get in and get out. You have benefits that cover rehab. The whole package available to you."

"That makes sense. I will." He seems sincere and weary. Weariness and exhaustion may be an advantage here. Relief to hang it all up might be enticing enough to get us to the next step. Josh drops me off at work. He is rather dashing in his navy suit. I say before exiting the car, "Sara will pick me up today. Wrap it up neat."

Josh smiles back. "I know." The window rolls up. He drives off. I go into work and take on my patients.

. . .

CROOKED BOB

For many of sixty-some years, Mr. Hauser enjoyed life being over six-feet tall. Not anymore; spinal stenosis has caused a drastic neck curve and rounded shoulders. It causes his head to stick out like a peeking turtle. This kyphotic posture is not why he seeks treatment. His inpatient stay is based on a slow healing, post-surgical, rotator-cuff repair combined with a high risk for falls. His chronic, deteriorating, cervical posture is not the diagnosis of payment, so no one is treating it.

"How long has your neck been like that Mr. Hauser?"

"Call me Bob. It's been years; crept up on me. One day I didn't recognize myself in a photo. I had therapy before, but it didn't make much difference."

I examine his shoulder. His right scapula droops like a curtain sliding off a loose rod. Bob can raise his right arm about 60 degrees, less than half-way. A person needs at least half-range to shave or hair wash. Bob rates his shoulder pain a 7 out of 10, and his neck pain a chronic 5 which comes and goes. He started using a cane a few months ago because his balance became unpredictable.

"Bob, treating your shoulder without addressing your postural alignment won't get us very far. Your posterior musculature is weak and not holding your scapula in place. This causes your right shoulder to droop which in turn causes the left hip to hike up as a compensation, and that effects your lower back. Meanwhile, your upper back rounds forward causing a protrusion of your head. You probably strain your neck just to look up and have a normal field of vision. No wonder you get fatigued and lose your balance."

"What the hell did you just say?"

"I said you're crooked Bob! Tired and crooked!"

"Tell me something I don't know! Look here. I can straighten up for a little while." He lifts his chest and his chin to demonstrate.

I deeply sigh. "You are not straight."

"What ya mean?" Bob lifts his flannel chest more by straightening his docker pant knees. This causes his toes to come off the floor. "I feel like I'm going to fall backwards when I do that."

"Your center of gravity is off because you keep your head forward. Middle for me is with my head over my shoulders. Your center is a couple inches in front of you. The rest of your body is adjusting."

"I guess that makes sense," he says with a purse of his lips.

"Bob, you can't just lift your head to correct everything. You need to grow tall along your whole spine from your tail bone to your head." I demonstrate. "Pull your shoulders down; activate your abdominals. Pull the knee caps up. Then, push down through your heels like this—wait a second." I wheel over a full-length mirror and guide Bob into a more erect posture. Turns out his kyphosis isn't as set in as it appears. "See," I proclaim, "there's a suit and tie stance in you."

"I like it! The arm feels better, too. Got any glue to stick me this way?"

"I have some ideas, but it could get weird. I had special training for stroke patients with motor planning and alignment. I also taught both yoga and Pilates. Lucky for you I love a healthy spine." A wide grin flashes across my face.

"I don't need my legs to go behind my head, just my arm. Can you do that? Scratch your head with your foot?"

"If the itch is annoying enough; not trying to brag, but I can do scorpion pose. It's the same as doing a handstand, but on your forearms. Once in the forearm inversion, you lift your head up while curling your back like a scorpion tail and touch the top of your head with your toes."

"And you want me to get weird?" Bob cradles his right arm on his lap. With many elderly patients, the *fear of pain* is second only to the *fear of falling*. Bob has both to fear. He twists his mouth in thought. A slight lift of his checkered sleeve reveals a faded tattoo—some kind of rope knot with a blurred date.

A lack of confidence shows in his down-turned eyes. "Listen, we can decrease the pain in your arm, possibly your neck, too. I can't promise you'll be six feet again. But you'll get to comb your hair."

"All right," he says. "I can handle weird."

Bob sits on an adjustable high/low mat with a rolling table tray in front of him. We warm up his upper body muscles with some towel slide exercises. Then I get my secret weapon.

Bob declares, "That ball is about as big as you."

Holding the jumbo, apple-red ball I climb onto the mat and explain. "You're going to lean back into this therapy ball. It will support your whole spine and head while I hold it steady. We're in this together; you, me and the ball."

"We're talking to a ball now; nothing weird about that," he says to one of the other patients who pleasantly nods at his comment.

Kneeling behind Bob I sandwich the therapy ball between his back and my front. Using my thighs and body, I press the ball into the curves of Bob's spine. "Lean into the ball," I say. "Press up from the mat." Bob straightens his arms. I externally rotate them at the humerus. Rotating the heads of the humerus brings his shoulder blades nicely towards the spine. It also lifts his rib cage and promotes spinal elongation.

"I feel like Frankenstein, but in a good way."

"Bob, drop your head back to touch the ball, like you're doing a back dive over it."

Bob slowly presses his shoulders against the ball, but his head and neck betray him and strain to stay upward. "Am I there yet?"

"Almost, roll your eyes back. Look for me behind you." Shifting his gaze backwards initiates momentum from the top cervical vertebra. Success! Bob's entire spine arches over the ball. The back of his head makes contact. He is in the complete opposite posture of how he walks around all day long. This exaggeration exercise will help his body find the correct middle-ground.

"Great job. Relax and breathe into the stretch." Bob does as he is asked before steadily returning upright. We repeat this exercise three times, at which point a straight posture feels somewhat comfortable to him because we broadened his range of movement. Not once has he complained about his shoulder.

Sitting side by side on the edge of the mat, it is time to add some function to the session. This is the "occupational" part of occupational therapy. "Bob, I want you to slide you right hand across your lap. Walk your fingers up your shirt and touch each button."

Bob slowly finger-walks up his belly, button by button.

"Pinch your shirt collar Bob. That's it; demand some strength from your shoulder…let go of your collar. Wave… bigger wave from your elbow, good. Now slide your right hand up the back of your neck." Bob's aged hand touches the nape of his neck. "Get tall…rub the back of your head."

Bob's palm brushes back and forth over silver military cut hair. "Look at that. I can't recall the last time this hand touched my hair. Glad I still got some."

Time to achieve a functional goal. We do this again with a comb. Incrementally Bob raises the plastic comb to his right temple. Then Mr. Robert Hauser—former basketball coach, military vet, husband, and grandfather—combs his hair!

Bob slides his arm down to rest on his lap. A cold pack wrapped with a towel is draped over his achy shoulder. Reluctant emotions rise to the surface. He confides. "I haven't been able to brush my teeth properly. My wife has to shave me. It's embarrassing."

"I understand."

"Sometimes that's why I don't want to eat. I feel like a baby trying to feed myself." Elderly Bob grits his teeth. His left-hand pats the right arm in a manner of consolation.

"You were getting by with a difficult injury. The progress you made is yours to keep. Tomorrow you might be sore, but that's okay. Soreness—okay; pain—not okay."

Before the rehab aide wheels Bob away, he points toward the center of my chest and says, "Thanks kiddo. I like weird."

LUNCH TIME; brought my favorite: tuna fish on a croissant. My cell phone flashes. *Why is an auto body shop calling me?* Intrigued, I answer. The male caller asks if I am the owner a Nissan Pathfinder. At first, I forget that I recently traded the Kia for a new Pathfinder. "Oh, yeah, that's my car."

"There was an accident. The police came. The Nissan had to be towed. Your husband is here. Don't worry, he didn't need to go to the hospital, but he doesn't look well."

Still processing here…Josh…accident…my new car. I manage to utter, "*He* is my *ex*-husband."

"I thought he said, well, my mistake. Anyhow, the tow driver noticed that he seemed confused; saw your ex-husband walking around in circles. Maybe he hit his head."

"Interesting. Did you see any blood on his head?" I already know the answer. This question is simply for my amusement while my tattered mind sorts out which emotion to feel. *Round and round the emotions go. Where they stop, nobody knows.*

The tow yard guy responds. "Did I see blood? Ah, no, not that I recall. He's across the room sitting on a bench. The car ma'am, is pretty bad. You'll want the insurance company to take a look. It's in the lot. They might total it. I think your husband, sorry ex-husband, needs a ride."

Faster and faster the emotions churn. A maelstrom is coming, there's nowhere to turn.

Sara picks me up at work. She goes aghast with the totaled car news. Kindly, Sara allows me borrow her car for a pressing errand: to run my ex-husband over. A junkyard full of wrecked cars is the last damn place I want to be weeks after my father died. After *they* died.

I arrive at the tow yard. Stepping across another gravel car lot with the same crunch under my feet takes me back. Images of my father's macerated vehicle reel like a sick movie trailer. My steps quicken to an angered march. A hanging bell clangs as I storm through the office door. The sharp noise alerts the owner of this sparse workshop. Josh is still sitting on a wooden bench wearing a full suit. A floor fan whirs in meek effort to cool the room. First, I approach Josh. His reddened face glistens with sweat.

"Your head looks fine to me; how fortunate."

"Jess, I'm so sorry."

"Don't—" It's a swift twist of the heels.

At the counter I bluntly introduce myself to the owner. He immediately takes me back to my car, parked in front of a barrage of other beaten down vehicles. The entire hood is completely smashed. The passenger side is bashed. The windshield cracked beyond visibility. The grill and bumper are barely hanging on.

"Your, ah, friend doesn't seem well. Maybe he should—"

"Have his head examined? Yeah, I know."

Exhaling I take one final look at what used to be my new car. Back at the counter the necessary information gets exchanged. Josh and I are free to go. It is a brisk, mute march back to Sara's car at the furthest distance possible from each other. Josh slumps into the passenger seat. I sit stiff and erect pressing firmly against the back of my seat. My hands white-knuckle the steering wheel bracing for impact. A time bomb ticking at my core is about to—

"You totaled my car!"

"I did."

"Engine parts are spilling out!" My hands make a dumping gesture in the air. "I can literally see the engine through the hood."

"I know."

"One day—you only had to hang on for one fucking day!"

His locked stare is at the dashboard. Sweat beads off his shaven jaw.

"You were supposed to close-up shop. Get in and get out. Keep your benefits, then go to rehab so something like what just happened, does not happen."

"I know. This is bad."

"Remember how much shit you gave me when I kept your car keys? I protected you and society. What did you do in return? Accuse me of controlling you and belittle me behind my back. And now, I'm the stupid one, because I loaned you my car. I'm the fool who trusted you. I was trying to help," I start counting on my fingers, "help keep your job, get sober, get into recovery, have a family, have a friendship with your ex-wife; all of that with some dignity. But all you can do is lift a little finger?"

"You were being helpful. You gave me a chance to handle things without interfering. I-I screwed it up."

"You need help Josh. You can't do this on your own."

"You're right. I thought I could handle this."

"You're not handling it."

"I need to handle it."

"Stop parroting me! I know how that fucking works! How come you're still alive?"

"I ask myself that same question."

"You could have killed somebody! You could be in the back of a squad car on you way to jail."

That put him at a loss for words. Well, I want blood from a stone. My palms bang at the steering wheel as I scream from my gut at this pathetic man. "How come you get to walk away from a car accident and my father doesn't?"

Nothing; I get nothing.

I am so out of here. The car door slams behind me. Back and forth I rage around this fenced in junkyard. Angry dust clouds trail behind me. Hapless stones are kicked in front. Round and round I circle like some wounded, raw-headed, vulture ravenous for its next meal. There is nothing to pick at because...

My dad is not here. He is not here! I want to walk into his living room and say, "Hey Dad, it's me!" From the computer room I hear the wheels of his desk chair turn away from playing too much Skyrim. He pops out of his computer room wearing a white undershirt and dress pants. He sees me, lights up and says, "There's my girl!" His chest is big and broad from years of weight lifting. His arms stretch wide waiting for his daughter's hug. I bury myself in his chest. The moment his arms wrap round me I feel small, safe and loved. This is the father I lost. This is the father that doesn't get to come home again.

My trail of crazed dust clouds blow through the chain link fence. This directionless hurt has no end. There is no pulling the plug on this pain.

Back inside the steaming heat of the car, I turn on the ignition. His blue dress shirt is drenched. He looks like a cornered rabbit. I know exactly how that feels.

Sara's car churns gravel as I spin wheels out of the parking lot. My humanity feels dead. My ego shot. Compassion got pummeled into weakness. Shattered is my moral compass. Even my humor deflated. I try to label this crazed state to get some kind of footing. Is it pure sadness? No, I am beneath the salt of my tears. I am beneath a desert where nothing will grow. I am beneath rock bottom.

The mind is a curious conundrum. It must decipher where logic fails. My mind unfolds to a vision: a high school science classroom. In the corner hangs a skeleton. Its purpose is to serve the students and the instructor. Every year in good fun the class give the hanging skeleton an ordinary name, like George. On athletic game days, George holds a cheerleader pom-pom in his hand of bones. Christmas time, George wears an elf-hat a top his skull of empty sockets, bare teeth and locked mandibles. George gives the impression that he is smiling. Do not be fooled. George doesn't give a shit. George had his heart removed. He does not feel anything. My dad is dead. CJ, a woman I loved and admired, who would help me through this is gone. I am stripped to my core of cores. Only two things remain: anger and, believe it or not, courtesy. Since I am such a fucking polite person, anger can decide what happens next. I won't even blink about it. I am a skeleton of myself. I am George.

BACK HOME JOSH immediately disappears into the basement. Under a blanket he curls on the sofa. Downstairs I follow only to grab his suitcase by the washer.
"I'll pack your things."
"I will just lie here. I won't move."
"Whatever."
I dart upstairs; begin shoving his things into the suitcase. What does not fit—the suit on a hanger, dress shoes, an electric razor—gets stuffed into a trash bag.

Well, Devine universe I cannot fix my husband. I am not your right-hand angel of service. I am neither hate nor love. Turns out I am just plain me, and I quit.

I call my mom to come over and watch the kids. I ask Sara for another favor: help me drop Josh off at a hotel. Sara is a tried-and-true friend. Before Josh's deportation, the kids and I share a Hawaiian pizza.
Jolie asks between bites. "Where's dad?"
"He's in the basement trying to be invisible." I do not tell the kids about the car; another day.

"Okay." Jolie refocuses on her triangle of ham and pineapple. Sara and my mom arrive at the same time.

"Mom, pizza is on the table. Sara, come with me."

Standing over Josh still hiding under a blanket I supply the necessary information. "Your stuff is packed and in the car. Sarah's car that is. Mine is totaled."

The blanket remains at his ears.

"Sara is here. Time to go."

Josh replies, "It is hard to move. I think I may have broken my ribs."

"Call a doctor from the hotel."

Sara has joined us. Her arms are crossed.

"What hotel?" he bothers to ask.

"A cheap hotel in a busy town; you can walk where ever you need to go."

Sara chimes in, "Don't make things harder Josh."

Still, he does not move from the sofa.

"Josh, if you don't get up, I swear I will call a cop to move you."

Slowly he rises. We escort Josh in a silent car ride to a clean, 2-star hotel room with a bed and a mini fridge.

"Here's your stuff." The suitcase flies out of my hands. It lands hard on the polyester bedspread. Sara drops the garbage bag. Tossing more things from my purse, "Here is your wallet with everything intact." For a moment I want to take his credit cards. He will buy alcohol, the rope from which he will hang himself. But I don't. Out of my back pocket comes the last of Josh from my life. "Here is your toothbrush," slammed down the suitcase, "and your grandfather's watch." That I place on the dresser.

Josh has quietly parked himself on a corner of the bed. His blank stare is at the floor. Sara reminds him, "9-1-1, if you need it."

Click, I take a final mental picture. There is a telephone pole transformer out the window and Josh at the end of his rope. This bland generic room is where we will find his body, days from now, face down on cheap hotel sheets, alone.

"Good-bye Josh."

He peers up at me. There is nothing to say.

I leave him not so he can drink himself to death. That is his choice. I am walking away so he can sit with every single moment he belittled me and know he got it wrong.

"Take care," Sara says. She was once one of my yoga students who blossomed to have her own studio. She kisses Josh on top of his head. In the hallway Sara whispers, "I feel sorry for him. I think he's going to die in there."

"Yup."

Briskly I move down the corridor. His death is not my fault. His choices are not my problem. I am George.

10
BOTTOMS UP

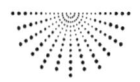

Day One: Do nothing. Do not check on him.
Day Two: Numb
Day Three: A tenebrous night; vast darkness mixes with a moonless sky of roaming satellites, constellations, planets, asteroids, black holes…is anyone else out there? Is this an existential crisis? Where does it all end?
Day Four: The fog of numbness protecting me has evaporated. The mourning period of a daughter grieving the loss of her father has lifted. Rage scrubbed off the judgement, grief, loss, anger, foolery, and exhaustion of a failed transactional, albeit caring, relationship with Josh. My epicenter has a sense of neutrality and calmness. I am still. I am without ego. I am okay. These are my small steps forward.

It is lunch time at the Atrium. I abandon my stint of solitude and rejoin my fellow OT's. Gathered around a treatment table covered by a hospital sheet, we open our home-packed meals. Loosely I explain the events leading to my ex-husband currently rotting in a hotel room. Six, female stunned co-workers offer their support:

"You did everything you could."

"Aww, Jess, you're driving CJ's car; playing her Simon and Garfunkel CD."

"He won't call an ambulance."

"Maybe, you should call the hotel?"

Sitting directly across the cotton sheet Marleen chews on her Kung pao chicken. Not yet ready to speak, a boney index finger goes up to her mouth. Marleen is an easy to guess 71-year-old. Batman gives her the easier patients. Occasionally we engage in fun banter; she is more stoic than I. One time Marleen and I entertained our lunch comrades by upping each other with alcoholic-spouse stories. I said my ex was belittling. Hers was mean. My husband was neglectful. Her husband wouldn't come home. I had to call the police. She called the police, too. I had a SWAT team on the lawn (top that Moh-leen). Marleen had a helicopter circling her house. Well, since I did not have the National Guard on my roof, nor a tank in the driveway, she won the game that nobody really wants to play.

Marleen wipes her mouth and squints. She always squints when she talks despite wearing thick glasses. "My ex-husband died on the streets, alone, like a bum. He lost connection with us for years. But the police, they still call you. I told them, *thanks for calling* and hung up. I got nothing to say about it. He was married, had children, and in the end, no one looked for him." And with that she spears her next piece of kung-pow chicken.

Well, fuck all Marleen! Is that what my children will have to live with, *No one even looked for my dad?* And by "no one" I mean all fingers point toward *me*?

This is the moment to rise above the salt. Translation: to come out of self-centered thinking, now that I am fine, and view the perspective of others. My experience with their dad is different from theirs. If he dies, would my children feel guilty? Burden themselves thinking they should have done more? A wheel of hypothetical outcomes spins in my head. Would my children be forever emotionally stuck to some fucking degree of either grief, anger or apathy? Maybe, it would be just one kid stuck in two of those feelings? Or two kids stuck in only one emotional nightmare? Or, do all three just go a little dead inside and stop caring while eating Kung Lao chicken?

No combination of this Pu Pu platter is acceptable. I want to ask Marleen, *when did everyone close their heart?* And *does your heart stay that way—always ready to close again?* I understand why Marleen sips from a tall glass of apathy. It is a cool drink on a stubborn, hamster-wheel kind of day.

No sooner does our lunch pow-wow finish and I come out from under my rock when my cell phone rings. The screen says Carl is calling. "Hello."

"Hi, Jessica…" Carl is quick to articulate why he is calling. He and Eddie had called Josh after he did not show to a couple of meetings. Josh told them he was in a car accident and staying at a hotel. Carl goes on to say, "We've been with him a couple hours. He's really thin–holds his jeans when he walks. He doesn't walk very well."

Okay, so he's skinny and tilts. How is he even alive? I tapped out from saving him; it was my stoic ending. That said, Josh seems to have weaved his own life line with Carl and Eddie. These two grown men are willing to step up on his behalf and help. They are asking me for guidance. This is an honorable intention before me. From within I release a deep, deep, I'm talking ravine deep sigh. "Put Joshua on the phone."

In the background I hear the crack in his voice. "She wants to speak to me?"

"Hello?" he says spoken softly.

"Hey there."

"Can I come home?"

Home? He never called my place "home", nor hinted that I gave him a sense of home…was a sense of home. *Wanting to come home* feels like a humble, vulnerable moment. It seems akin to a soldier's longing to go home when he's not sure what he is fighting for anymore. When nothing makes any sense anymore.

My home is not what Josh needs, a sense of home, sure, to feel safe and loved. "Josh, where do you really need to go?"

"I'll go to rehab. I *want* to go. I will happily do so."

"That's where I will take you, rehab. The place we looked into before. You thought it was okay."

"I trust you. Whatever you think." Josh puts the other guys back on the phone.

"He looks pretty bad," says Eddie. Lots of vodka bottles around."

"I'm sure. Stay with him till 4:00. I'll line up a rehab place. Hopefully, we can get a bed for tonight."

"You got it kid. We'll stay with him till you get here."

The stars align; the rehab center has an opening. As I go back to treating patients through therapeutic activities, my mind dances…*They have an opening. Josh is going to rehab. He has a team!*

I leave work full of positive energy. Driving to the hotel I call *the team*. Maybe they can get Josh to shower before I pick him up. Today is going to be a good–

"What do you mean he's gone?" I yell into my cell phone. "You only had to watch him for a few hours! I've babysat Josh for days."

Eddie and Carl explain in tandem over speaker phone how their concerns grew. "Josh thought he was having some kind of chest pain."

"So, you took him to the hospital?"

"Maybe he was having a heart attack."

"Did Josh look like he was having a heart attack?"

"Not really."

"Did you wonder if Josh was avoiding rehab?"

"Actually, I didn't think of that. Did you Eddie?"

"Yeah, I thought so."

Carl lowers his voice at Eddie, "Why didn't you say something before we drove him there?""

"Josh is a doctor, right?" Eddie inquires.

"He's a head shrink gentlemen, not a medical doctor."

"He said he broke a rib," explains Eddie.

"A bunch of ribs," adds Carl.

"Did he say, 'Pain is shooting up my arm?' Or did he show you a bruise on his chest in the shape of a steering wheel? Shit—I almost ran a red light. Guys, at any point did my ex-husband stop breathing?'"

"No, but didn't he just have a car accident?"

"Four days ago. Did he tell you it was my car? He totaled my car."

"Damn! He did not mention that. Things make a little more sense now," Eddie declares.

Carl defends his actions. "Jessica, I did call my sponsor. He said we should take him to the hospital."

"Why didn't you at least check with me first?"

"I don't know," Carl says. "We went with the sponsor."

Do not send a scout to the battlefield when a Ranger is needed. "Which hospital?"

Usually getting to speak with emergency room nurse can take forever, except when a patient disappears. The receptionist knows who I am describing. She hustles back to the nurse's station. A tall, male nurse in his mid-thirties emerges from a cluster of blue scrubs. He introduces himself as Chris. He leads me through the waiting room and out the double glass doors. Chris relays that Josh pulled his leads off and snuck out of a curtained ER room not long after arriving. He asks if I would enlighten the situation. I supply the briefest synopsis. Chris admits, "ER rooms are not equipped to be detox centers. Patients are very disappointed when we cannot give them meds to help with their detox symptoms. There is a gap of where to go for help."

On the down-low I attempt to gain a sense of Josh's condition. Without putting Chris in an awkward position, I ask, "What if a patient "hypothetically" received an EKG and a chest x-ray? It would be helpful to "hypothetically know" if there are any broken ribs or a heart attack in progress?" Chris bites his lower lip ever so slightly. He shakes his head side to side.

Driving up and down low-rise city streets I search for the A-wall patient not having a heart attack, until I am back at the hotel. Once I explain to the clerk this is a wellness check, she lets me into his room. Josh is not there. His suitcase is open, lying on the carpet. His clothes are barely unpacked. A dried banana chips bag is rolled up on the dresser. Empty vodka jugs sit inside and outside the trash can. There is no wallet; no watch. I grab his things and check him out. The AA guys do not even call to see how things are going.

Back home it is cheesesteaks for dinner with the kids. I make no reveal about today's debacle. The rehab center calls to ask if we are running late. I break the news. "Unfortunately, my ex-husband is not coming today."

Before sunset, the doorbell rings. Two young men in their late twenties stand a good distance from my front door, perhaps to seem unthreatening. "Excuse me but are you Jessica? My name is Jim and this is Alec." Their grey sedan is parked at the curb. Suddenly, the back car door opens; Josh awkwardly stumbles out. His face is sunburnt.

"I see you found our missing person."

Josh grins and waves with one hand; the other hand is behind his back. His plaid, button-down shirt is untucked. He staggers towards the driveway, then disappears into the backyard. *Go hide your bottle Josh.*

"We saw him floundering around ma'am, but we kept driving. We talked about him. Alec and I thought he was lost or something. Later, when we drove back, he was in the same spot! I know this sounds weird. He asked us to take him to this address. Is this okay?" The whole time they are sure to keep their distance, one further than the other.

"It's okay," I say. "It's pretty rare someone would help out like you guys did."

"You sure? We're doing a good thing right?"

"It's fine. He's in a crisis situation."

"We were worried." They step backwards towards their sedan, caution on the faces. "This felt like the right thing to do." Then two men and I wave good-bye as they drive off.

Every time I burn out, another supply of fuel arrives. This mini rescue was Josh's serendipity; I had nothing to do with it. Josh won't even remember these angels, but I met them. The fact Joshua is clearly being given another chance is bigger than me. I humble down and chill. I make the decision that I will link the father of my children from point A to point B; further assistance would interfere with the natural consequences he needs to face. And I am not turning my back to serendipity. Surely the last 4 days have been some version of hell for him. Most of it will probably get blacked out; nonetheless….

Josh totters away from the shed holding a fistful of his jeans by the waist. We sit down on the wooden steps of the back deck. He gazes at me. Joy seems to light the remaining crystal blue in his eyes.

"Well," I sigh. "You are not missing, and you are not dead. You sure know how to charm a gal."

"You look so beautiful. Somehow, I forgot. Even if you are mad at me, you're like an angel."

"You're lucky. I'm too tired to be mad. This is so pathetic."

"I know." He sighs.

"What happened to you at the hospital?"

"Aw man, nurses started running tests. Put leads on my chest. Doctor said he couldn't give me anything for the shakes because "they know". They could tell I'm an alcoholic. I told them I just needed enough to get past the detox part. They said, 'They can't.' It's so fucking hard. They left me alone. I ripped off the lines and snuck out." Josh rubs his hands together. "I want to get better. I honestly do. Did you know withdrawals can kill you? I can't get meds to help with the detox, but if I go into cardiac arrest because of the withdrawals, they'd be all over me which would be more dire and more costly."

"I agree. There isn't much offered between a twenty-thousand-dollar rehab or sucking it up and doing it at home with serious risk."

"If they could give me something to get thru the next few days."

"Josh, getting through the detox period is not the finish line. It's the starting point. There's a physiological and mental process that takes months and months. You need guardrails to keep the course. Rehab centers help put those long-term rails in place after detox."

"I'll do whatever you say."

"We lost the rehab bed."

"I'm sorry. I am trying, minute by minute. Withdrawals feel like your body is literally, painfully going to crush itself to death."

I put my hand on his knee. "Consider taking a shower. Your hair looks like a troll doll." Tufts of his blonde hair shoot in all directions. "I'll get some aloe vera for your face."

"Thank you."

"Hopefully, we'll get a rehab bed tomorrow."

Or we won't. A rehab bed can go faster than a new pair of Jordan sneakers, especially if they don't think we'll show. Josh holds his determination to stay sober with dug-in fingernails. Knuckle heads Eddie and Carl finally call. They feel bad Josh missed out on rehab. Every evening as we wait for another opening (and for the rehab center to trust us), Carl and Eddie come by and take Josh to an AA meeting. The following week our friends Mike and Ellen get involved. Ellen gives me moral support. Mike interjects into Josh what a committed father should do. Mike and the two AA guys get organized and huddle around Josh as we wait; they make sure someone takes Josh to a meeting every day.

In the meantime, the car accident was an acceptable excuse for Josh to keep his job and take some time off to recover. The painful alcohol withdraws pass; the weening beers helped. Josh returns to work. It takes all he has to manage his job cognitively and physically. By evening, it is all he can do to eat, go to a meeting, and review his workload to stay on top; he is still learning the ropes. Drained, Josh goes to bed by ten o'clock. He gets through both night and day without a drink. Once in a while Josh needs my help to problem solve something for work. He trusts me to know his thinking isn't clear. We talk it out. When it's time for an evening meeting, Josh is always ready and waiting for his ride. He likes the groups; he likes what they have to offer. "Some of these guys have been sober for twenty years. Those guys I want to listen to."

Josh is pleasant and caring around the kids. He is not so much a parent, more like an uncle. We begin to enjoy one another's company, again.

After three weeks the rehab facility agrees to waitlist Josh. The next available bed is his. When Josh and I double-checked that the rehab facility does accept his insurance we learned some bad news. We had assumed Josh's benefits kicked in after 30 days of employment. That was Hawaii old-school. His insurance benefits kick in after 90 days; Josh was worked sixty-seven. The math: another twenty-three days in my house, plus weekends. Come on! —I was mastering *boundaries*. Guess I have new lessons to master on *flexibility* and *release of control*. When the wind blows fierce, branches that hold firm break. Reeds that bend weather the storm.

Plan B

Josh earns another 30-day recovery coin. He picks Carl as a sponsor. This is odd choice, because Carl has barely over a year in recovery. I am not surprised Josh picked him; Carl is too green to call Josh out on his shit. In support of their budding friendship, the kids visit Carl's house. Apparently he has a double-bay mechanic's garage that is cool to see.

One day Carl comes by extra early to get Josh who is not home yet. Carl seems to have done this on purpose to spend time with me. In our private conversation I learn how enamored Carl is with Josh. He surprisingly tells me, "I never met anyone with three PhD's before."

"Three! Josh told you he has three? Come on!"

"Are you sure he doesn't?" Carl asks looking at me as if my eyes were swollen and I could not see clearly.

"Carl, I was at Josh's graduation. He got a doctorate in psychology. That silver watch with the university logo was a graduation present from me."

"He never said it was from you. It's a beautiful watch."

"Josh doesn't tell anyone it's from me, not even my kids. He has an image of me to portray. He admitted to me, once, that I was his 'smokescreen.'"

"I can see that," he says. "Josh throws a lot of blame at you. Some of it doesn't make any sense; I don't ask."

Regardless of the latest stories of grandeur, Josh wants to follow the AA 90-90 plan: attend ninety-meetings in ninety-days. Josh is already a month in with success. His life has a predictable rhythm of work and meetings. Our home is an alcohol-free environment. Refreshing to me is that Josh has ownership about having a drinking problem. He does not have denial on replay. He is following the lead of the recovered guys he admires. They address alcoholism upfront. They say it takes power away from the addiction.

But at last, a rehab bed has become available. Josh, however, feels there is a choice to be made: continue along the 90-90 path or enter rehab. The AA guys are not opposed to rehab, but they say the 90-90 program can really work. They support Josh's thinking, or excuse, that rehab could affect his job. Due to Josh's recent progress, there is a high chance rehab is only approved for a week, maybe two, then he is right back here at this same spot. I consult with Mike and Ellen. Mike talks to Josh about rehab. Carl, on the other hand, supports Josh's preference.

I call a family meeting. Both options are explained to the kids. Each kid has a say in the direction we go as a family. They know Dad would need to continue living with us. We are his half-way house. We are stabilizing. We don't keep alcohol in the house. When Josh's disease is not running the show, he is not pissing any of us off.

Connor and Nicky are willing to give their dad the chance at the 90-90 program. Connor offers, "The second that's not working, it's rehab."

"Dad, you can stay in my room," offers Nicky. "We can talk about rent later. Like a dollar a day, maybe." Nicky crosses his arms and nods his head.

Jolie and I gravitate towards rehab first, then the 90-90. "It would give you more strength," Jolie says.

Everyone was heard. Now we listen to Josh who speaks in a sober, heart-to-heart manner. He lays out his network of support, his routine, the 12-step program he is working, and how the meetings feel. He does not claim to be born again; however, he feels having a spiritual aspect in his recovery is working for him and makes a difference. He agrees he needed rehab before, but at this point he can function.

I know that he dove into AA to avoid rehab. Sometimes a

detour from dread can give a push towards other viable alternatives.

Privately Josh and I speak. "This is doing me good. Rehab would feel like a step backwards at this point," he says. "I don't want that other life. I'm doing this for me. Of course, you and the kids matter. But first, I have to do this for me."

"Where do you want to live during this critical time"?

He hesitates. Rests his fingers across his mouth. "Being here is my stability. I would like to stay. I can understand if you don't want me to. If you don't, I will figure that out. That is not on you. What will be, will be."

Josh rarely admits much of anything. When he does, it is a small treasure. This reminds me of when I pursued our divorce. He said he felt like *he was losing his legs*. I thought, *how could you treat me so badly, if underneath it all, you value me to that degree?* At this moment, his pedestal is gone or tucked in a closet somewhere. He is being vulnerable and honest and has created a support system outside of us. Most important, his actions match his words.

To the father of my children sitting beside me on the sofa that he has been sleeping on for a month (didn't want him too comfortable) I say, "You can stay here. We will support you."

Immediately his body sinks. "I didn't think you'd say yes." Restraining his relief, "Are you sure the kids will be okay with this? Is Jolie okay with this?"

"The kids want you to mean what you say. We want you to stay sober. They are learning to draw a line for themselves. Jolie and I have a different preference; doesn't mean we're right. Different paths can lead to the same place."

"I didn't always view alcoholism clinically, as a disease. There are etiology studies and imaging studies of the effects on the brain. I didn't realize the huge correlation of thinking and behavior patterns with addictions. I didn't put together that I have an addict brain behaving and thinking certain predictable ways."

"Sounds good to know."

"I never thought what it was like for you."

"How could you not? That's what partners do." His words were a mix of hurtfulness and validation (and stupidity and selfishness). "What do you think I was trying to say all those years? You neglected us. You belittled me. I'll leave it at that. Drinking made everything worse."

"I didn't see how my drinking made things worse for you. It was my drinking issue, not yours"

Part of me wants to shove a volcano of moments into my ex-husband's tiny aperture of awareness. However, he is becoming a sober man. We are building trust. And, as much as he used to go off on emotional rants, he is not doing that. He has not, comparatively, since his efforts to come back. Make no mistake, bullshit still flows, and he would sell me out behind my back for free. I will keep my healing separate from his healing. Our kids being around two healing parents, is a lot better than two fighting parents.

In good humor I say with brevity, "Good-luck with your new pint-sized landlord."

Josh laughs. "I don't mind a landlord who smells like a teddy bear."

11

SHOWDOWN AT HIGH NOON

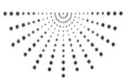

*H*ere at the Atrium sub-acute center it is fairly common to treat a charismatic or colorful-personality type. But two showmen at the same time–that is rare. Wearing pressed pants, starched shirt, onyx cufflinks, Mr. Cavaletti still carries the look of his former tycoon days even in his late seventies. Mr. Cavaletti retired over a decade ago, although "stepped down" might be more apropos for the mafia. Every evening Mrs. Cavaletti, wife number three, visits with a homemade dinner neatly packed inside a Coach tote bag. The stylish couple play cards and watch TV until their evening kiss, then a driver takes her home.

Mr. Cavaletti was hooked to a ventilator for over a week following a cardiac procedure. He still requires 3 liters of oxygen and use of a walker. His PT goal is to ambulate with a single point cane. His OT goal is to perform activities of daily living (ADLs) without an oxygen tank. His personal goal is to smoke Cuban cigars again.

"I'll quit on my own damn terms," Mr. Cavaletti points at Donny Mac's chest. "There is nothing, I tell you, like when my lady and I sit on the back porch in our rocking chairs, smoking a hand-rolled cigar with a glass of Blanton's over ice. Not the small cubes Donny-boy; one, big cube. It opens up the whiskey just right."

"Light up near that O2 tank and you'll blow you and the Mrs. right off the porch!" Donny-boy charms his warning with a laugh.

"Then do your job sunny boy, and I'll do mine." Mr. Cavaletti gleams a full set of squared teeth from his wheelchair.

"Yes, sir!" Donny Mac salutes unfolding a walker, "I can tell, you are going to stand a full two minutes today. We almost had it yesterday."

Donny Mac and Mr. Cavaletti proceed to do standing trials for fifteen-second increments. Batman repeatedly visits their session and chats it up for two reasons: (1) it creates a distraction, so Mr. Cavaletti stands longer, and (2) provide any backup in case Mr. Cavaletti's knees sink south.

My patient, Rex, was bred in cowboy country. He may not be city polished, but he carries a fierce sense of independence and manners; he also enjoys acknowledging the ladies. His stories paint vivid pictures about growing up as a cattle rancher. "Riding my fastest steed, I could lasso a run-away calf from 300 feet," Rex says with a wink and a nod. "Little fella would be roped and tied before he knew which side the sun come up."

Rex is a couple years older than Mr. Cavaletti. Combine their ages–that's over 160 years of machismo. What is Rex's rehab goal? Get the hell out of here and go back to feeding the squirrels that visit his modest yard. "Those furry critters come right up to the back door," Rex claims. "One-time, this little fella left me a nut right on the stoop." Rex may have been pulling my leg, hard to read him. Rex speaks out the side of his mouth as if the other side is biting down on a strand of hay.

Although they lived polar opposite lifestyles, both men share a few common threads: masculine independence, old-school charm and a gentlemen's code, *do right by me, get loyalty in return.*

Despite the character similarities, there can only be one rooster in a hen house.

"I don't like that guy," whispers Rex with a squirm in his wheelchair.

"Why?" I ask writing a treatment note next to him on my clipboard.

"Look how clean his hands are. You can tell a lot about a man by his hands. I bet that guy never had a callus in his life."

"You sizing him up."

"Is that a bad thing?"

"No," I say. "But I prefer not to assume anything. Besides, some men are more brain than brawn."

"Sweetheart," he says, "if brains were sticks of dynamite, that guy wouldn't have enough to blow his nose."

BACK IN THE REHAB GYM, when Mr. Cavaletti achieves his two-minute standing mark. Rex pushes himself to stand for two-minutes and ten-seconds. When Rex independently climbs up and down three steps, Mr. Cavaletti accomplishes five. Their competitiveness becomes the spontaneous focus at our next staff meeting.

Around a conference table packed with therapists, the physical therapist treating Rex recommends treatment throughout the weekend. "Rex likes to wander around in his backyard and feed the squirrels. He needs to be safe on the grass."

Concerned about Rex's cognitive status, I throw my professional opinion in the ring. "In the evenings, Rex needs someone to check on him. He Sundowns and may forget to turn the stove off. Or, he might leave the house one the evening to look for some lost, imaginary cattle and not find his way home."

"Rex has a grandson," announces the PT, "he often checks in on his grandpa."

Batman glances up from writing notes on his clipboard.

"Get social work to order a home care evaluation. I'll see what kind of commitment the grandson will make. Next is Mr. Cavaletti. Let's advance him to a quad-cane next week. "Colleen is he safe in the bathroom?" Colleen is our OT team leader.

"Yes, they already have grab bars and a shower bench in their bathroom. He says he still makes a good marinara. I'd like his balance better for carrying items in the kitchen."

"Donny anything else for Mr. Cavaletti?"

"Eight steps to get in the house, then everything is on the first floor including his humidor room. Mr. Cavaletti personally invited me to come over and smoke a cigar with him."

"That's good since you haven't got any friends," remarks Batman without so much as a glance from his clipboard.

Donny Mac puts a hand over his heart. "I'll ignore that, because I know you are my friend."

"Next Sunday can be his last session," says Traci, the PT supervising Donny Mac.

"Hey Jessica," across the table Donny Mac spins on his stool, "what if we have Mr. Cavaletti and Rex go against each other."

"What, like a duel?" I ask.

Batman points his pencil up. "Mob boss against Dirty Harry. Like it."

The professionalism around the conference table downgrades to high school level jeers. *Do it! Have them race around the cones. No, Rex would win. Basketball shots! No, Cavaletti used to play street hoops. How about standing poker? No, needs too much recall. Standing Black Jack? Boring! Ball kicking? Did we ever find the ball? Activities upstairs borrowed it. How about a balloon toss? Oh yeah! That's the one!*

I interject. "What is it with men and their competitiveness?"

"Come on! This will get all the juices flowing," Donny Mac pleads. "They'll be back in the ole days having a street fight, the kind that's all talk and no one gets hurt."

My pen taps away. "Am I the only one trying to protect the egos of these men?"

My co-workers all throw back, "Totally. Absolutely. It's just you."

Batman overrides the chatter. "This is what builds a man's character. Perhaps you're worried Donny boy's city slicker will kick your cowboy's ass."

The gasp from my mouth is well heard by this cajoling crowd. I throw stink-eye at the smug faces of Batman and Donny Mac. "Oh, it's on." I put my arm out and drop my cheap pen on the table. "Balloon toss. Tomorrow. High noon."

Batman whispers to Donny Mac, "You're welcome."

Balloons at Noon

"What's that again?" Rex asks between tuna fish bites served on a rolling bedside table. "You want me to play volley ball with a balloon against Mr. Softy hands?"

"Technically, you'd be side-stepping and reaching out of your midline-comfort zone to stimulate a balance reaction." I demonstrate this by tapping an imaginary balloon.

"You want to waste everybody's time." He pokes a plastic fork at a rock-hard tomato wedge.

"It's not a waste. It exercises your righting reactions, your standing tolerance and your balance. You need these things, and so does he. It's only fun for everyone, if it's fun for you two hombres on some level of testosterone I don't quite understand."

Rex rubs the facial scruff on his square jaw.

I kneel down beside his recliner chair. "Besides," I whisper with a quick lift of the eyebrows, "you will crush him."

"All right, go ahead. Make the deal pretty lady. We do this after I take my nap, and before his."

Friday before lunch, and before anybody's nap, we meet in

the gym, between the practice stairs and the stationary bikes. From his open-door Bat-cave, Batman can view our half-circle of patients in wheel chairs paired with therapists counting weight reps, returning tossed bean bags, and laughing at stories the patients tell, patients wearing sweaters or sweatpants, or sadly both at the same time. Donny Mac and I clear space in front of this half-circle for what is about to go down.

Rex's long-term memory begins to time travel. Back at the ranch, Rex returns from riding the mountain side. Reins in one hand, Rex trots his mare back to the stables. He uses a pocket knife to scrape the field dirt off his cowboy boots. His jeans hold the smell of leather long after his chaps and gun slinger are hung back on an iron hook. His black, fringed vest matches the cowboy hat tipped over one eye. This is how it's done here in the ghost town of dementia, where the wheelchairs become bridled horses, the therapists are saloon ladies, and the bartenders serve Patrón tequila shots instead of strawberry Jell-O cups.

Mr. Cavaletti time-travels to the streets of New York. The boss wears pinstriped suits, custom made from Italy. His smooth face is blade-shaven by the steady hand of a local barber. In this city the wheel chairs are Cadillacs, the therapists are mistresses, and the vanilla ice cream with a wooden spoon is replaced by a dirty martini garnished by a speared olive.

Donny Mac strolls out to the center of the gym. He proceeds to blow up a cherry red balloon and tie it off. "Gentleman, your one job is to hit this balloon hard enough to pass the blue tape line Marta just laid down. Thank you, Marta. The balloon must be kept in the air. If it touches the ground on your side of the tape, the other team gets the point. Jess and I can help, but we cannot take more than two steps. If we happen to end this friendly game in a tie, that is O-O-kay."

"What are you a pansy?" shouts Mob Boss. "There's no tie."

"One man left standing isn't a tie, punk." Dirty Harry chews at his straw.

"Okay, good talk." Donny Mac retreats toward Mob Boss. He then bows at Rex and I, extended balloon in hand. "Would you two like to serve, or shall we?"

Dirty Harry gives a crooked smile. "You can serve; ladies first."

Mob Boss grabs hold of his walker. "Don't worry shit-hole," slowly he rises, "I like being called pretty. It keeps me humble."

"Doesn't your pecker already do that?" Dirty Harry slings it back with an impeccably straight face. He, too, stands without speed, my hand on his walker. Donny Mac and I cue both men to step their feet apart wider for a steadier base.

The men face-off, their walkers twenty paces apart. Both gents have a pink, striped gait belt around their waist. The belts are for the therapists to grab if either man loses his balance. Rex's flannel shirt is tucked into black Carhartt pants. Mr. Cavaletti wears a tan cardigan closed with silver buttons. The slacks match the sweater.

The red balloon floats toward the cowboy. Rex reaches forward with a stumbled lurch; he swats the balloon over the line. My hand hovers near his gait belt. Rex's shot has speed; it banks too low for Mr. Cavaletti. Donny Mac takes a swing and misses.

Traci, a senior physical therapist yells, "That's one for Jessica's team. First one to five points gets a prize. I hear its homemade banana bread." Beside Traci is her patient, an elderly, rotund, grandma riding a stationary bike. Grandma is pedaling so slow that her foot fights gravity on the down push.

Dirty Harry tips his hat towards his adversary. "If you spent less time in a barber's chair gettin' pretty, you would have made that shot."

Mob Boss throws an icy stare. Donny-boy holds out the balloon. Mob Boss whacks it high. The balloon soars across the tape line. It arcs towards Dirty Harry's hat. The cowboy draws his right hand—too slow, he misses. I fail to reach around fast enough to save it. The floating tomato lands on the floor. The city slicker team scores.

Mob Boss promulgates to Donny Boy over his shoulder, "I hear squirrel meat makes a nice stew. Know anywhere we can get some fresh squirrel?" Mob Boss kisses his fingertips with an air of *bon appétit*.

"Keep your focus," I mumble into Dirty Harry's ear. Marta hands me the retrieved balloon.

Traci announces, "The score is tied: 1 to 1." On the stationary bike grandma has fallen asleep; it is not the first time.

Dirty Harry steadies himself to place the swollen-red latex in one hand while he draws back with the other. It is a forceful hit. The balloon sails right between Donny Boy and his boss. Both must have thought the other guy would swat it. Neither took the shot.

"Oh-h-h!" The crowd of patients and therapists jeer at the sight. An elderly lady pulling TheraBand across her lap smiles a flirty coo at Rex. He winks back at her.

"The score is 2 to 1," updates Traci.

Donny Boy holds up the volley ball filled with his own hot air. Mob Boss whacks it over the line. Dirty Harry shoots it back. Mob boss return swats with a curve. I stretch and manage to tap it up. The balloon is primed for the perfect set up. Rex commits with a mighty, slow swing. It helicopters to the other side. Where will it land? The energy in the room has shifted—we are having fun! The cherry bomb banks left. Donny Boy kicks it out of bounds.

"Aww," says the crowd. The score is tied.

Mob Boss recovers from his lost point by shouting, "Nice hat cowboy. It will look good on my lady when she's wearing it and nothing else."

Dirty Harry responds without missing a beat, "Don't be upset when she shouts my name instead of yours."

Mob Boss lifts his chin. He takes a pause. "That's a good one. Mind if I use it?"

"Sure slick. It'll cost you a fancy cigar."

Mob Boss gives the nod, "Done."

The showdown continues. Each man is back to his prime in the playground of the mind. In reality each man is struggling to return home with a sense of dignity; without the fear of falling; without their lives held back by a single misstep. As therapists it is our mission they succeed and that everyone gets a slice of banana bread no matter the score.

12
COUNT TO NINETY

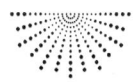

The psychological raft Josh built has navigated sobriety for over two months. Every day he attends a meeting. Sundays are his favorite. That is his *home group*. Members rotate duties such as reading the opening prayer, setting up the chairs or, most popular, brewing a strong pot of coffee.

My curiosity gets the better of me. "What's so special about the Sunday group?" I ask at the end of a pasta dinner.

Josh picks at what's left of our fettuccini entwined with lemon chicken, shaved parmesan and asparagus. The kids have already left the table. "A lot of the guys are ten years sober, even twenty. They live a lifestyle I can imagine. They have grandkids. They have family around them. Other groups have younger guys dealing with legal issues and court orders. Those members are fleeting; it limits the friendships. There's strength in numbers." Josh soaks up the lemony-chicken broth with some French bread. "Don't worry, I still get something out of every meeting, even if that is to keep my head down and let another day be."

"I have a compliment for you. Don't take it the wrong way."

He rests a piece of French bread on his plate. "I will try."

"You seem more cognitively with it; your problem solving and memory. Also, your mood doesn't have the, uh, extreme end ranges it used to. I find it way easier to be in your orbit. It was tough before, know what I'm saying?"

"Yes, I was difficult to be with. I made your life difficult, perhaps unnecessarily."

"I'll take that rephrase."

Josh brushes bread crumbs off the table; dumps them onto his dinner plate. "My thinking was to keep plugging away, no matter what."

"Did you ever think your issues effected the quality of my life?"

"No," he chuckles, "I didn't think about how things affected you. I do love you."

"There is not much *why* behind that, which means your vision of me is shallow. We have no in-depth conversations, unless it circles around you. You still don't ask anything about me, my day, my feelings. I'm glad you've stopped the round about insults you used to sling, which is a ridiculous low bar of appreciation." My fork digs into the carbs. "I think you say, *I love you*, because it's a good thing to say. Women should jump when a man says it, right? It's the fairy tale line to get the girl. It's a line item to cross off."

"That sounds pretty harsh," he says. "I'm not a robot. We had good times, didn't we?"

"Of course, we did." Swirling layers of pasta cover my plate as I try to explain the double-edged sword. "I feel as though you haven't thanked me for supporting and running this family for the past two years. Instead, you say, *I'll give you money*—the insulting word there is, *give*. You *give* money to charities. You *give* money in exchange for nothing. Raising kids is not nothing. Since raising this family is most of my life, it's fair to say you don't value me."

"I'm looking at you right now." He smiles and puts his hands out. "I think you're adorable."

"You just handed me a dollar bill," my disgust rises, "but you think it's a twenty."

"If I hand you a twenty, it's a twenty."

"Really? You asked about getting back together while intoxicated. That is not a relationship I deserve. It's not any different from what failed us. You and I both deserve more than a hamster wheel relationship."

"I don't do the hamster wheel thing. I had some slips, sure."

"Dude, you totaled my car!"

Josh stares at the unfinished pasta. "I'm pretty sure those guys who hit me in the truck were smoking pot."

"It was one guy, and YOU hit HIM!" I show one finger. "We got and read the police report together. You know Josh, I had to switch insurance companies. They were going to double my rate even though it wasn't my accident. I had to get a new car. I had to take off work to detox you without pay. Don't you get it? I lose nineteen dollars of myself when I take your twenty to the bank of reality."

"The police report did not say how fast the truck was going," Josh declares.

And we are back on the hamster wheel again.

I respond with my inside voice. "The accident happened on a round-a-bout. How fast could a truck be going on a circle?" My index finger makes rapid, tiny circles in the air—bing, bing, bing, bing, bing, bing, bing. "If you can't own causing an accident, or remember it, that's one thing. Flip it to being the other guy's fault is something else. I am not trying to cause shame. You just should not forget how bad things snowball, so you never go back."

Josh pauses in thought in his own peculiar stillness. His dinner plate is clear. He seems to be letting his defensiveness wash away. "In AA meetings they teach that trying to manage the idea of never having another drink is too much. *Break it down,* they say. *Manage a day without a drink. Go to a meeting instead of drinking.*" Josh places the fork and knife on his finished plate. "It is manageable for me to string along parts of a day where I don't need to have a drink. Some guys have to break down not taking a drink before dinner, during dinner, after dinner. If they viewed not drinking for an entire night, it would be too much at least in the beginning."

"How is it for you?"

"Fine. Some days I realize I hadn't thought about it, no urges. Other times, I acknowledge the thought, the desire, and then say to myself, *nope,* and skip over the moment." Josh picks up his plate and rinses it clean.

HE DID It

Total astonishment. Josh actually achieves 90-days of sobriety. (About damn time) The shine off that ninety-day sobriety coin is beautiful! I want a coin for being his detox center and half-way house, the kids too. There really should be a family coin, just saying.

This milestone earns Josh a turn to share his story at a meeting. It is part of the healing process and part of the giving back. Josh does not invite the kids and I to this open meeting which surprises me. Somberly, I quell my deep disappointment. The AA path is his lane; I need to stay in mine. His decision is not for me to judge. Besides, I am not a fool. His story will veer from reality. Both Carl and Eddie have mentioned absurd things Josh has said about me. No surprise, I am still a scapegoat. I did ask Josh, *what is something you mention at meetings?* Josh said *he didn't know where he'd be if his parents had not taken him in. He might have ended up homeless.* His parents were his entire thank you list. It is probably for the best I am not invited. I thought he could inspire the crowd by letting them know ex-spouses can step-up. He could say how he was given many opportunities to re-establish his relationships with our kids. Where is the sign-up sheet for 90-days free of narcissism?

Josh returns from speaking at his special meeting with a rare aura of joy and humbleness. According to Josh everything went well. He felt supported and felt that his story contributed to the bigger picture of sobriety.

Later, while I am putting my folded laundry away in my bedroom, he pops on down. "Can I show you something?" he asks bright-eyed and soft-spoken.

"Sure," as I put down a pile of folded jeans.

Josh lines up his sobriety coins on my dresser: the 1-day, the 30-day and the 90-day. He picks up the latter. "Here, you should really have this. You deserve it."

The 90-day coin glistens between his thumb and finger. This is a full-valued twenty-dollar bill at the bank of amends; a high gesture sincerely offered. I stare and smile playing it cool. Inside, however, I swoon for this coin! I want to hold it and kiss it and run around the house for a fucking victory lap! Whenever the sobriety door slammed shut on his face, I held that door open and kicked him back over the threshold, again and again. I gave him a seat back at the family table. Our kids welcomed him with arms wide. Josh made some serious amends; many faultmakers do not. I gave his amends and intents more value than his personality sell-outs that targeted me. I let him return *home* so he could be independent again. Maybe, in return, he would lift our lives. Those two things are not contingent upon one another because I don't need him.

Josh rests the precious coin in my hand. He looks more at the coin than me. The golden disc covers the center of my palm. I give it a once over, taking in its beauty and the numbers 9-0. *Breathe.* I reach for his hand and give the 90-day sobriety coin back. "It belongs to you, next to the other ones. You earned it. It's your personal vault."

Josh gazes at the coin now resting in the center of his palm. He grabs the other coins and puts all three in his pocket.

Now what? Does he start looking for an apartment? Nope. My dating life has been on hold. It added more stress than anything else, but I do miss companionship, intimate companionship. Lightly, I discuss the topic of dating with Jolie, age fourteen. I wanted a feel on her current thoughts. She says without hesitation, "Mom, how are you supposed to date anyone? Your ex-husband hanging around is a cock-block."

Uh-h, yea my daughter said this. She has a valid point. Guess I should stop putting myself on hold.

The days continue to fly past 90. The winter holidays are approaching. Josh does not voluntarily talk of moving out. I care that his financial savings grows, so he can feel on top things. But the moving out ball has got to start rolling. I mention apartment hunting. Josh grimaces as if he took a silent punch to the gut. He explains it is hard to find time to look for one.

The man is sober. I am getting child support. The welcome mat will stay until the new year. Then it will be time for Josh to go. I do not discuss this plan with anyone. I am head of this household, and this is what we are doing.

It's All in the Execution

I am about to swallow a really big pill without water.

"Hey Josh, if you stay here past New Years, I think you should pay some rent."

His head snaps. "What? I already pay you child support. Now, you want rent. How is that fair?"

Using my inside voice I respond. "When you lived at Rodger's, you paid rent. If you move out, you'll pay rent.

Continuing to live here should include, at a reasonable rate, some rent."

"The overall situation is you collecting more money."

Thats the pill: Jess-i-ca is an unfair, money-collecting, bitch. Better for Josh to think all that, then feel kicked out. Or, hurt that his family expects him to leave. The preference here is to play it extra safe on his behalf. Of course, it is reasonable he gets his own place, but "reasonable thinking" does not often hang on our Christmas tree.

Fueled by irritation, as I had planned and expected, Josh begins the search for an apartment, his ego intact. He mentions a dry town about fifteen minutes away. Sounds good to me; however, he can only find places that are too expensive. His pace to find a proper apartment slows way down. So, I pick it up and find a place, priced right, comfortable, and in the dry town he mentioned.

Josh gets on board with the place. The walk through is scheduled. It's an old building on the verge of being run-down, but the apartment is clean. He likes the apartment enough, especially when he upgrades to a 2-bedroom balcony. It has a view of a nothing fancy river. After the tour we head to the office. He is ready to sign the contract…but his spotty work history and credit review is not pretty; it sucks. They will not let him sign a lease agreement without a co-signature. Josh is not going to qualify anywhere else. My credit is intact because we maintained separate credit cards during our marriage. Both the guy behind the desk and Josh wait in silence to see what I am going to do. I wonder too.

Once upon a time, Josh and I found a house on a whim and bid on it within the same day. We began raising two children there. At our best times, we know what's at stake. We do not need to talk it over. We need to decide. The ball is in my court.

My reluctant signature hits the paperwork. He thanks me, sincerely. Anyone, I DO NOT recommend holding someone else's legal bag. Even so, I believe one's home environment matters. A home is a self-reflection. Josh deserves a decent home that reflects dignity. That dignity can begin within the woman raising his children to see him that way…to a certain degree.

 Josh shops for furniture, picks out bed sheets, lamps…. He has created a comfortable, mildly executive-type themed apartment living space. On moving day the kids and I bring over a giant peace-lily. Both my arms circled around this pot. The house warming plant reminds me of the time when Josh and I met in Hawaii. He brought a trailing, ivy plant for me and my roommates' house warming party. He was the only guest in a house full of invited psychiatric residents who did.

For this New Year's dinner the kids and I are invited over to Josh's new digs. As we step off his apartment elevator, there is the reek of pot for the entire length of the hallway. This totally amuses the kids. Connor has brought his first girlfriend.

 Josh roasts two chickens. We have a lovely dinner followed by all six of us walking along the river path. Afterwards, Nicky and Jolie make-the-bed-up in Josh's spare bedroom for their first overnight stay. The next morning the kids say they woke to homemade pancakes served with Canadian and maple butter gifted by Grandpa Caleb. Sharing days and moments like this is how our divorce was supposed to go. Time has a way with these things.

13

APARTMENT, RELAPSE, ENOUGH

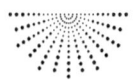

*G*od damn it! One month alone and he's drinking again. The tells—? What he doesn't say, the excessive smiling, bursts of explanation, chewing gum…one clue follows the rest. At least our communication is respectful as he admits to sliding off the rails. He simply wanted to have a beer with dinner, thought that would be all right. Dinners with a beer turned into dining with a six pack, then a bottle of wine. It became an embarrassment and bothersome to have cans and bottles pile up and continuously go back to the store. Hard liquor was the justifiable solution to quench the beast.

"Josh, this time, it's rehab."

He shook his head. "I need to get back to my meetings. That's where the cracks started."

My palm pops up like a stop sign. "Every relapse hits you harder and faster. Meetings are not going to cut it. Your body picks up where you left off."

"If I can't get back on track with meetings, then I will go." Spoken like a dummy through the ventriloquism of addiction.

"I will not drag you there."

"You won't have to. I don't want to lose my job. You will see me go, peacefully."

"Fine." The beast wins the round. No matter, I will not go back in the boxing ring for his sobriety. Carl signed up for this battle, not me.

Another week passes. Josh functions as normal. Then, he drops off the radar which could easily mean blackout periods. Carl texts me that Josh is not responding to his messages. Carl is on Team Josh which I appreciate to a degree. Carl is a novice; hence, I agree to meet him at Josh's apartment for a wellness check.

Indeed, Josh is there instead of work. He is surprised, albeit happy, to see us. We are invited into his living room where Carl and I sit at opposite ends of the sleek sofa. Our host triangulates across from us in a swivel chair. Josh, regressing to a kid who cut school but thinks the parents don't know, asks, "What brings you guys to visit me?"

Carl speaks with concerned inflection which is better than my fed-up tone. "I was wondering where you've been pal."

"I've been here. I've been there." Josh's inebriation and lack of time is palpable. "I even went for a walk."

Carl looks at me, raises the eyebrows he barely has and says nothing. Carl took this gig to be Josh's sponsor, then he hit-on me. Now he is next to useless.

I scoot towards the coffee table, hands tucked under my lap. "Josh, I'm sure none of this is easy for you. We're here to help you figure this out."

"Hmm," a curled finger presses against his lips as he ponders. We wait. And wait. Casually Josh blurts, "It's not going great."

"What do you want to do about it?" asks Carl.

Josh shrugs his shoulders. I shrug mine with a grin. He mirrors my expression.

"When did you last go to work?" I ask.

Again, he shrugs.

"Was it yesterday?" asking with a playful head tilt, "Or, maybe, two days ago?"

"I went today," he affirms.

My entire body deflates at the nonsense. "Josh, it seems very unlikely you worked today. I'm home because our census is down; staff is rotating turns to take days off."

"No, really I went to work." Josh perks up like a prairie Meerkat. His infectious energy pulls in our attention. "I woke up. Got the French press. Made coffee." Josh raises ceramic mug in hand. "I got completely dressed in a suit and a tie. Went out that door," his free hand arrow chops toward the exit, "I drove straight to work. When I got there," his eyes wide, "not a single car was in the parking lot. The building was locked. I was thinking, *Is it Saturday? Is it a holiday?* I had my watch on–this silver watch. Aww, Jess, you remember this?"

"Yes, I gave it to you when you graduated."

"You did. Thank you! This watch told me I was two hours early," he holds up the peace sign, "I drove ALL the way back home, took off my suit and tie. I set my alarm for the right time, and went right back to bed under the sheets."

Josh breaks eye contact drifting in a mental pause. Sips his coffee. Swallows. "Next thing, my alarm goes off. I do it all over again! I make another cup of coffee, put on the same suit and tie. I drive back to work. Cars are in the parking lot everywhere! I stroll inside; head straight to the bathroom; wash my face. In the mirror I can see I look horrible: my face is gaunt, eyes are bloodshot, like, I didn't even know how bad." Josh leans forward continuing a whisper. "I walked out the front door like I was nev-ver there. Noo-body saw me."

The tale is not yet done. "I drive back home. Repeat hanging up the suit. And I hang up my tie–can't forget to hang the tie. It's pressed real smooth on a wooden hanger, really. You guys can go look in the closet if you want. I don't mind."

Josh presses his lips against the mug's smooth edge, sips his coffee completely unfazed by the dump truck load of hot mess surrounding him. He is in over his head and about to lose everything. Josh shows no sign of concern; no sense of urgency to dive back from the brink of this dire situation. He should be asking for help, seeking help. Instead, he is acting like a reality game show host without the reality. That my friends is the definition of batshit crazy. It is interesting, funny and sad on the outside, but a brain's disconnect or misfiring is on the inside. Reality has moved do a different plain. Problem solving stretches above the pay grade.

My eyes roll around the Ferris wheel. Josh reads my face. "I know. I know," he says. He gets up and weaves toward the kitchen.

Carl looks appropriately dumbfounded. He shakes his head and rubs his hands together. "You had quite the day pal."

The approach I take is different. "You need to call out of work," I holler.

"Oh, they don't care," Josh hollers back.

Darting to the kitchen, the smell of fresh roasted coffee fills my nose. He is pouring a refill. "Joshua, and I say this with all sincerity, you are going to lose your job, then your apartment. You already have family in three different countries no longer willing to let you stay with them. More dominos are ready to fall, unless we fix this today."

Josh looks over my head and sighs. Steam from a dark Colombian bean rises between us. His gaze drops to my thick-soled Doc Martins. He peers up my faded jeans until landing on my fitted tee that reads, *Yoga pants don't lie*.

Josh mutters, "All right."

Suck-it ventriloquist beast! Side by side on the sofa, laptop in hand, we search for any human resource email; he needs to properly "call out sick". That progress moves forward like sap on fallen tree bark. Josh frequently finds reasons to stall. I push through transforming his stammering words into a cohesive

HR email with a cc to the boss...*feeling ill...will know more after a doctor visit...yada, yada.* Click. Send. Job saved.

Next, secure an intake appointment with our one-choice rehab center. Josh is handed my phone already ringing. The receptionist politely asks, "Why are you calling?"

Josh shoots a pinched eyebrow glare at me. "I have a problem," he says in a husky voice, "with alcohol." As Josh sluggishly departs toward the bedroom I hear him murmur, "I can't control it."

At this point Carl begins an uncalled for good-bye. He mentions loaning Josh twenty-five bucks. He wants me to repay it. At 6' 3" he looms close over me. This passive-aggressiveness will get zero satisfaction. I flick out the cash as if no-matter money for a toll booth. Josh and I don't need him. Carl leaves without a good-bye to Josh.

The rehab center has a 6:00 evening slot—time to pack! I buzz around with the task at hand like a diligent bee in a garden. Josh jostles like a wilted flower which is to say not all, slumped in his bedroom chair, legs splayed, both hands cupping that same mug filled with "coffee".

"What's with the flat face?" I ask. "And where's your suitcase?"

Josh rubs his temple. Sips his drink. With a loud sigh he gets off the wood spindled chair to retrieve his luggage.

Must think. Josh may be absent from this apartment for a while. Food in the fridge must go. I exit the bedroom. Perishables are tossed into a garbage bag which includes the vodka bottle he has been tapping from the freezer. The kitchen has already been kept clean. I buzz back to the bedroom for a peek — Is this dude for real? Piled high and wide, slopped all over the bed, is a ridiculous mound of clothes to which the suitcase cannot even be seen.

"Yo! The receptionist said, 'pack five items each', not fifty!"

"I heard the spiel." He spins around to address me directly. "Let's be rationale and talk about this intelligently."

Here we go. "Ya know what, Josh? I'll be right back." I dash toward the kitchen to play bartender stirring a tumbler with my signature drink: faucet tap water on the rocks mixed with a splash of vodka from the garbage bag. Back in the boudoir I lean against the doorframe with a *hello darling* expression, cocktail in hand.

With a mere hint of hesitation Josh accepts his drink. He takes a sip…swallows…winces…then lets the pontifications rip. "Let's sit down and seriously talk about the prospect of going through with this silly idea of yours."

"Sure," I tap the wooden chair, "pop-a-squat. I will listen and tweak this, ah, laundry pile of yours. We do need to shut the suitcase." Quickly my therapeutic hands sort and toss. My back faces him. It is mu only shield against the boomerang of manipulations set to launch.

Josh articulates, "There is a fine line between a helpful person and someone who is controlling. People pay to listen to me; they take notes. I am a helpful person. Which one are you?"

My hands stop shoving clothes into his suitcase. The burrs of his words are penetrating my skin sinking deeper than my psyche wants to admit. So, I welcome them and turn his attempt of manipulation into fuel for my intelligence. His gas lighting words are supposed to ignite me, so I strike the match and seemingly cause everything to blow. The flames are a blame trap. I end up burned. He walks away somehow the victim.

Ice clinks in his tumbler. "Jess-i-ca, do you really know what you are doing? Think about that."

I do not even turn around. "I'm wondering Josh if you really want to burn your last bridge."

It does not matter how much gasoline he pours. Power lies with me because I no longer have to kick this man out. I will be a safe distance and far from cause when his addiction sets flame to all he built. Right now I could walk. I could threaten to leave this precarious situation as an ultimatum. Or...

My vibe shifts. Thoughtfully I am folding and arranging his clothes in the now visible suitcase by the foot of the bed. I represent the other side (the life he wants). Josh can choose to cross over. Nothing shall be forced nor rushed. Momentum will not be thwarted. I will flow with the flow so my inebriated, manipulating, reluctant, scared, ex-spouse standing on the edge of losing everything can feel...comfortable. There is a caring man behind the narcissism; the narcissism must be put at ease. Believe me, I would rather Hulk-smash this man and this stupid suitcase into my car, then drop-off his wasted-ass with sticky note to the forehead that reads, "When annoying, give guitar-peace out!"

Another sip clears his throat, "What are you doing?"

"Counting to five," five-folded underwear are slipped into a zipper pouch. Five-balled white socks are snugged to one side. "There is a lot to consider here, Josh. Is it okay I put ice in your glass?"

"Yes, you didn't need to. I know why you did."

"You are a smart one." I quick step by to the bathroom. Grab toothbrush, razor, no mouthwash—all liquids are forbidden. Back at the bed, he watches me. His dark denim legs are crossed. A Harley Davidson t-shirt wrinkles at his waist.

"Should we pack a belt? I don't know if you still like wearing them."

"I am wearing one now."

"Great! We're done." The suitcase slams closed and zips with ease. A sequestered quiver in my chest heightens. I am alone with him. He is serving mind-fuck cocktails while his blood-alcohol content rises. I pull is suitcase to the living room; park it by the door. On the sofa lies his laptop. I neatly wrap the computer into a circle. Turning over my shoulder I casually mention, "If you'd like, I can keep your computer at my house. It's up to you."

Josh steps outside the bedroom, empty glass in hand. He does not respond.

I paste on the politeness. "Do we leave your laptop, or take it?"

"Bring it. What about, uh, this?" He wiggles the empty tumbler.

Our pathetic dance continues. I cross the room and push the Dell computer into his chest. "Here, you carry your laptop. The vodka is already packed."

In the kitchen I sling the kitchen garbage over my shoulder. His apartment keys get shoved in a pocket; the perishable bag tucked under my arm. Marching straight to the exit my free hand clutches his suitcase. "Would you open the door, please?"

His grey hiking boots approach. He is not quite six-feet with them on. His breath is just above my head. "Are you sure about what you are doing?"

I drop the suitcase, twist the handle and press my back against the presently wide-open exiting door. Josh remains still. I wait. I wait. Josh clenches his jaw. He grabs the suitcase. He elongates the pull-out handle elongates with a snap. Marching out the door my ex-husband pulls his suitcase down the long, putrid, weed-smelling hallway to the elevator.

Upon a final glance of his living room, I pick-up the peace-lily with my freed arm and prop it on my hip like a fat baby. En route to the elevator, I open the grimy chute and toss out the garbage, a chunk of my patience leaves with it. Rehab intake is T-minus three painstaking hours.

AT HOME, the kids and I become a collective front after a family huddle in Nicky's bedroom. I mention their dad is nervous and fearful about being admitted and consequently is hounding me;

distraction efforts are requested. The kids are on board. They cajole him outside. "Watch our scooter tricks Dad." The boys take turns on the ramps out back. Connor spins the scooter base before he lands. Nicky squats down as he sails off the ramp's edge.

Momma bear announces to the crew, "Ah, I need to return a book to the library. Back in a bit." Instead, I go next-door to Gabby's house. From her back deck I can watch over the kids, and Josh, who is sitting on the grass next to Jolie watching the boys scooter ride.

Ellen is expecting my call. "Girl," I whisper into the phone. "I still have to get him into a car."

Ellen, my experienced confidant, laughs at my escalating situation. "Jessie do you think I wanted to go to rehab? I was planning my exit strategy the entire ride there. Rest assured, deep inside, I knew I needed the help. Josh does too." Ellen had mentioned that in AA they do not recommend taking someone to rehab alone. She knows Josh will be more reasonable with some form of witness.

"Will you drive us?"

"Absolutely," Ellen responds. "You only needed to ask."

3...2...1

Blast-off time for the alcoholic express! This should go as smoothly as a one-legged duck landing on a frozen pond—not well, not pretty—and if there's a crack, he is goin' slip on through. Gathering in the living room, Jolie wheels his suitcase next to the stone fireplace. By stone I mean a DIY stone stacking kit. If across the street basic Bob could reface his fireplace, so could I...burned through three hacksaw blades custom cutting the rough stacking stones. Turned out to be a professional looking fireplace.

"Dad, are you bringing any books?" Jolie asks as she squeezes into the cloud chair beside Nicky who is playing Castle Crashers.

"No," Josh says sitting beside Connor on the sofa. "You're not allowed. Only approved literature. They don't want anyone triggered from something they read."

Nicky offers his reassurance. "Maybe you'll find some new books to like."

"Maybe."

From our gathered circle Connor speaks with delicate directness. "I know you can quit Dad. This program has shown a lot of people make it. If you put in the work, you can too."

His Dad continues to focus on the coffee table in front of him, then nods. Connor breaks the clumsy silence. "I don't want a drunk dad anymore. You had a great, professional career. We had a great home. I appreciate all the things you've done for us. You have a chance to pull it together. It's hard to see you blow it."

His father gazes up with soft eyes acknowledging that his son spoke from the heart. Josh lifts up his arm. Connor leans in for a hug. Josh whispers, "Thank you. If I do go, I'll be a good student. I've always done that right."

"Oh, you're going," simply vomits out of my mouth; couldn't stop the words if I tried.

"Did you remember your toothbrush, Dad?" Jolie asks on point.

My cell phone pings. Ellen's text reads, "I'm here. Just get him in the car!"

"Kids say your good-byes; Ellen is out front with the car running. I'll meet you outside Josh." Out the house I whiz with suitcase and purse in hand. The emergency kit is already packed.

Ellen's sedan window rolls down. Her spiked-blonde hair is stuck as usual in a 1980s Duran Duran video. "How's it going in there?" She inquires while chewing some gum.

"Well, I know he won't give the kids a hard time. They'll hug him out the door."

"Ah, here he comes." Ellen gives a queen's wave out the car window. "Hi Josh!"

The craftsman door closes. Josh stands on the edge of the porch observing us. Ellen redirects her posture toward the road. Her window rolls up. She is not here to placate. I remain at the curb beside the back passenger door. Josh shifts his weight, places his hands in his denim pockets. He stares my way, perhaps in search for an angle to work me over.

A leather purse hangs from my shoulder. It contains the emergency kit. Here it comes…a chilled can of beer rising up over my head. I give the can a little come-and-get-it wiggle. I throw a little flirt with the eyes signaling, *it's so good*. Josh's hands fall from his pockets. The car door is opened for him. The beer wiggles again sending its wanderlust. Amusement washes over my ex-husband's face, yet he does not descend the steps. Young bewildered faces glued to the kitchen window watch as this scene unfolds. Connor shakes his head. Jolie flips her palms up. Nicolas is too young to say, *what the f—*surely thinks it.

Pressing the aluminum can to my cheek I call out, "Oh my, it's so cold on such a hot day." I close my eyes, arch my neck back, and sensually roll the refreshing can of golden hops along my nape from jawline to collar bone. "You know you want some."

Josh descends the steps, saunters over to the trunk of the sedan and stops. A furry, blonde eyebrow elevates on his mildly entertained face; this sends the telepathic message: *Jess-i-ca, you don't really know what you are doing.*

Pop! The aluminum tab releases all that built up tension. The beer is outstretched before him. His shoulders relax. He shuffles forward. Slowly he seizes the tiny-tinned, six-ounce shorty from my hand. He comments dismissively, "This *thing*," he gives it a twist, "doesn't count as a real beer."

"There's another one for the car ride."

Josh takes a sip and folds into the backseat.

Ellen has turned cherry red from sequestering laughter about the beer bribe. She squeaks, "Ahem, what music do you want? We have satellite radio. Pick anything you'd like."

"Jazz." Josh settles into the backseat with another sip. The back door remains open.

Ellen hisses, "What are you twelve? Close the door."

Josh yanks it shut. Politely, he asks, "So ladies, where are we going?"

"Look at that Ellen, my ex-husband does have a sense of humor."

Ellen offers, "We have a few jazz stations. What's your preference?"

"I like classic jazz—not the fusion crap. Jess, remember all the Coltrane CDs I used to have?" Josh locks eyes with Ellen's in the rearview mirror. "I had a lot of jazz CDs before you-know-who threw them out."

"I did not throw them out."

"Yes, you did."

"No, I didn't."

He insists. "Jess-i-ca, you tossed them when we were chucking stuff out in the dumpster. Remember the dumpster in the driveway? I was helping you throw our lives away?"

"Did you actually see me toss your jazz CDs onto a pile of trash in front of you? And then what—you didn't say or do anything?"

Josh finishes his beer. "Where are my CDs?"

"In the basement, in a box with other things like your favorite kitchen utensils, books, a suit. I saved them for you despite—whatever." I drop it. We ride in silence as a jazz horn section scats from the speakers.

Josh says in a huff, "Thank you for not throwing them out."

I huff back, "You're welcome."

Ellen turns up the radio. "This is going way better than I thought it would."

"Thanks Ellen." My sarcasm is dry as toast.

"No, really," she laughs, "I'm missing a free Zumba class for this. It's totally worth it."

A perplexed Josh distorts his face to ask, "What the hell is a *Zumba*? Did somebody mash a *Zoo-sa-phone* with a tuba? And get a Zumba?" Josh leans forward putting a hand on the front seat. "Ellen do you play the Zumba?"

Pushing his hand off of the seat I adamantly declare, "You cannot combine a sousaphone with a tuba."

"What! Of course you can." Josh persists.

"No, you cannot."

"Why the hell not?" He yelps from the backseat.

"Yeah, why the fuck not?" Ellen double downs. "A Zumba could be a "sousaphone" and a "tuba" smashed together."

"Because a sousaphone is already a modified tuba. John Philip Sousa—the instrument was named after him—wanted to design a tuba that was easier to play when marching. Hence, if you combine a sousaphone with a tuba—you're back to a tuba!"

Josh tilts his head. Scratches his chin. "That makes total sense."

"Does it?" Ellen pinches her face. "Why do you know anything about Philip Sousa?"

"Because, I was in a marching band."

"Did you play the sousaphone?" she asks.

"She played the Zumba!" Josh proclaims. "And, uh, I'm out of beer."

"Did you play the Zumba?" Ellen proceeds to whimper like a puppy, "Please, please tell me you played the Zumba."

"I'll have you know I was drum major for the Lion's Pride Marching Band. I stood on a podium with my white cowgirl boots, a big 'ole cowboy hat and a white cape that I handmade on my mom's sewing machine. I conducted the entire marching band including the tuba section, which was Paul."

Ellen snickers. "Ah the high school years. You were conducting high notes. I was getting high and drunk."

"Me, too," adds Josh, "well, just the drunk part."

Further along the drive, Ellen offers Josh some reassuring tips which he seems to appreciate. He asks about a typical day both in and out of the detox phase. Past the fields and farmlands Ellen shares her own story offering comfort and compassion. Eventually, behind a row of pine trees lies the ranch style compound. The admissions building is in the back. This is not a simple drop and go. Josh is whisked away for an intake interview while Ellen and I wait for almost an hour in the conference room. There are plenty of snacks, coffee and pamphlets.

The intake wraps up with insurance approval. Ellen imparts to Josh, "It will be worth the sacrifice to let it all go." She gives him a strong hug. Face-to-face he thanks her for the ride and for waiting around.

"You're welcome," she says.

A counselor with a handful of keys waits by the door. Next is my turn. Josh gives me a partial, one-arm hug. He asks if I would bring him cigarettes. Ellen's jaw drops.

"You, ah, don't really smoke."

"I know, but it will give me something else to focus on."

"Okay." Still waiting for my gold star of appreciation. *Don't you see me?*

"Well, bye," he says with a slight wave and exits with a counselor in tow.

Ellen's face is squished as if she just sucked a lemon. "He didn't even thank you. Like, I'm waiting for him to say it, and instead, he asks you to bring him smokes!"

"I know." My head goes down. "I'm the messenger of what he doesn't want to hear."

"Oh, I get it. But as your friend, I wanted to slap him."

"When you were dropped off at rehab did you say, *Thanks for bringing me?*"

"No!" Ellen snorts. "I believe I said, *Go fuck yourself!* And slammed the car door."

"You were quite the gem."

"Why, thank you."

"In the OT profession we have to teach skills when patients don't feel like doing anything; they're sick, injured, tired…but if we don't get them moving, they stay stuck and dependent. Maybe that qualifies me as a professional pain-in-the-ass."

"Or, maybe that is what makes you truly special. Wait till Mike hears you got Josh in the car with a shorty. The look on his face was priceless!" Ellen clears her throat. "Josh was right though; that wasn't a real beer."

14
FAMILY WEEKEND

Donny Mac and I are in the wheelchair closet sorting through a plastic tub full of mismatched wheelchair legs. Reunification of these parts is near futile but try we must. It is not a good look to have elderly patients hold one leg out while being pushed in a wheelchair. That would be like taking lessons from a surf shop and finding all the surfboards are cracked; it does not build instructor confidence.

Donny Mac holds up both a short and a long, right-sided foot-rest. "Why are there so many right-sides? Who's stealing left-sided ones?"

"Who would steal any of these?" I fling a footplate to the discard pile. "They're rusty and janky."

Donny Mac deepens his voice to the bass of a Barry White romance song. "I've got something for you babe. It's not rusty or janky?"

"No wonder you're separated. One day you're going to put your key in the front door and its not going to work."

"Hey, hey, our separation is just a phase." He tilts his head back. An expression of reflection strikes his face. His fingertips do that spider-doing-a-push-up thing. "Maybe, it's not a phase.

It's likely not. She did seem pretty clear." He chucks another janker to the pile.

The cell phone inside my khakis pocket vibrates; it's the other kind of rehab calling. "Yo Swanks, I need to take this call."

"Go do you," Donny Mac says, then shakes his head mumbling, "This place has got to get some new wheel chairs."

While my cohort sorts his metal and mental bits, I try to sort out why a case worker is bluntly telling me to come pick up my ex-husband. Apparently, Josh has decided to sign himself out. This feels like a wet finger in socket.

"Are you kidding me? It's been less than a week!" I gape at Donny Mac who's mouth is open as wide as mine. "The kids and I are coming this Friday to the, the, what's it called, the family thing."

"I know ma'am. He is sitting right here." The flat-toned caseworker provides the mildest, exasperated explanation. "He prefers to leave. He wants a ride."

My voice lowers. "Did you try, I mean really try, to get him to stay?"

"Yes, a few of us explained that we feel this is too soon. He disagrees. We need to arrange a pick up for him."

Donny Mac pinches his fingers at his mouth; pretends to toke a joint, then passes it to me. I take the hit and flick it. "Put Josh on the phone."

The caseworker iterates in the background, "Jessica wants to talk to you. Do you want a ride home? Then talk to her."

"Hey," Josh says. "What's up?"

"Seems you think it's time to discharge after five days."

"I can finish the rest at home. I feel fine."

"Let's review how that might work out. You go a week, or two, without a drink; your body is naturally repelling it anyway. Then you decide to have just one drink. That drink spirals into a bender. Your benders keep hitting harder. Everything you worked for will be at risk, again. It's a sticky cycle."

"I hear what you are saying. I can go to meetings."

"Imagine how much stronger you could be, if you double-down on where you are today?"

To this I hear the silence of reflection.

"Josh, the kids and I are participating in the family workshop this weekend. They write you a letter; you write them a letter. It's part of a healing process, which quite frankly, they deserve. Can you just give it a few more days—until the event?"

"I don't think my insurance will cover it."

A counselor spits out from the background, "Your insurance did approve."

"Three days Josh—you lived in my house for six months. Give yourself a chance to see what happens if you stay longer."

"I really prefer to go."

"You're a mental healthcare worker. How often do you say to your patients, 'You'll be cured in a week, and you'll love every minute of it?' Never; it doesn't work like that. You don't have to like being there. It's not their job to entertain you. It's your job to get something out of it, every hour, every day. Can we please turn this around?"

"I am not claiming to be cured. I don't think this place is right for me. No offense," he offers to whoever else is in the room.

"Then make it right for you. If you don't want to stay for yourself, then stay for your family. It's fair we ask that you try your best."

"I'm doing good here, right guys?" Josh proclaims to his audience. "I haven't missed anything they tell me to do. I talk to everyone here. I give away more cigarettes than I smoke. Jess, I'm trying."

"Would you try until we see you as a family this Friday? We can reassess the situation then."

His offers an elongated silence. "Okay," he says.

Whoosh! A counselor jumps in stating, "Josh, we'd like to confirm that you are staying another week?"

"Yes," Josh sighs, "I will stay thru the family weekend thing."

"We have to let the insurance company know to keep your spot. Let's do that right now." The counselor is no fool. Josh is sandwiched between me and his word; he jumped on it. Another voice asks Josh to accompany him.

"Bye Jess. I have to go."

The phone gets passed. "Hello," a counselor says. "We will continue things on our end. We'll see you and the kids this weekend."

"Hold up! Your boy was about to go AMA (Against Medical Advice)."

"Yes, he was."

"I got him to stay." What does a woman have to do to get a gold star around here?

"You did, thank you. Josh seems to think he should be supervising all of us."

"Ah yes, he knows more than all of you put together. Good luck draining that tank of gas."

"That would be something," he replies.

Seriously, if Josh lost his addiction and his narcissism at the same time, what would be left? He can't give up drinking and have his grandiose, protective shield get whacked too. Those shield defenses wove into his dura matter a long time ago. They are not unwinding at this juncture. Whatever—we all want Josh to cross to the other side and live his best life. Maybe he will…maybe.

THE REHAB CENTER had provided us homework: constructive questions to answer for the family members to express themselves. Some of the questions help shape a letter to their Dad about how his drinking affects them. Sheets of lined paper and three envelopes are spread across the glass table top. In the center a folder bulges with stapled information packets and instructions. This feels good. I explain to the kids sitting around the table, "We need this done for Friday's visit." I smile at the boys in their Hollister T-shirts and Jolie wearing a shirt with a melting face; but none of them move.

"Okay, let's get started."

So they start to moan, "We don't want to go."

"Excuse me?" This was my superhero moment. These kids are stealing my cape. "Connor? Jolie? Nicholas? None of you want to go and support your father?"

Connor speaks first. "We'd lose a day of school and a Saturday. It's his problem not mine."

"I have band practice," Jolie chiming in, "I shouldn't miss it."

"I don't really want to go," Nicholas says either from sibling observation or mere disinterest.

"This doesn't make sense." I am miffed. "There will be other families there and speakers. It's good for you guys, too."

"We'd have to miss school," whines Nicky.

"I don't like that part either," I admit. "They are giving us lunch. Did I mention it's a buffet?"

Connor's face has gone taut around the mouth, much like his dad's when frustrated. "I don't want to talk in front of anybody."

"Mom," Jolie makes her plight, "it's two-days. We have things ta-do!"

This is where being a single parent without back up gets tough. My perspective feels under pressure. "It was a game changer for me to hear an alcoholic speak his truth. It gave me a deeper understanding. It's an angle your Dad can't speak from, yet. Perhaps, you might hear things you never knew could be helpful."

"It's good it helped you mom," says Connor, "but we don't want to go."

Weighing on my mind is another reason they should go. My

kids are more likely to have a drinking problem. Attending maybe of some future added benefit; I don't know. I opt for a more indirect approach. "It's likely that one day you might have to take a friend to rehab, or someone close to you. You'll have experience to offer. You'll be that solid person."

The kids are not forward-thinking on this; they are in the moment. I listen until it is time to compromise. We read over some literature from the packet of facts about alcoholism and recovery. I slide over their questions to fill out describing how *drinking behaviors* effect them. The compromise presented is that the kids don't have to go if (1) they fill out the questionnaire and (2) write the prompted letter to their dad. I will attend the family weekend alone and deliver everything. This sounds reasonable to me, but resentment arrows zoom from their quivers.

I don't want to go. I hate writing. It's his problem. Why should we do his homework?

Blah, blah, blah-h, their complaints bounce off the mom shield. My retaliation is three pencils laid out before them. They pull back and launch more arrows.

What good is this going to do? I don't know what to write. Come on, Mom.

"Ready," rhetorically spoken. A yellow highlighter swipes which questions each kid will complete factoring their ages: 16, 14 and 10. Their pelting continues.

Are you going to do one? This is stupid. What if I hurt his feelings?

Gently I press a fingertip upon my lips, "Shhh." The same finger pushes a white envelope toward each obnoxious child's writing stations. "Your father is worth twenty minutes of your precious time. Part of his recovery is to take in what each of you have to say. Your voice matters and my efforts deserve your support without the crap." Briskly I leave the table with the parting words, "I will set a timer."

Pissed off and alone I hug my knees on the bathroom floor

and rock. Their dad will never know the crap I'm left to handle while he cocoons up in a self-centered bubble. He thinks I am competent of nothing. Moreover, I am also pissed and upset that I can't tap out. I don't have a partner. Shit gets rough with teenagers. I don't know what's right every time. Leaned over at the sink, the cold water on my face washes my pity-party away.

Peeking around the kitchen wall, things at the table are not as bad as I left it. The kids are totally quiet, deep in thought, writing, nonstop. The pause button is pressed on the watch timer. One by one the kids seal their envelopes. I rejoin them at the table. With a welcomed level of calm, Connor, Jolie and Nicky each express one final though: *I don't want you to read it. I said what I had to say. Hope he gets better.*

The letters stack in my hands. "I will give these to Dad."

The mood in the air is solemn, raw. My oldest says, "I told him I believed in him."

"I said some things he needs to know," says Jolie. "I also told him I think he can do it."

Nicky puts his arms around my ribs and squeezes. Love wipes a pity-party clean, too.

Going It Solo

Buzzing around Target I search for the perfect shirt. What does the ex-wife attending "rehab family day" without "the family" wear? Guess I'll know when I see it…ah, found it! Yaz-z —the blue t-shirt with a big S on the front. Superwoman.

Josh is disappointed the kids did not attend; a light in his eyes immediately turns off. We sit among ten tables of family and attendees. I take notice that there are no kids here. After a couple hours of speakers, Josh quietly accuses me of manipulating him and not bringing the kids on purpose. This is said under his breath to me while a counselor speaks at the microphone.

I whisper back. "They have school. They filled out their forms and wrote you letters. Do you think that was easy for them?"

Josh takes the envelopes I waved off the table and places them in his notebook. When a break comes for table chatting, Josh introduces me to his counselor. He seems embarrassed to admit his kids did not come.

The counselor reassures Josh this is understandable. "I'm impressed your kids wrote you. You have teenagers, right? Their thoughts and feelings are in those letters. It's a big deal."

Josh nods. It does not seem to matter I took the day off work and showed up. No one else brought kids here and I bet they did not write any letters. Screw Josh's mild tantrum. I am choosing to get something out of the family program. Every speech about what recovery looks and feels like has value, because for too long I lived in an opposite world of fake lip-service. Out of twenty families attending, I am the only ex-spouse here. My Superman T-shirt gets a lot of nods and brightened faces. Even my ex-husband smiled when he first saw me.

Josh completes the rehab center's recommended time with stellar compliance. Upon discharge, a partial day program is recommended. Josh thinks he does not need it.

15
POOR PLUTO

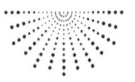

When I attended school, Pluto was the ninth planet of the solar system orbiting way out in the back of the galaxy. The littlest guy did its galactic thing. It had a comfortable existence. Then physicist Neil deGrasse Tyson reassessed the situation. Poof! Pluto gets kicked out of the club for noncompliance. The stretched point here is that knowledge can empower change. While banning Pluto from the planetoid club did not alter my life, I appreciated that world scientists collaborated, unified and handed us a truth, instead of letting it be. It was worth getting it right.

At this point I feel that I have held up my end of a spiritual contract with my ex and my family. This brings renewed energy to perform a healthy scrutinization of my own lifestyle. If I do not then I would be a walking hypocrite.

Where does one begin a self-renovation? Nothing like a cringe photo of non-defined, hotdog arms and a missing waistline to make that clear. Everything about me in that particular photo appeared blah—my body, skin, clothes, hairstyle, my creative spirit. It was as if part of me inhabited Pluto, existing comfortably, yet not engaging with the big leagues. When I side-stepped myself for a non-uplifting partner, a feminine piece of myself bowed out. That loss was an important source of power.

Well, *bonjour Pluton!* I am off to discover, harness, and deliver my potential, because that is worth getting right.

Physical Health

Building the upgrade starts with detoxing the body. At my reduced weight of 133-pounds I still get heat rashes, sweat pants are my friend and at night I have to void 2 or 3 times which is a sign of insulin resistance. Many cultures practice fasting. A proper *intermittent fasting* (IF) provides the body and mind a chance to do wonders. One benefit of IF in the morning is extending nighttime cortisol production. The morning is where I start.

First week, I push breakfast to 11:00 am. I have headaches; but they clear. My first meal is pasture-raised eggs. Second week, my first meal pushes out to 1:00 pm. This is not too difficult. The bigger challenge is to stop snacking at night. If I am real about it, I snacked whenever I felt like it. That is hard to quit, but an absolute must to get a change in body and discipline practice. Even a little snack limits the full benefit of the fasting system especially tapping into the stored fat which is ketosis. To boost the IF benefits, I drink shots of apple cider vinegar (ACV) with water. It helps adjust the gut pH to foster healthier gut bacteria.

As my nutrition improves, I break under the trying 130-pound mark—fortitude is found! I stop eating after 7 pm. This puts me in an 18-hour fasting zone with a 6-hour eating window.

Initially, this feels strenuous (more mentally than physically).

But soon it becomes somewhat natural. My energy, facial skin, and sleep improve. Becoming bolder I increase the fasting to 20 hrs. At this point...check out my waistline! Before there was a pair of back-fat side-rolls on each side. Now there is only one cocktail-size Weiner-roll per side; I can live with that in my late forties, if I must. The bathroom scale displays...a sixteen-pound weight loss! 127 is a fine weight for 5' 2" although, I most definitely was 5' 3". Must have lost an inch of spine in the divorce.

Another benefit of an IF and a ketosis-eating lifestyle besides feeling great and visceral fat leaving my body: hormonal rebalance. The mild hot flashes I randomly had completely stopped; when I re-eat sugar and carbs to the point of gaining a few pounds back, the mild night sweats come back. Some hormone re-balancing is possible.

Moving forward I maintain this current weight without the strict, extreme eating windows I had needed to get the change going; my body is more efficiently. Next change: match my environment with this 2.0 version of myself.

Home Health

Enter the right book. *The Joy of Tidying* movement is changing lives. Mari Kondo's cleaning and organizing methodologies are a game changer. From Japan to China, Canada to Australia, and certainly across the USA folks are dumping all their clothes into a pile, holding a once beloved shirt and asking, *do you still bring me joy?* Like an old high school flame, if that shirt does not spark joy: break up with it! Thank the item for its service— *Thank you flannel shirt for keeping me stuck in the 90's*— and toss it.

What remains are joyful expressions of myself through clothes. My wardrobe is sorted by item type then color and refolded like origami. These origami clothing pieces are tucked back into the drawers like a bento box creating evermore space. Clothes are easier to find and select. This organization sparks into the rest of the house...sorting books, kitchen gadgets... eventually re-organizing the entire house until everything has its categorized place, value and function. The total result: luxury of space, easy cleaning, a peaceful sense of pride and sparks of joy everywhere.

Financial health

I read advice from financial gurus Suzie Orman and Dave Ramsey. They teach strategies on how to eliminate debt, achieve financial security then build wealth. First move is to cut up credit cards except: the one with the most cash back and one debt card. I had to get a new wallet; the old one held the fatter shape. Reduction to managing one bank statement gives a fuller-picture of the cash coming in and the cash going out. All my reward points are redeemed in cash. The small wins add up.

My *cash only* perspective decreases overall spending and keeps my goals in check. The goals: no debt, 3 months of living expenses saved (for emergency); then investments. If I work my ass off for a year with extra OT work, I can pay off the new car and be debt free. I was never bad with money; but I want to be successfully great at it.

The lifestyle changes are in play. I need less, spend less, weigh less, feel better and look better. My credit score soars from a low 700 to a high 700. With money from my father's estate which was only the value of his car split with Greg, I will expand the gardens and add a porch to the front of the house.

The 2.0 goals have not yet been completed and already I desire incoming visions of my 3.0 version. Secretly, I want to reach 120 pounds; I did try but could not. How about an 800-credit score? Could I write a successful second book? Sheesh, it took 8 years to write the first one. Will I ever earn a million dollars? Is a love-life better than my dreams even possible? I do not know these answers or where I will land. There is a thrill to that because it means I am evolving...learning from better mistakes...going outside my comfort zone. Perhaps there is no limit on the versions that lie ahead.

16
TRENT

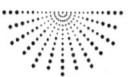

Florescent streaks of pink taffy and orange sherbet scream across a Floridan sky. A sea breeze infuses the air. Another coastal sunset drifts into the shades of twilight. This is the salty taste of St. Petersburg. Here is my spur-of-the-moment vacation to escape the dutiful version of myself in exchange for…anything new.

My Airbnb accommodation is a basic bedroom with shared kitchen and living spaces. The super host, Kelly, turns out to be super cool. She kindly includes me with her evening plans for a bicycle ride with her "special group". Whether coincidently or serendipitously, she belongs to a sobriety group led by her best friend, Trent.

Kelly and I arrive at a former-commercial store that has been converted into a recreational center. Trent manages this recreational center; he also lives there. Next to a handful of bike cruisers, Trent loads a milk-crate-sized speaker onto a bicycle trailer. We exchange polite introductions. He and Kelly pack snacks, frisbees, bean bags and mason jars of strange concoctions into the trailer. In our chit-chat Trent casually remarks, "People who don't drink are boring."

"I wouldn't say that's true."

Trent peers over circular rimmed glasses. "It's true."

Feeling a little defensive I retort, "Well, I don't need to drink, and I'm not boring." Admittedly, this is a weak claim (unless we're talking about playing with kids, then I crush it). Trent does not challenge my claim; he seems sagacious about these things.

Bagged homemade cookies lie on top of the full cooler which Trent slides next to the speaker. He flicks a button from his pocket. The hitched bike and trailer pop alive with strands of twinkling lights. A dozen individuals recovering from addictions have gathered on the sidewalk with their bikes. Let's ride!

I am feeling pretty cool that within hours of disembarking my plane in a new city, alone, without a plan, I am riding a pale-blue beach cruiser past outdoor shops and restaurants in a make-shift mini parade. Kelly, wearing an illuminated baseball cap as bright as her decorated bike, is our illuminated leader. Effortlessly she weaves around parked cars and the grids of touristy down-town traffic. Her bushy, brown curls blow carelessly behind her. Woven into her cap above the brim is a mini-electronic sign. The words *Sobriety Society* flash across her head like a stock market ticker. The changing lights on her wheels create mesmerizing circular rainbows. The bike parade snakes through crowded tourist filled streets. At the tail end Trent blares techno dance music. Patrons dining *al fresco* wave and smile. Pedestrians waiting for green lights to change dance on the street corners as we ride by. *See, I'm not boring; look at everybody waving at me.* Of course, I am riding on Trent's coat tails.

Our parade destination is an expansive circle of Adirondack chairs within St. Petersburg's new 26-acre waterfront pier. Recently, the pier had a celebrated reopening after a grand renovation. At the city's celebration, artist Janet Echelman unveiled her arial sculpture, *Bending Arc*. The sculpture is a massive five-story canopy made of ropes and sails.

Bending Arc is composed of 1,662,528 knots and 180 miles of twine. Covering a portion of the park, it spans 424 feet across and measures 72 feet high at its tallest point. The monumental sculpture billows and collapses with the ebb and flow of winds high above the Pier. At nightfall, colored flood lights illuminate the shifting choreography as the coastal breezes shadow-box with the shifting sails and slapping knotted ropes. Underneath *Bending Arc*, families, kids, dogs on leashes and lovers (some on leashes) stroll the park grounds. Countless pristine yachts dot the waterscape much like the pointillism of a Seurat painting.

Our bicycles come to rest against towering palm trees. Tanned legs from our group stretch out on the Adirondack chairs. Thick grass offers a revitalizing tickle for tired feet. Trent, the consummate host, pulls out a half-gallon mason jar filled with a homemade concoction of mango and coconut juice infused with *kava root* and powered *kratom leaves*. He pours and passes. Everyone accepts the big red drinking cups with gratitude.

Always happy to educate Trent answers my inquiry about the concoction. "Kava root is found in Hawaii. It has calming properties; it relaxes. Kratom takes the edge off addiction cravings. It also helps to manage pain."

Kelly chimes in, "The Kava lifts your mood. I can feel it."

"The kratom helps with my back pain," someone else adds.

"Kratom has a lot of healing properties," Trent confirms. "It's why I serve it at my sober center. The biggest part I miss with drinking is the camaraderie. My mission is to make being sober...sexy. There's no reason it shouldn't be." His chiseled features, wavy hair, and lean physique remind me of a European soccer player. Trent does not bother to fuss over his appealing looks. He has a candid and calm demeanor that would definitely offer an addict *losing his shit* a sense of comfort. Offering wellness beyond comfort, Trent runs three successful shops selling kava and kratom. He himself takes kratom three times a day and a kava drink as needed.

Kratom is derived from a sister plant to the coffee bean. Trent deals directly with a local distributor in Indonesia. He claims, "When you open a package of my kratom, it releases Indonesian air."

"What does kratom do for you?"

"Kratom targets the addiction urges and the Kava decreases detox symptoms; both act as mood stabilizers. Someone cannot sit through an AA meeting if experiencing the shakes from withdrawals. Over the years, I have had 3,000 customers. Only 10% dropped out from meetings in their first year."

The passion Trent exudes about recovery intrigues me. After my 15-year marriage to an alcoholic, I find his honesty and intensity about recovery refreshing. Being the therapist that I am, I ask about his past.

Trent's origin story does not begin with a tragic childhood. He grew up wealthy and loved among many siblings. At age sixteen, he first smoked pot with his friends to kill the boredom. "It was fun," he says.

Trent's father worked long days for many years to become a self-made millionaire. Frank, Trent's father, at age 10 landed odd jobs for a printing press. Over the years Frank learned the business well enough to start a company of his own. Trent recalls seeing his father layout screen printing work in their basement. Fifteen years later his dad had over 300 employees. The business was so successful that Frank bought a castle with an underground fortress. If the world had an apocalypse, Trent and his nine siblings would be safe.

"Dad was nuts about being protective," Trent recounts. "Our family was part of a documentary called, *The Doomsday Preppers*. It was about rich folks and their extreme measures in case the world goes to shit."

Visions of becoming a millionaire, like his father, entered

Trent's teenage entrepreneurial mind. Unlike his father, Trent was not willing to take years to accomplish self-wealth. "Screw that! I was going to be a millionaire by age 21."

Trent's foolproof plan was to sell drugs which Trent describes in hindsight as a sure path towards self-destruction. His father's fortress could not protect his son from hurling towards an absurd, and I mean an ABSURD, amount of alcohol and drugs. Trent explains. "In my young, male brain I thought this plan was brilliant and flawless. I knew people with money, a lot of money. If I conducted myself in a proper, upscale manner and did not smoke into my profits, I was set."

"Did it work?"

"It was working, but at too slow a pace. So, I expedited the plan; sold harder drugs for more money. Figured I was safe, because I didn't touch the hard shit. I actually thought those who did hard drugs had some kind of weakness. That line of thinking separated me from being a drug user. I just sold them; I didn't use them…much…hardly." Trent raises his eyebrows into his messy bangs.

"Were you a millionaire by 21?"

Trent nods affirmatively. This is an impressive feat.

"And by twenty-four," Trent says with a grin turned down, "I lost it all. I lost everything."

"What? How?"

Trent laughs. "I was snorting what I was selling! Cocaine to go up. Ketamine to come down."

"We're you drinking too?"

"That was the least of my problems." His eyes roll back for a pause. "Eventually, I tried prescription drugs to get off illegal drugs, but they're designed to be addictive too. It was impossible to get out from under."

Trent hustled to make another million (the same way). He self-swore not to use this time. Well, he lost that fortune (the same way). It took until now, age forty-nine, to remain clean and sober for 18 months. Steadily he is on his way to another million, this time honorably selling kratom and kava to prevent addictions.

A COUPLE DAYS after the parade adventure, I am back at the Sobriety Society House returning my e-bike; Trent loans and rents bicycles. Following a personal tour, we sit on an L-shaped gaming sofa in the empty lounge. Trent makes me a small kava tea, and himself the usual: a kratom veggie smoothie in a glass jar. I have an itch to scratch from our conversation the other day; something seemed a miss. "You mentioned opening a kava/kratom shop years ago, yet you've only been sobered for 18-months."

"Yes," he leans back into the sofa. "For a long-time I was an active addict helping other addicts. Arrogantly, I thought I wasn't like my clients. I wasn't *a real addict*, because I was selling stuff to *help addicts*. I had it under control; my clients did not. That is what my addict brain told me. I believed this even though I could not stop using. The lie I told myself was that *I could stop, if I really wanted it.* Meanwhile, my life was unmanageable, and I was stuck in a vicious cycle: things would fall apart, I'd quit drugs for two or three months and rebuild everything. Each time I started over I thought, *it will be different this time.* Then, I'd fuck it all up again."

"Sounds familiar and exhausting. You definitely pulled some head games on yourself."

"Remembering all the shameful things messes with your head. With blackouts you forget how bad things got. There were times I'd be wasted when someone came into the store for help. That person had to leave, because an addict can't watch another addict losing it; it's not helpful.

"At my kava bars we educate and self-empower clients to tweak their own dosages. We teach them how to make their shakes or homemade power bars…we teach it all. The millennial generation is open to this. They don't like going to AA meetings. AA wasn't dealing with opioids at its inception."

My curiosity has peaked. "There had to have been some kind of turning point. Something that happened 18-months ago?"

Trent takes a long, deep breath that draws out his past, and brings it here. With piercing brown eyes, he utters, "There was."

Rock Bottom

A striped bath robe lies over Trent's worn Zeppelin t-shirt and loose jeans. He makes use of a weaved blanket draping over the sofa to wipe his wire rims clean. He keeps the back story simple. "I was running a five-year bender on oxytocin and alcohol. It's bad when you drink alone and use alone. I was doing both."

"How bad did it get?"

"I was snorting 30 oxytocin a day."

"Thirty—snorted? I didn't even know one could–wow!" Trent exudes no humor or lightness despite that we are surrounded by his arcade games, a fuse ball table, and furniture set up as a conversation pit. "What made you finally quit?"

His life's turning point was on July 4. Trent explains, "I kept dealing with heavy depression. Often, I woke-up feeling like I was in a dark cavern and couldn't escape. It felt like death was coming for me. This was when the depression got overwhelming. Nothing I did nor took could the depression from coming again. But this time, I figured out a way to fix it. If I did something that was the complete opposite of how I felt, that would have the power to turn everything in my life around.

"The 4th of July was right around the corner." His arms lift up in declaration. "I decided to throw the biggest party ever! Bigger than any party I'd ever thrown, seen or couldn't remember."

I smile at the grandness. "That is quite the opposite of feeling depressed. But Trent, in essence you were planning to do more drugs."

"I was going *to share* my drugs. To the brain it is different if you are sharing. This party was going to be the best and the last time I ever used again. So…

"I book a huge suite at the grand Hotel overlooking the ocean. I get five bottles of Tito's and, of course, enough cocaine for everybody." Trent stretches his legs. He looks out to a window. His voice drops to a whisper, "And then."

Briefly, we share a view of clustering palm trees. I ask, "Then what?"

"My girlfriend cancels on me; just blows me off. She doesn't pick up my calls. I go to her house. She isn't home. I'm hurt and angry; I feel like a failed partner. It's the final straw that sets me off. Fuck everybody! —I call all my friends and cancel the party. I go to the hotel room, open the Tito's. In the course of the night I drink all the Tito's and snort all the cocaine. Whatever pills I had, took them too. It was the most I ever ingested at one time in my entire life. It should have killed me."

This blows my mind— Blows my mind! But I remain as neutral as a journalist doing an interview. I do not want to come off as a judgmental goody-two shoes. I ask him, "Did you start vomiting? I mean it must have made you sick."

"All I did was pass out. When I finally woke-up, I couldn't believe I was still alive. There was only one reason I was breathing," Trent up points a finger, then turns it to point at himself, "I had become the biggest addict ever. Consuming all that would have killed anyone I knew, but it didn't kill me. That is how much of an addict I was."

Trent twists the mason jar in his hand. He drinks the green liquid to the near bottom. "I passed out again. The next time I woke up, I was suicidal. Never did I have that before. Drug overdosing is many things; this was different. My own thoughts were hijacked. There was a mission in my head to kill myself by my own hands. It was unnerving. You can't shake it off. You can't talk yourself out of it."

My head whirls with everything he says. "I can't imagine. It sounds like an altered-state."

"My thoughts were not mine anymore. All I felt was deep failure. My brain kept replaying every negative thought I had."

"Like what?" My mug of tea is still warm. It tastes of ginger and honey.

Behind the coffee table Trent crosses his legs. Cut-off jeans fray around his pockets and ankles. He reveals, "I felt I wasn't a good father to my daughter. Felt I had lost all my friends. I kept losing my businesses and screwing up my relationships. My girlfriend didn't want me. Each failure connected to suicide. Killing myself was the only thing left to succeed at. I grabbed the hair dryer attached to the wall and wrapped the cord around my neck. I pulled it over the door and tried to hang myself. The cord broke away. I later researched, those cords breakaway at 20 pounds of pressure for that reason."

Trent's mason jar rests on the table, a bit more is still at the bottom. "Were you relieved when it broke?" I imagine Trent will answer a *hard yes* to this question.

"No, I was not," he replies. "Failing at suicide became another failure on the list. This made me more determined. So I took the iron cord and wrapped it around my neck. I threw it over the curtain rod. The rod broke. I tied it to the ceiling fan. The fan broke. The room was a destroyed, suicidal mess. My mind got worse and went berserk. I thought, *only the biggest loser of losers fails at suicide.* My harshest judgment had been at someone who couldn't turn their life around, then chose to kill themselves and failed. I mocked them in my head. I pitied them. Here I was…a hypocrite. I had pretended not to be an addict. Yet, I had dumped more drugs and alcohol into my body than any person should and survived. Why didn't I die?" Trent raises his glass jar.

"Because I was the biggest, mother-fucking addict ever, so big that I couldn't even over-dose myself; what a fuck-up." Trent lifts the mason jar to his lips. He drinks until there is nothing left.

I search for something to say. Nothing fits except to hold space with him, listening, heart to heart.

Trent continues. "Every bone in me wanted to jump out the window and end it. I hurled a metal ice bucket at the center of the glass. The bucket bounced off. Over and over I violently smashed at the window with the ice bucket…then I threw a chair. Double-proofed hurricane windows do not break. Twenty dents went into that window. Thank God I didn't have a gun or I wouldn't be here. Access to a gun in that state of mind equals game over. Overdosing on meds where a side effect is suicidal thoughts is a one-way ticket."

"At this point do you think to call someone for help?"

"Not a chance; I had to succeed at killing myself. I was not going to die a hypocrite. I had to succeed at suicide. Living at this point was not an option. I left the hotel to drown myself."

Trent's Beneath Rock Bottom

Trent walked toward the water planning never to return. Everything that mattered had been stuffed into a backpack–money, laptop, phone, personal items–all to weigh himself down. His hotel de horror was next to the pier during its Bending Arc renovation. In the search of a tenebrous location to drown himself, Trent stumbled upon a 9-foot *johnboat*. The painters used it to stand on while painting the pylons. Trent waded out to the pylons. The johnboat accompanied him without any claim. He tied the thick wet hemp rope tightly around his waist. Dragging the weight was meant to speed up the exhaustion in this Kamikaze swim to end his life.

"I thought it was pretty smart to pull the boat," says Trent. "Without it I might not drown."

"If I may suggest, perhaps the boat symbolized your failures. You're a self-made man. You tried to keep a code. Perhaps the boat, bound to you, was an extension of your assumed failures dragging you. Or it was symbolic of the addiction you were tied to."

Trent sinks back into the cushions. "Maybe; I see the symbolism in hindsight."

"I'm trying to picture this. Are you swimming up the coast? Out to sea? How far did you get?"

"I kept swimming back and forth from a rock point to the pier. I swam for two days straight, from July 5 to July 7."

"Two days! I know you had drugs in your system, but you should have gotten exhausted and drowned."

"That was the plan. At night I didn't leave the water, I sat on some rocks. There was a lightning storm, wild as hell the first night. I remember it vividly; drugs will do that. If I were just drunk, I would have blacked out."

"What were you thinking all that time?"

"Every negative thought. They kept coming, so I kept swimming, and waited for death. The second night, maybe I slept a little. I thought, *how long is this going take? Why won't I just give up?*"

I found this wording intriguing. "Hmm, that's a different angle than thinking, *why won't I just die?*"

"Huh, I don't know. How so?"

"I think the exact words someone chooses to pinpoint a core thought matters. *Why won't I give up,* is different then, *Why won't I die?*"

"Explain." He extends a hand out.

"The answer to *why won't I die is…*because you won't give up. *Why won't you give up…*is the real question to answer. I think your mind was sorting itself out. It seemed as if part of you was fighting."

"Swimming was all I could do. Workers kept showing up to the pier. Each shift men pointed to the crazy guy swimming back and forth pulling a boat. I guess they didn't realize it was their boat. On the day of the 7th, as I approached the pier, one of the workers walked out onto the rocks and waited for me at my turn around spot. He called out, 'Hey man, do you want some water?'"

"This guy looked me square on. He offered the most basic act of kindness." Trent opens his hands as if holding a gift. "I stopped swimming."

"It is amazing what a strike of kindness can spark."

"That positive sparse spark was all I could allow. I thought, *at the very least I deserve a sip of water*. I untied the rope, took the bottle and drank. Once I started, I could not stop. I was so fucking thirsty. This guy didn't say anything; he didn't judge me.

"I decided to lug myself out of the bay. My legs were chewed up and bloody from the rocks. The skin on my hands and feet was like shredded coconut meat; they looked wrong. Another guy gave me a ride to a nearby store. I bought a couple of Gatorades with wet money...sat in the parking lot with my book bag...stared off into space with complete absence of time. I began to think, *I have to do something different. I have to do something different. I HAVE TO DO SOMETHING DIFFERENT*. My phone and laptop were drenched. No one could call me, but I took it as no one wanted to call me. No one noticed I was missing. The world will not suffer if I am gone.

"I looked pretty sketchy sitting outside the store–a tall, lanky dude who hasn't eaten for days, shredded to shit, sunburnt, bloody, ragged t-shirt, and shorts falling off. Someone called the cops. Eventually, six officers were on the scene. Cop cars were scattered everywhere. They offered to take me to the hospital, but I didn't want to go. I explained that I sold kratom, and that it helps with addiction cravings. Told them I had to go back to my store and get some, so I would not use again. Only one cop offered to take me home. His name was Ernie. Riding home in the police golf cart, everyone starred at the cop with the freak.

"Ernie did not say a word he whole time. When we got to my store Ernie asked, 'Do you know why I offered to take you home?'

"Told him, No.

"He said, 'Because kratom saved my life.'"

St. Petersburg has a youthful, downtown district. It bustles with tanned fit bodies wearing chunky sandals and high-end sunglasses. Among many art galleries, a Chihuly Collection Museum sits as the crown jewel. Inside tourists can find massive handblown glass sculptures and large-scale chandeliers made of the vibrant colors found on Latin skirts swirling to Spanish guitars. Cafes sell kratom. Coffee bars offer shots of kava and kratom.

Trent recounts what happened when he got home. "I put a sign outside my store, *Business closed until the eighth*. My home was my business at the time. I figured I probably pissed off all my customers by not being there for two days. I spent the next day sleeping and contemplating about what I had to do different. I put a sign on the door that I'd open on the 8th"

"No doubt," I mention, "two-days of letting shit go had to be cathartic." The kava-infused ginger tea I've been sipping has brightened my mood.

Trent details his first step was to stabilize his mood and cravings with botanical solutions. Refreshed with sleep, nutrition and clean clothes, Trent opened for business. He expected no one to come. However, when his shop doors opened that next morning–

"There was a line around the corner. My customers were waiting to see if I was okay; they weren't just there to buy product. They were worried," Trent says with a cracking voice. "I never had so many people in one day. Broke a sales record: $1200 worth of business in a day."

Instead of being in a box at his own funeral, Trent was the hearth of a community welcome.

"That night I went to an AA meeting. The only reason I could sit through it was because kratum held off the cravings. After three days of hearing about the 12 steps, I thought it was the best self-help option out there. I decided to become a member and not do it alone. Wish I had learned about it in high school as a reference. Kids might need it to face all this addiction that society is leaving behind for them to walk into. I went to meetings every day for the next 90 days."

"I know about the 90-90. How are you doing today?"

"I drink kratom three times a day. I go to weekly meetings, and my new "high" is to be part of someone's turn around moment."

Trent leans toward the coffee table and points for emphasis. "I've seen kava calm down the body, and the brain, time and time again. That has to happen, first, so you can start making those immediate good decisions. Take it as you need it; for example, if someone's mom suddenly dies, your recovery is at risk. This plant gives another option to cope. It also helps manage pain which gets people off pain killers. There are 25 strands of kratom, but the top five are branded into colors."

"What did I drink the other night? It gave me the jitters for a couple hours like coffee, but without the heart palpitations."

"You had a mix of green and white kratom. You had too much for you."

"Makes sense. I can't drink a full mug of coffee without jitters; I'm a tea gal. The kava didn't get me high like marijuana, and I don't crave it."

"I've had 3000 clients and only 10% have relapsed. We give them constant education, so they are in the driver seat. Pharma companies failed to pass a bill to make it illegal, so they smear it. Meanwhile, they legally fill scripts for addictive drugs. People should be able to at least try and see. Nobody loses everything because they are drinking kratom."

Trent's 4th of July turnaround plan did work; it was indeed the last day he did drugs. It was for the best he partied alone, keeping up with Trent would have killed somebody. Swimming tirelessly in the ocean tied to a boat, he was a man trying to kill himself and save himself at the same time. The separation began with a spark of truth: *I am worthy of...a sip of water.*

Trent wants addicts to experience the freedom of leaving an addiction behind, thus he shares his story. He also listens to other people's stories. They serve as a reminder that he is only one drink, one pill or one snort away from a repeat trip to beneath rock bottom.

17
SHE CAN'T KEEP HER HANDS OFF ME

*J*osh makes it through winter without any clinical follow-up. Spring…not so much. He is right back to where he started and I am right back to asking…

"Did you call the rehab center?"

"Couldn't get through." He pours fresh coffee into a travel mug.

"Leave a message; it keeps a spot on the rehab waitlist."

"Yes, dear."

Ugh.

Later, Josh texts me at the Atrium that he left a voice message. Did he though? Certainly, I am exhausted by his relapses, isn't he? My mom mentioned the average visits to rehab before it sticks is four times…these are my distractions sitting in the bat cave trying to appear productive. While Batman visits his Bostonian family I cover the department, hence no patient treatments. The bat cave serves as my privacy shelter, that is to say, until Donny Mac saunters in.

"Hey, boss lady. Thought we had you today." A boyish grin creeps upon his mouth. He leans a single arm onto my desk.

"Guess I'll have to do whatever you say, boss. Feel free to get wildly creative."

"You really should wear a pin saying, 'Excuse me, I still have a bullet in my head—*dain bramaged.*'"

"I don't get it." He plops onto a wooden chair.

"See, *damaged* starts with *D*. And *Brain* starts with *Br*. So, when you switch the—"

"I'm kidding." He points a finger-gun at me.

"Good thing you're so dapper."

"Thank you. So, what's the latest?" Donny Mac leans back into the chair spindles lacing his hands behind his head elbows out wide; it pulls the sleeves back to show the biceps.

"Don't ask." My heavy head gets propped up on my hand. "Feels like I'm swimming in deep water without a life vest again."

"Are you wearing a bikini? Because I want to picture this just, right?"

Goofing and chatting like adolescent friends is kind of nice. We know when to push our immature humor to the wayside. Donny Mac listens to my predicament with care. He smacks his forehead asking, "What is your ex-husband thinking?"

"I don't know. My mind is bewildered."

He ramps to a flirty tone. "You know, if you were my wife–"

"Speaking of wife, how's paradise going for you?"

His expression recalibrated. "She and I are still taking a family vacation together. We're going to Disney."

"That sounds promising."

"The wife told me I'm sleeping with the boys. She will room with our daughter."

"Yikes! That's super blunt."

"It's all right. It's all about the kids. I plan on having a good time. Do you think Josh will go to rehab again?"

"Sometimes Josh is willing to go, but the rehab center is leery and dragging their feet. Josh didn't do their follow-up recommendations. I can't babysit Josh every day to make sure he calls. If I had a male sounding voice, I could simply pretend I was—hmm."

My eyes lock with Donny Mac. His eyebrows pinch down. My brows arch up. I chin-nod to the *yes*. He mouths the word, *no-o-o*. I mouth the word, *yes-s-s*.

"Okay," he says. "I'll do it."

Double-fist pump! "You're the best!"

Donny Mac wants some data points. "All I must do is leave a message, right?"

"Yes, unless a receptionist picks-up. In that case tell them you have a problem and that you want a bed. Josh will do the actual intake later."

"How should I sound, excited? Wait, no. I should be overly polite, so they take me?"

"Dude—neither! To capture the true, situational essence of my ex-husband one must sound ambiguous and mildly depressed. Follow this up with a subtle sense of superiority, as if they called you—then snap! In the midst of their confusion, you decide to bless them with your presence and surrender full compliance."

"I better practice this conversation." Donny Mac sits tall and adjusts his waistband with both thumbs. He closes the office door. I hand him the conference phone from the desk. He holds the phone to his ear and crosses his legs. With a stretch of his neck Donny Mac clears his throat to make *the pretend call*.

Sitting regal as well, my hands folded over the desk, I am ready to critique, though I'm sure Donny Mac will do great. Whenever he starts. Yup, this mock call should happen any second now…the phone receiver is literally on his ear

"Mac-man, what are you waiting for?"

"It's still ringing."

"Oh, for crying out loud."

"Shhh," he sheepishly says behind a finger to his lips. "Ah yes. Hello there."

"Your voice is too high," I interject.

"Ahem—hell-oh-lo. Hell-lo-low, there. I am calling you because I have a problem; a very, very serious problem. It's my wife. She can't keep her damn hands off me. I could really use a break. Do you have any–ouch!" he yelps from my kick-to-the-calf.

"Would you be serious," I scowl.

"Okay. Ahem—getting low. I am calling to see if there are any rooms available. My wife thinks I have a problem. But I'm thinking *she's* the problem. What's your opinion?"

"Donald, I will run you over with a stationary bike, so help me."

"All right, all right, no wonder he drinks."

"You are sooo NOT funny." I fixate at the ceiling to contemplate. "Say something like, *I know I'm supposed to call at ten o'clock. So, I'm calling at ten o'clock.* Repeat yourself a little. Don't mention your wife. He will sell me out later."

"Why? You're helping him."

"Dropping an addict off at rehab gets an *f— you*, not a *thank-you*. You have to take the hit."

Donny Mac shakes his head. Phone to face again, he begins. "Hello. It's ten o'clock and...." He nails the voice of chronic despondence; rehearsal over.

At 10:00 a.m. my pretend ex-husband leaves an actual message. The next day he leaves another voice message, and the next day—still no bed. Donny Mac hops on a plane for The Magic Kingdom. Does he continue calling a rehab facility across the country on a family vacation despite the time difference? Yes, he does this while in line for *It's a Small World*. It works. Donny Mac gets the father of my children, a man he has never met, another chance.

. . .

Just Get *In The Car*

The elevator to Josh's apartment opens on the twelfth floor. The smell of marijuana smacks the nostrils and bonks the eyes faster than spelling out B–O–N–G. The only flicker of design meandering this corridor of doors is a four-leaf clover wreathe hanging two-months past the Ides of March.

Norman, Josh's new sponsor, has already arrived and answers the door. He is a construction union guy; early sixties; salt and pepper hair; all-salt beard. We exchange appreciations.

"I found Josh wondering around outside by the trees." Norman then yells over his shoulder as I remove my sweat jacket, "Right buddy? We were taking a walk."

"Yup," Josh puts down a chunky handled mug and a Montreal baseball cap on the dining room table. Sunlight cascades into the living room through the sliding glass doors.

"Josh seems fine to me," Norman says softly, "he's just been drinking coffee.

"Uh-huh, he wasn't fine when we spoke last night." Behind us I hear Josh microwaving his coffee in the galley kitchen. "Hey Josh, glad you're feeling better. You have to call the rehab place at 10:00 a.m. sharp to confirm your bed."

Josh speaks flatly as he re-enters the room. "You said they already had a bed."

"You know the drill. Confirmation is part of the process; you in particular, because you were there four months ago and didn't do any follow-up."

"You told them I didn't do any outpatient?" He nods at Norman who looks clueless as to what to say.

"No, I did not. The outpatient clinic told them. They brought that up to me as I further pleaded your case to get you in again. They need to know you're invested."

Coffee steam mixes with his thick, blonde hair as he sips without urgency. "Invested in what exactly?"

"Your…sobriety."

"I'm gonna go," Norman announces with a finger tap to the temple. "I'll see myself out."

"Stay. I shouldn't be the only one here rooting for sobriety."

Josh puts his mug down, leans on the dining table. "Jessica do you actually know what you're doing?"

Here come the hits.

"They will assign me some kid doctor, not even a real doctor, whom I could supervise. What can they offer me that I cannot offer myself?"

This is a big breath moment. I smooth out my pink sweater and respond. "Inspiration that quitting can be done and you will be better for it. As you know, speakers tell their personal stories. There is ZERO access to alcohol, so you can move your life forward. Shall I go on?"

A bark creeps into Josh's throat. "Do you know how much money I have to pay you? I can't make that much. I never made that much. You made everything up in the divorce." Norman watches us volley; he is neither a ref nor a ball-boy.

"This again? The court used your W-2 forms and paystubs. I can't make that up. In the end to run this family was *less than half* of your pay and you put up *zero* responsibility. *All* my pay is used and I have *full* responsibility for three children. The judge even commented on record, I could have asked for more. You did not HEAR this because you were HIDING OUT in another country." I cross the room to the sofa. No more swings. No more games. This will only lead to embarrassing Josh and blowing whatever cover story he told to this sponsor who is obviously here to help. I anchor myself on the sofa and squash a throw pillow. "I am not your enemy Joshua. I never was."

Josh begins to pace. "I can't keep paying that amount. It stresses me out."

"You can get the amount readjusted." This, of course, is public knowledge.

His pacing halts. "What do you mean?"

"You file a motion on the first floor of the courthouse. I know where everything is on the first AND second floors thanks to you."

"Would you really do that?" Norman asks placing his hands together. "He mentions this issue a lot."

"He brings it up because it's a distraction. I'm the scapegoat. He probably didn't mention the amount is so high because it includes almost 3 years of back-pay at this point. Did he mention that?"

"No, Josh, I don't believe you mentioned Jessica was going it alone for years."

Josh sits on the sofa, triangulating each of us. "I wasn't working." He rests his coffee mug on the table.

"You quit working to avoid paying; that's abandonment. You also can't keep a job because you can't stop drinking."

"I left to avoid you."

Norman slides his plaid sleeves up his arms. He looks at Josh and says, "Filing a court motion sounds like that would tackle a big stressor for you. And it sounds like Jessica is on your side to do that. I've been divorced twice. My wives didn't do that. I never heard of any ex-wife doing that."

My ex runs his fingers through his hair.

"Josh, you need to get real," I implore. "If you can stay sober, hold a job and enjoy our kids, than please, take me to court. I'd be happy to stand by your side. I know you are not making the same amount you were before. I don't want you in a hole where you see no way out. That said, coaxing you to go to rehab is quite frankly above your intelligence."

Josh stretches back into the sofa. He tightly folds his arms across his chest like someone refusing to wear a jacket when it is clearly freezing outside…igloos, dog sleds, a polar bear ice-fishing. Reality seems pretty clear from my standpoint.

Norman glances at his watch. "It's ten o'clock." He takes the smallest step possible towards Josh and plants his feet wide. "We need to call."

Josh unlocks his arms. "Fine. I'll call."

"You can use my phone." I tap the rehab number from my recent call history. The phone is placed in his hand already ringing. Clutching it with a frown, Josh walks off into the kitchen.

Sun rays bounce across the surface of his coffee resting on the table. I take a sip...alcohol creamer confirmed. I take in the view through the balcony glass doors. Beyond the balcony rows of trees follow the curves of the river. There is a pedestrian bridge nearby...I think about how a person can be like a bridge by helping people cross troubled waters.

Norman steps close to whisper above my shoulder. "You'd really do that for him?"

"He stands; I stand." I toss the squeezed throw pillow back to the corner. "By the way, did you know there was vodka in his coffee?"

"Really? I didn't check. I didn't see anything in the kitchen when I got here."

"Did you check the freezer? Or the oven? Or the top cabinet where someone five foot three like me would never think to look?"

"No, I use to hide my whiskey in the garage behind cleaning bottles. A jug of Simple Green can hide a lot."

"I should be near him while he's on the phone. He may still try to get out of going."

"You probably don't need me here anymore. I will just–"

"Is he in the car yet?"

"You think he'll really give you a problem?"

"How long have you been in AA?"

Norman clears his throat. "A long time."

"Glad to hear that for you. Is this your first time sponsoring someone?"

"Yes, how did you know?"

"Just a guess," I say and press my lips together.

"Josh asked me. We talked about it; decided we could definitely make it work. I still check in with my own sponsor."

"No offense, but that's why he picked you."

"It was a mutual decision."

"He's a psych doctor, a very good one. He picked you, consciously or unconsciously, because you're not seasoned. You should have guessed there was vodka in his coffee; I knew before tasting it. You still think he'll walk out of here without a fight or a play. He's sacred. He has to go today while he can still call out of work for not showing up which he won't do himself; he's getting more drunk as we speak. If they fire him on abandonment, he loses the insurance to cover rehab. It we compress this crisis situation into a manageable marble and roll Josh out of this apartment and into my car, then Josh could get admitted."

"I never met anyone like Josh. He impressed me. We talk about cars and people. I never met anyone with three PhDs before. I was flattered."

"What! How many PhDs?"

"Josh told me he has three: psychology, ah, physics and I forget the other one. Was that a lie?"

"He has one Norman. He has one well earned, PhD."

"Are you sure?"

My face goes full night owl. "I was at his graduation! He wears the watch I bought at his university gift shop, not that he tells anyone it was from me. Would you please stay? In fact, I would like you to drive with us to the rehab center."

Norman looks bewildered, but I do not sense him a fool. "I'll call my girlfriend," he says pulling a cell phone from his loose denim pocket.

I already learned from Josh that Norman's kids don't talk to him. Josh doesn't realize he is walking the same path as Norman and many others with adult kids who won't talk to them.

Quietly I scamper into the kitchen to make my presence known.

Over the phone I hear a woman's voice listing all the things Josh must pack...*5 shirts, 5 pairs of socks...no books or magazines, no mouthwash....* Josh mouths to me, *Really?* I open the freezer door, point to the vodka, and mouth, *yes.* Josh does a slight slump of shame. Soon he is off the phone. He unzips the suitcase with ease; lays it wide open on the bed.

"I'm having trouble," he says sinking into a desk chair.

"Trouble with what?"

"Thinking," he tells me.

"Do you want help packing?"

"Yes."

We agree: two-pairs of pants and three-shorts into the suitcase. "Do you want all white socks?"

"I'd like some coffee."

Norman walks in and asks, "Do you want me to heat up your mug?"

"Yes, thank-you," Josh says with a puppy pleased look.

"Add more coffee, please," I side mention.

"I get it," says Norman on task.

Soon he returns with a hot handoff to Josh who appears to be incapacitated. Norman leans against a bedroom wall. There are no pictures or windows in here. Norman announces, "The General at home cleared me. I am down for the road trip."

"Great," I say. "Departure needs to be in a half hour to make the appointment. The suitcase is ready except for the shirts. Josh, pick five t-shirts."

Josh stumbles to the drawer, pulls it open and stares. Norman and I are both feeling the *enough is enough.*

"Why don't we let Jessica handle the shirts," Norman says escorting Josh back to the chair.

In an effort to have Josh feel part of the process, I pick out two t-shirts and ask, "Which shirt do you want? The green Maui surfboard or the white North Shore?" The Maui shirt was always a favorite of mine.

"North Shore," he says. North Shore goes into the suitcase.

I hold up a plain aqua-blue shirt and the Maui surfboard. "Which one?"

Josh ponders. Slowly, he points to the aqua-blue shirt. It goes in the suitcase.

Next, I hold up two black Harley Davison T-shirts. Moving as if he was a robot losing power, Josh points to the newer tee with a small logo.

"Great choice! Three down, two to go." I tuck the latest into the suitcase. Cleverly, I hold up the Harley Davidson T-shirt that he did not want and the Maui T-shirt I like. Josh sips to the bottom of his liquored coffee. He tilts his head and touches the previously, unwanted Harley T-shirt.

Opening the bottom drawer I pick out a wrinkly, button-up, old, plaid shirt and hold it next to the lush, tropical Maui surfboard T-shirt with the curled wave emblem over the chest. Josh places a single finger to his parting lips, squints his eyes, and points to the wrinkly, plaid shirt. I twist it into a ball and stick it in the suitcase. Josh is packed.

"Holy shit!" blurts Norman, who has been in a petrified stance this entire time. "That was like watching a fat kid climb a skinny tree. I didn't know who to root for, the kid, or the tree."

As I zip and turn the suitcase closed, the Josh exits the room. I reopen the suitcase, pull out the original unwanted Harley T-shirt and shove the Maui shirt inside. Norman, who kindly waited for me, smiles. I flip the suitcase closed with a proclamation. "By the way, I'm the tree in that scenario."

"You think so," says Norman. He reaches for the suitcase. "Who's doing all the work?"

I hand him the suitcase I just packed for Josh. "Me," I sheepishly respond.

"Who is sweating his balls off? The fat kid or the tree?"

For a moment I swallow my defensive justifications.

Norman leans towards me. "Don't worry Jessica. Josh will have to bend, but he won't break. You're doing a good thing that few would do in your shoes. It may take a while, but one day he will appreciate what you have done for him."

"At this point I don't need or want anything from Josh. I am doing this because I can. Because beneath it all, he trusts me. And for what its worth the life we built, we did it together. He got some things right."

Josh enters in the car willingly with Norman and I. The drive is calm and quiet.

AT THE REHAB receptionist desk Josh's suitcase is immediately placed in the back. Josh is whisked away by a counselor. We wait in the familiar lounge with conference tables and a vending machines. The room is empty except for me, origami-folding paper napkins, and Norman playing solitaire on his phone. I hope Josh gets insurance approval. I don't know what else to do.

Forty minutes later the lounge door swings open; a white paper crane falls to its side. Josh ambles over to us, a counselor shadows behind.

"I'm going in," he says.

"Everything got approved?" I ask.

"Yes, they said they can give me meds to help with the withdrawals."

"Sure, they will. I'm glad. You'll get through them."

"I know it's my fault I'm in this position. It's not you." He fiddles with the leather band on his watch. He places it in my hands.

"Would you hold on to this for me. It was Zeta's."

"I know."

"One other thing; they said we can have cigarettes. They have to be new and sealed. Would you get me some?"

"I recall. I got them for you last time."

"You did? Hmm, I think I knew that. The cigs are like a method of communication. Something I can offer someone. Get the kind closest to herbal."

"I'm going to use your debt card."

"Fine."

"I'm also going to pay myself back for the hours I missed at work and our current child support payment. I mentioned this to you last time, you agreed–"

"I need to go. I get it."

"Okay."

"Norman," Josh extends an arm for a firm hand shake, "thank-you for coming over and for being here." .

"Do what they tell you. Everyone is here to help," Norman offers with an extra hand on Josh's shoulder.

Josh waves his hand up towards me and says, "Bye." The door swings closed. His absence of appreciation lingers, but it does not overshadow that we are here for the right reasons. I believe in the healthcare system and I believe those who walked the walk and gave their solemn word that a sober life is worth it. I have known Joshua for almost twenty-years. He matters to his children. He matters to his parents, his brothers and his profession. Perhaps he matters to me more than I realize; but, that's a bit of a cluster-fuck. In the eye of a cluster-fuck we meet our beliefs.

Family Day, Take Two

The Superwoman t-shirt rises again, but his time I am not alone. Connor agrees to attend the family weekend for one day. We are here with about fifteen others, listening to the morning program of speakers about alcoholism and recovery. Next, each family member has a turn to say why they are here and who they are supporting. Connor is age 16. He is the only minor in the room. He already informed me that he was not going to talk. Our table is last to speak. The counselor asks Connor if he would like to share why he is here. Everyone in that room including me turns to see what this young son of an alcoholic has to say. Immense empathy pools in everyone's eyes.

Connor speaks. "I am here because of my dad. I don't like to talk about it much. It scares me that I don't want to talk about it. I think he can get better. I think he should get better, as a father, to me, my brother and my sister. Ahem, sorry," Connor clears his throat, "I don't really know what else to say."

"That's okay," says the heartfelt counselor. "Thank you for showing up today for your dad and for yourself. It shows character and faith."

"Thank you, sir," says Connor. My son seems centered. The program now brings out the sponsored individuals in recovery. We break to meet them in the courtyard.

Josh and Connor sit together on a bench by some irises and a nearby water fountain. Josh talks calmly with Connor. When I join them on bench, Josh argues with me about why he doesn't need to be here anymore. Connor gets up and walks away. I listen to the onslaught reasons of why this highly reputable place is beyond inferior.

Josh and I go back to the group with pasted-on smiles. The younger wives in the group speak about fears of losing their home. I feel like shouting,

Ladies if you had to drag him here; if he is mad at you for being here, then sell the house! You deserve better and you are going to lose it anyway. And to the girlfriend over there I say, 'Run!' He will never hold you in regard when he's facing the wrong way.

But nobody asks for my opinion.

On the ride home Connor breaks our silence. "Why does he lie about things?"

"I know. It sucks. Grandiose thinking is another way to put it."

"Dad told me so many negative things about you. I shouldn't have believed him. It made me angry at you. I didn't question him. He's, my dad." Connor's voice chokes, "I'm sorry mom. I didn't know."

There were episodes in Connor's teenage years he was so angry or annoyed with me or his siblings. I couldn't unplug it. No matter how much I kept my kids under my wings, *someone* drove small wedges between us. Wedges are removable, truth refills the space.

18
COURT

Seven months have passed; Josh remains on track. I suggested at least twice a week visitation with the kids for a sense of routine, though he is welcome anytime. Besides attending the kid's athletic games, he only does the two days I suggested. He covers Saturday while I work a second job and Wednesday night. The latter gives me three hours of no responsibilities. My big night off is hanging out at a bookstore café and writing; sometimes, I see a movie by myself. When Josh visits, his parenting skills function more like a caring uncle. Homework is not done. He does not plan anything. One of our kids might go for a walk in the woods with Josh while the other kids are out with a friend or preferring to stay in his or her room doing their thing.

This band-aide parenting does not alleviate my guilt about not being more fun, or attentive or on-time. I want him to bring his own fun and deep attention with the kids. I want him to catch a ball I miss juggling 3 kids. Not for nothing, I also hoped he would see the kids more so I could gain some personal time for dating. Although, frankly speaking, that is a dead-zone. I have no time, and it is slim pickings out there. I lightly discuss dating with my fifteen-year-old daughter and mention that perhaps my mojo is stuck. She crudely tells me right there in the living room, "Mom, how are you supposed to find someone with Dad around as a cock block?"

Hell-o-o! More astonishing than what she said is that she's right. My daughter's observation pinpoints the molasses movement from divorced to freedom.

Momma is dusty sweetheart. Give me time.

As THE WEEKS ROLL ON, the family visiting arrangement actually becomes a nice groove. Josh rides the groove well enough to tackle a pressing goal of his: file a motion to lower alimony and child support. Now that he is sober-living it, my ex is taking me to court.

"Don't be alarmed that a lawyer may call," Josh informs me. That is the lead of how he tells me. "Please don't talk too long. The lawyer's rate is $300 per hour."

Does Josh think a lawyer will take his case seriously after speaking with me? I remind Josh, "We are a united front; you don't need a lawyer. I am fine with minor support adjustments. Adjustments are pretty standard…provide pay stubs, bill costs, etc. We talk with a judge in a courtroom full of other cases and get a fair decision."

"The whole thing sounds like a cattle call," he says. "I hate that. You're not getting a lawyer?"

"I meant what I said before. You have been holding your end. Our combined lawyer fees would equal months of child support."

"I feel like I will never get ahead," Josh remarks, "It is a suffocating feeling."

I restate the mission. "We will keep each other afloat."

It seems Josh and I may want the same thing. Obviously, less money makes things more challenging for me. But compromise is key. I have kept the family's lifestyle within a new level of means; I feel a sense of accomplishment about that. A mutually respectful arrangement is what should have happened prior to his abandonment, prior to our divorce, and absolutely before the gun incident. When we are afloat; the family is afloat. Glad we're on the same–

Is He on the Same Page?

Our legal motion had like four-pages to fill out plus addendums if needed. Josh and I do not discuss his motion which is fine. It was his job to fill it out and initiate the process, not mine. Once he files, a copy of the documents must be sent by certified mail to me. At that point I have the option to counter-motion.

Every day I check the mailbox to see what he requested; no envelope. Then, one fine day, I open my door to find Josh's motion has arrived by certified package. At the base of my doorstep is NOT a thin manilla envelope as expected. It is a new pair of winter boots cause things are getting deep sized box.

All you need to do is acknowledge the motion, Josh casually mentioned. The subliminal message was *you don't even need to read it*; uh-huh. Scissors cut through the priority packaging tape. Bubble wrap is pulled aside to reveal…a 2-inch thick, three-ring binder. *Damn–I just got served certified crazy.* This ludicrous, pale-white, plastic binder has tabs…not five tabs…not ten tabs. It has letters A through Z! Rarely am I speechless. But here I am mumbling, *bippity-boppity-boo.*

Ahem, Josh requested child support to be cut by nearly 70% and alimony by almost 100%! He does not contest that I have full custody, meaning it is not like he is offering to chip-in responsibility to off-set the reduction. The slashing is not even the best, or worst part, depending on one's taste for sarcasm. Josh wants to reduce all the back-pay to zero. Z-E-R-O as if the four of us never existed for three years. While he posted pictures of his motorcycle trips and ice fishing with his father, I raised our kids by myself and that is worth zero. I imagine that if Josh's brother had raised our kids, instead of me, and had said to Josh, *here's the bill for a portion of what it cost to raise your children while you played, drank and got your shit together,* Josh would (1) totally pay back his brother every penny and (2) thank him. But according to this alphabet-stew binder under tab E…I am *erasable*.

JOSH'S JUSTIFICATION in his motion is 'he was not working.' It was a simple scheme: *I don't work. I don't pay*. There is no mention as to why he was not employed i.e. revenge, aggression, alcoholism, disregard, abandonment of a six-figure job for the purpose of not making money, to look like he had no money, to escape paying any meaningful support.

My ex-husband is not the first irresponsible spouse to pull this maneuver. Every state has an agency for collection. One time when I was speaking with my case manager, I overheard a guy argue with his case manager about having to still pay $2/week for his kids. Look, I totally support that someone should not have most of their income go to someone else. Of equal concurrence, if a spouse was used to being totally taken care of financially, well, time to figure out making some kind of living. But Josh and I's motion is a screwball's turn from either one of those scenarios. It is pretty cut and dry what is fair at least to me.

What I am about to say is not easy to admit. I figured out what he did. At the tail end of our marriage, he ramped up making money, so he could abandon his family and sustain living under the radar for as long as possible while violently putting me under financially. If that wasn't hurtful enough, he took off to prevent our divorce from ever becoming legal.

Aware he had bunkered down at his dad's house in Canada, I sent him our divorce papers. He refused to sign. The existence of his children needing to be fed, clothed, housed, et cetera magically erased from his thinking and my value was nil. Josh's current motion is the same bullshit message.

Ha! —I know better. I collect myself and smooth out my plucked and ruffled feathers. My composure takes the lead. Painstakingly and carefully I fill-out my counter-motion, so I can divorce the same man for the second time.

We Shall See

Time for our day in court. A bailiff opens the towering oak doors. The hallway of defendants and plaintiffs pour into the courtroom as if church on a Sunday. We pack the pews like rows of shucked corn stuffed in a large pot of boiling water; we are all waiting to get cooked. Due to my history of having one of the crazier court cases, I am used to being near last on the docket; it spares everyone else's time. Assuming this judge has not received an A-to-Z motion before, I expect we are going last.

My seat is on the plaintiff side. Across the aisle Josh presents as polished in his dark blue suit with a light blue shirt, top button undone. His blonde hair speckled with new gray parts as usual–above the left eye–no hair gel. My mother is tucked beside me. An attaché case with court documents leans against my arch-supporting low-heel Clarks. The rayon dress is a sheen of dark espresso. I associated the color with coffee beans going through a grinder which is how I felt leading into this. A jeweled dragon-fly clip neatly cinches some hair at the back of my head. The sentimental clip is a gift from Jolie. She knows that a dragon-fly came to represent my deceased-father kind of "showing up".

. . .

Dragon-Fly

I was searching for a nature spot to represent visiting my dad as one would visit a grave site. He does not have one, so sometimes I just pick a spot. At random I pulled into an empty lot of a small historical site which was nothing more than an old stone barn from the late 1800s overlooking a lily pond. The bench by the pond was an ideal Zen spot for quiet time with an "O" magazine. Warmed by the sun I sat lost in a Q and A interview between Oprah and Paulo Coelho, author of "The Alchemist".

Coelho was discussing a time in his life when he had not yet fulfilled his dreams. To move past the hurdles he intuitively started paying attention to a *symbol* here, or *sign* there, until he could put the whole puzzle together and understand his quest in life. This reminded Oprah that the alchemist had taught Santiago, "Listen to your heart. It knows all things." The article side notes that at that exact moment "thunder claps loudly in the background." Coelho exclaims, "This is a moment. It's a sign." And then...

A dragon-fly landed right on the magazine, its shiny blue tail underlining the words, "It's a sign." The iridescent wings were inches from my thumb. Ongoing for minutes, I held the magazine and kept very still. Dragon-fly stayed. I thought, *okay, I see you.* Eventually, I had to move and shooed him away. I departed from my sweet stolen moment by the pond happily knowing I will keep this magazine forever. Then I drove several miles to the food store.

The lot was full as usual. I parked at the far end. Got out of my car. Hovering five-feet at face level was the dragon-fly. It was the exact size and shiny blue-color I had been staring at ten-minutes prior. That store has been my home-base supermarket for a decade. Never, ever has a dragon-fly been in the parking, least of all, waiting to greet me as I got out of my vehicle.

Perplexed and amused, I walked towards the food store. Dragon-fly followed maintaining a consistent distance. I thought, *no way. No. Way.* Car after car the winged creature did not lead, stray nor fall behind. *Okay, fine. What's the message?* At full-force I start analyzing the situation because I was not about to walk into the store with an emotional-support dragon-fly. To seek the right answer, one must ask the right question. *Break it down,* I thought. *Breathe slow-e-r. What exact-l-y is going on with the dragon-fly?*

That I can answer. He is literally by my side. Yup, I am still here, and he is by my side. *Dad...is still by my side.* And with that the shiny blue-tail dragon-fly darted off into a bright clear sky.

The cosmos did not stop bringing it there. At home the groceries were put away. Downstairs in my personal space I pondered…I second guessed. *Why a dragon-fly of all things?* I looked around my basement bedroom-living space as if there would be an explanation. My dad had enjoyed medieval art. He had collected medieval items such as swords, wizard statues and small pewter sculptures. I had kept some of his things…like over there were his dragon-head computer speakers. Or there, on my dresser were the pewter dragon goblets that CJ and I had bought him. The stems were dragon tails that curled into a heart when the goblets intertwined. Never had I viewed these items as a whole. I never realized there were so many—on my desk was a blow-dart the size of a flute. Dad had kept the darts in a black pewter box. The handle was a serpent-dragon with its fierce mouth opened. The bookends on my shelf were dragons. The realization set in…*I was surrounded by dragons.* Pretty good trick making a dragon appear…Dad.

BACK INSIDE A NOW EMPTIED COURTROOM, the judge has seen everyone on the docket except us; *called it*. We approach our respective podiums before the bench. A stenographer and an assistant rushing stacks of paper in and out for the judge are also present. The honorable judge begins with a softball toss to the defendant. "Why do you question the validity of your divorce?"

Oh, right—when I was rendered speechless by the epic alphabet binder, I failed to mention Josh suddenly claimed our divorce was "invalid".

Josh replies, "That is not my signature on the notice. It's not mine." Josh refers to the postal notice sent to his father's house; his place of residence after he left the country.

The judge speaks point blank. "I have to believe you were well aware you were getting divorced."

"That is not my signature. My handwriting doesn't look anything like that."

"This was not the only notice you received." The judge looks at me to ask, "Do you happen to have any proof of the certified mailings?"

"Yes, I do your honor." Receipts of both the regular and the certified notices that I sent to both his father's and his mother's house are handed to the bailiff. I imagine my diligence comes as a surprise to Joshua. I inform the judge. "Your honor, in addition to these various notices, my husband was served notice of the divorce in our home while we were living together. I could see him from the kitchen when the doorbell rang. He opened the door and signed for our divorce papers. I even saw him open the envelope and read it."

The bailiff takes my postal receipts to the bench. After a moment's perusal, the receipts are returned. The judge power stares at Josh.

"I wasn't there for the divorce," Josh meekly blurts.

"And who's fault is that?" The judge quips. "You were invited."

Josh's turn to be rendered speechless.

Now that our divorce is legitimate four-years later, the

motion moves to money. First order: Josh is requesting credit towards backpay for $11,000 he claims to have contributed over the years. His rhetoric to me, not on his documents, was that I stole it to which there is some portion of merit. Josh should receive credit for a negotiated $3,000 check, plus a couple of $1000 checks I squeezed out of him.

Another portions I say with embarrassment are small withdrawals I took, $300 here and $100 there ,during the months before he left. It was out of fear the floor was going to drop, which it did. He pulled the lever.

Half of this 11K was for my wages lost to detox him (twice) and the support money he owed me while in rehab (twice). Both times I ran the reimbursement by him; he readily had the funds from living rent free at my house.

The last 2K was a check written to me as a contribution toward Connor's first car. He and I agreed to contribute towards the car. Connor had to come up with a grand himself. Josh wants his car contribution to come off the back-pay even though it was not child support; it was our separate joint decision as parents, one of our few. If he is allowed to double-dip, that means I bought Connor's car.

At this point I do not care. I do not contest any amount of the 11K refund in my counter-motion. I had told myself it's a nice problem to have under our past circumstances; it is beyond my imagination that over $80K of back-pay will ever get repaid. I would be lucky–even grateful–to sacrifice the very last of full repayment. If Josh gets full-credit today, he leaves with some kind of win. I get my karma cleared on my ethically low choices. Bottomline, the message to my ex-husband is *relax*. There is no need to run, or fall off the wagon, or lose your meaningful job. The 11K goes to the defendant.

Issue of back-pay. The judge leans onto his bench and lowers his reading glasses. He questions Josh about the request to eliminate all the back-pay.

"Your honor, I wasn't working during that time," Josh claims. "If I wasn't working, how can I be paying?"

"Is that how it works?" the judge asks.

"I have supporting documents of jobs I applied for during some of that time. I wasn't making any money."

Josh supplies his more recent efforts of looking for jobs through an online job recruiting site. He has over a dozen jobs he attempted to get. Just saying, I too, could apply for a dozen jobs I'm not exactly qualified for, then claim, *I can't get a job; I can't pay for shit.*

The judge peruses the documents. "I can appreciate these employment efforts. These will be accepted. These do not cover three years of little to no payments. Your payments were based on income you were making at the time."

"I've never made that much money."

"Your income was determined by federal and state income statements. The court does not make up someone's income." The judge adjusts his metal framed glasses. "How long were you gone sir?"

"How long?"

"Yes, how long were you away from your family?"

"It was," he lowers his voice, "about 15 months."

"Fifteen months?"

"I think so."

I wanted yell out—22 months! With a couple of short visits that led to shit shows. But I don't interrupt. I already wrote a small explanation in my counter-motion which I am confident the judge read.

"Why did you leave sir?" The judge wants to hear Josh's explanation.

"Why?"

"Yes, why?"

Josh responds with earnest. "I didn't have a place to live. I wasn't going to have anywhere to go. I don't have any family here." His cheeks began to flush red as his tone quickens. "What was I supposed to do?"

The judge responds in turn. "You are a man with a PhD. You were making over six-figures. Leaving was your only solution?"

Josh doesn't once take his eyes off the judge. "There was nowhere for me to go. I had to leave," he says. "Otherwise, I would have ended up living under a bridge."

Did he just say–

From behind me I hear my mother's gasp. It is the only sound in a courtroom gone extra silent. The judge's face freezes in a stupor; it is one of the most validating visions in my life. Briefly the judge and I share a glance; we share *the stupor*. My mind flashes to a big-top circus tent. Inside the center ring I wear a striped tuxedo and bowtie because I am the Master of Ceremonies. Raising my top-hat high into the air I scream to the crowd, *ladies and gentlemen, welcome to my fucking world! Bet you can't guess what this world needs?*

It is an unspoken rule; do not touch delicate craziness. It is not worth the mess to anyone. That is how the judge handles it by saying nothing in response. He gives no attention other than his initial shock. This is the type of moment when the kindhearted and the wise lean toward compassion. That is what this world needs. The judge pivots to another matter. He announces, "The defendant seeks to lower child support for the three kids as well as alimony."

My counter-motion addressed this asinine reduction by providing a breakdown of our cost of living and the precariousness of Josh's newly acquired sobriety. Much of our story does not matter to the courts; it's all about facts, proof and legal algorithms. I admit not having a lawyer makes it difficult to offer information. I notice my hands shake when I look thru my documents; it is different being up here than it was in my head. My counter-motion summation stated that I did not expect Josh to be capable of his prior earnings. I felt a 35 to 40% decrease was fair.

"Further reduction then what I suggested is beyond what reasonably keeps our family afloat," I tell the judge.

After further review of other documents, etc., the judge states from the bench, "Let it be noted, the court recognizes that the plaintiff has significantly been able to increase her earnings since the divorce which is admirable. It is to her credit for doing so while maintaining full custody of their three children."

Whoa! A little applause under the big tent for the judge and the plaintiff. Did you hear that Mister Under-a-Bridge?

The judge continues his wrap-up. "The defendant does not seek any custody rights of the children nor visitation changes." In my heart and gut I know that is best for the kids. But still, that is just plain sad.

The judge mentions nothing of Josh's alcohol problem and its relation to employment; I was kind of hoping he would. The judges finishes our alphabet soup by asking me directly, "Do you have anything else to add?"

Standing alone with my mom behind me, my dad—in theory —beside me and my kids counting on me, I answer the judge. "I believe that you have taken the time to read over what I submitted. My concerns were expressed in my motion; the request's of my ex-husband would put me under. My suggestion is based on what it costs to raise our family. Thank you." I give no dramatic pleas. I am not here to embarrass anyone. The fairness is there. The judge can find it.

With hands folded over our motions, the judge closes our session saying, "I will not make any changes today. You will both receive notice by mailings. Court is adjourned."

The delayed decision surprises me because most other cases got their judgement on the spot. Guess our motion was a lot to digest. Back at the pew, Mom squeezes my hand. "You did great, honey. The judge really spent a lot of time with you guys."

"Thanks Mom. This whole thing is unsettling."

"I know. But it's done ow we can have some faith." She walks ahead of me towards the over-sized doors.

Josh and I cannot help but meet in the aisle. His expression seems pleasant; kind of neutral. His voice softly spoken, "Hey."

"Hey."

"I guess you're happy," he says. "You won."

Smack! The confusion stops me in my tracks. "Are you claiming that I won?"

"Well, I didn't," he says. "That is okay. The judge made a lot of sense. You won. It's okay."

"Josh, I got *un-insulted*. That is not winning."

Josh stares blankly. His expression to me reads, *does not compute*.

"My mom is waiting for me."

"Okay. Should I stop by the house later?"

"Not today," my head still shaking as I exit the courtroom doors.

A WEEK later the court packet containing our future arrives in my mailbox. It is a thin manilla envelope. The results: child support and alimony are to be cut in half. To off-set this cut, his *back-pay repayment* amount was increased. My job covers medical benefits. College is not mentioned; envisioning that was too far ahead for me. Full-custody of Connor, Jolie and Nicholas remains with me. That issue was not on the table. I just really like saying it.

19

TWIST ENDING

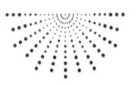

In 2008 when I fell victim to domestic gun violence, 1,800 women fell victim to homicide. From that eighteen-hundred 34% were murdered by an intimate partner. This means 1 out of every 3 women killed had shared both meals and a bed with her future killer. These stats do not capture the near misses, like mine.

Through hindsight binoculars I visit the distant memory… the moment when my husband threatened me with a 9 mm Glock. How close I came to death never hit home; his story that there were no bullets in the gun had something to do with it; police reports made no mention either way. This belief drained our world-of-suck to a broken heart's misdemeanor offense. I get that many would not be fooled. If someone brandishes a gun, the bullets are usually included.

The benefit of an ugly truth is that it offers clarity. Looking back at myself I can see both the fool and the warrior. I gained wisdom from wearing the fool's cloak. Wisdom does not grow without such experience. The compassion of my younger self felt like a superpower; however, at times it limited my ability to set boundaries. Empathy may have been the better choice; it has more interpersonal distance: you do you, while I do me, over here, so I can thrive because addiction does not play fair. It takes side with a bad idea like the fallacious, ugly idea that erasing the existence of a spouse or co-parent will solve everything. That is a cowardly, stupid, fatal idea in which everybody loses including the perpetrator. Josh did not fire his weapon and still faced a possible seventeen years of prison. My escape saved both our endings on that day in the shadows of our kitchen… standing beside the butcher's block…my husband ten feet away…he pulled that 9 mm hand gun from behind his back; pointed it at the ceiling. The moment of taking witness is the moment the body won't move. Whether I *live or die* was about to condense into a single point of time: he cocked the gun.

GET OUT! My leg muscles exploded registering the sound. I darted to the basement. Took a hard bounce off the wall and fly down the steps then leaped at the bottom landing to all fours on the concrete. I sprinted out the door; slammed it shut. This was in hopes of stealing better odds from Father-Time. Once in the backyard, escape meant bounding up a steep slope of brick steps two at time. I ripped open the pool gate. Every cell in my body commanded, *Run!* I took the risk to back-track directions and bolt across the pool yard. As I did the basement door went wide. Josh bellowed my name as I ran past his view.

The exit gate was before me. I kicked it open and ran across the manicured lawn darting past the old Sycamores and a flag pole that waves 50 stars and stripes. Sprinting toward the street there was no looking back. Josh had been a marathon runner; he was fucking fast. He set a town charity 5K record, a race he didn't train a single day for. Frantically, I searched the streets for a spot to disappear—a thick hedge. Porch bushes were not meant to fit a person inside them. But I got small, so minuscule as to hide deep within my own chest listening to the sound of my own lungs pounding. My heart suffering bruises and ache from betrayal.

The time was daybreak. The yards of colonial homes with slumbering owners were desolate. Scanning the streets there was no sign of him, but the relief seeped in slowly. An eerie calmness crept around like some kind of a damp, sea-mourned fog. The town echoed an unbelievable calmness. That calmness was so completely detached from my fucking situation.

At long last my instincts rang the *all clear*: it was okay to leave my encasing thicket. I snuck inside a neighbor's back door...called the police. Safety at my house was elusive until the police came...and the SWAT team. Only then with shields raised did the nightmare end.

Nevertheless, let us play out possible alternatives.

WHAT IF...

This time in the darkness of the corridor instead of aiming at the ceiling, he aims the 9 mm gun at me. What if all I could do was think— *Please, don't.*

First shot. He fires over the butcher's block right at my chest. It throws me back against the wall. Blood splatters the colonial wallpaper of delicate flowers right above the wainscoting. Shock pierces me more than pain. He fires a second shot because his adrenaline demands it. This bullet burns my chest with a stabbing heat. Blood pours out from the wound saturating my carefully chosen white t-shirt. My plan had been to ride my bike to the station to make a report, because he had stolen my car keys, license, credit cards, phone...he fires a third shot. This time he needs to be sure, because beneath a blackhole of thoughts, hidden inside the recesses of his mind, this man sees no other way out.

  Sliding down the kitchen wall, my torso begins to slump. It is difficult to breath. My options on this cold hard floor are slipping away. Slowly his footsteps approach. Standing erect he casts a twilight shadow over my bleeding, soon-to-be corpse.

Appear dead. Maybe, he will stop. Maybe, I still have a chance. Maybe becomes the space where my heart waits for his remorse...to put pressure on my wounds...call for an ambulance pleading, *Come quick! It was an accident. I didn't mean—* Only homicide makes the news; remorse does not.

After the killing, self-preservation kicks in. My husband pulls down a shower curtain and wraps my body up neat and quick to contain the blood. When we moved to a different state, he never re-registered the gun. This overlook now created plausible options which his inebriated mind explores as he wipes the floor and wall with a bleach solution. He is thorough; there is no trace a body was ever lying there, fighting for breath and life. Perhaps, what happens next had already reeled over and over in his conscious mind like a pleasant obsession.

The woodlands behind the house—where I often enjoyed a trail walk–make a solid choice *to disappear a body*. In our backyard the fence privately opens to these woodlands/soon-to-be graveyard. No one notices him slip into the woods carrying my plastic wrapped body. The dense overgrown landscape of vines wrapping trees allows my killer's actions to go unseen. He unrolls the blood-stained shower curtain dumping me atop wild ferns, fallen branches and knotty maple roots. He throws some leaves on top to cover me, to cover his guilt. Briskly, he walks back home brushing the wild rhododendrons with a balled-up shower curtain under his arm. He already thinks the town will believe and cry out his formulated ruse: *My wife was walking the trails in our beloved town...she fell prey to a random, unfortunate act of violence.... Please, my family needs privacy to mourn.* My husband rinses off the bloody curtain. He thinks it is better to hang it back up.

BUT WHAT IF...

All my years of a slowed down heart rate from practicing yoga paid off?

Lying in the forest against a maple trunk, haphazardly covered by a bed of leaves, I remain cognizant. These woods are familiar. It is nearly daybreak. Hikers will come with their curious dogs. A sense of hope sparks. I feel the life of the forest around me. Above me the gentle glow of dawn seeps through the canopies. Light glints off the nearby pond where we used to ice skate with our kids in a blanket of winter. The incoming sun rays tell the curled-up seedling, *it is time to get-up*. On hands and knees, I creep over dirt and brush until reaching the trailhead. The meek opening empties into a dead-end street. Crawling to the curb I see….

Already at his car, a neighbor is about to leave early for work. From the corner of his eye, he notices my attempt to push-up from the curb and stand. The neighbor rushes over. While in horror at the bleeding he recognizes my face. He asks, *what happened?* A tragedy held within his arms. Already we are accepting, *I may not make it.*

Decisions must be made without haste. Knowing I might soon perish from my kids' lives, could I save them from losing both parents? Do I tell this good Samaritan, *it was an accident?* Make-up a story about some old guy in the woods. Confabulate the old guy got confused…thought I was an attacker from behind. The old man carries a gun. He did not mean to…he got scared and took off. Would such a story close my case? Allow my children to stay in their home and keep one parent? The wave of sorrow headed their way I cannot stop. But in my love for them could I lessen their pain? Josh will find a caring woman to raise them.

Leaning together against the neighbor's car the neighbor and I wait for the ambulance to arrive. This is when I ask my final friend for paper and pen. He finds this in his car. I tightly fold the note, beg that he give it to my husband. The ambulance arrives. Hurriedly I am packed onto the stretcher. The siren noise fades from my street and I think lying there in the back of this ambulance, *I hope the siren didn't wake my kids.*

The good neighbor does as he promised. He raps the brass knocker of our door. Josh answers notably tired. The neighbor breaks the troubling news of finding me shot and bleeding to death, his woe evident with somber expression. Joshua listens. The handwritten note is gingerly placed in the hands of my bewildered husband. Josh thanks him before closing the door. A Grim Reaper's hush falls heavily over his world.

My husband reclines in his black reading chair; the note held tight in his hand. Beside him the window overlooks the boxwoods and brick steps that bound up to the pool. With little hesitation Josh unfolds the squared-up paper; the tremor of horror only visible to the naked truth. Written with my dying hand were three sentences meant only for him.

I forgive you. Raise them right. Stop drinking.
Sincerely,
Your wife

There it is. The death of a noble martyr; her final sacrifice.

Unless...

I decide my life is worth the fight. After he dumps my bloody body, I writhe to a tree, dig my nails into the bark and claw myself up. The old trunk holds me steady. My legs regain their strength to carry. I stumble out of the woods and onto the street. The strong-bodied neighbor runs over to me, concern in his eyes. He catches me around the waist. Gasping for air I rasp, "Drive me to the hospital."

"It's okay, you'll be okay," he whispers. "I'll take you there."

Our eyes connect. I grip his shirt saying, "My husband did this to me." Releasing the truth turns my pain into an anger. I use it to survive.

Nurses swarm around the operating room as I am prepped for surgery. They stick leads on my chest; IV drips in my arms. Above me shines the brightest of lights. The surgeon arrives—cap, mask, gown—she blocks the brightness offering a gentle presence. I grab the hand of this woman who will save me. My weakened voice rises for everyone to hear, "I have three children. I am not done."

20
ALOHA

The Hawaiian word for love, hello and farewell.

Beneath the soil leaves twist and unfurl from deep hibernation. The iris, tulips and an awakened peony bathe in the sun's golden light with their fullest expression. Nature gives all bursts of color a turn to reveal its story. As the shrinking petals cascade into a final bow, the garden fades to yellow with no regrets.

Time has spanned only the weeks of yolk-colored daffodils and Easter tulips since our wintry day in court. Josh's sense of usefulness to his family has already waned. His focus has shifted elsewhere. He seeks a new beginning. Perhaps he seeks to escape gardening a family? Or, the boundaries of his precarious sobriety? Whatever it is, Josh is wilting here. He is actively pursuing a clinical position in Hawaii—as in half-way around the world, Hawaii. Location Diamond Head, Oahu is actually where we met. I was twenty-five; he was six-years my senior. Soon after we were raising two kids by one of the world's prettiest beaches, Kailua, before moving back to the mainland.

Why does Joshua wish to return to that far-away tropical island? Is the answer in the question? His answers to me are that he finds himself somewhat bored and stagnant. He does not feel of much use. That is all I got.

Back in my mid-twenties when I relocated to Hawaii, I was avoiding all the influences I had outgrown, such as, my home life, my routines, the same society, eating the same foods…. I wanted to carve my own adult path. Bold and young I drove my two-door Nissan Pulsar across country, shipped it from California, and relocated to Oahu by myself. There I fell into harmony with the *mauna* and the *maki*, the mountain and the ocean of Hawaii—whereby lives the *aloha spirit*. My OT career blossomed at Queen's Hospital, a major trauma-center for the region. I gained diverse friendships. Hiked five of the Hawaiian Islands. Completed a mini-triathlon. Found a life-long love for yoga. I even learned to pronounce the Hawaiian name of the state trigger fish: Humu-humu-nuku-nuku-apua'a.

Regarding Josh's plan to relocate, I make serious effort to view it from his perspective. He is a partial outsider to his own family. I am not his wife. Revolving around the kids while I run the show probably leads to boredom or who knows what. Quite often our teenagers prefer their friends, sports, hobbies, or phones over hanging out with Mom or Dad. I see his side.

ON THE OTHER HAND…

What a dick! Take the court-awarded financial windfall and run from responsibilities on spindly sobriety legs no less. Yes, parenting is hard to figure out at every twist and turn. Suck it up buttercup! Learn to do it better. He is bored while I am exhausted. Nicky just got a sober dad at twelve-years old. But hey, if Josh cannot step into being a father for Nicky in his upcoming teenage years, then I do not want him near my son.

The two of them can figure out their relationship when Nicky is an adult. For the next six years he can go through me.

In addition a move to Hawaii ditches all the stability he built up. Relocating puts him at high risk to drink again. Maybe, he still wants to do. I share these truths and concerns with Josh. He appears to appreciate my thoughts. He consults with his own network of support about whether to move away or not. Final decision? His furniture goes up for sale.

At my suggestion as some form of good-bye, Josh takes Nicky on an overnight camping trip before leaving for whatever he seeks. His Hawaii departure date is a month before Connor graduates high school and Nicky sixth grade. Connor recognizes his dad will miss his graduation and is very disappointed. He accepts the decision with calm maturity expressing that is not what he would do if he had a son. Connor loves his father, but does not admire his choices.

This is where I learn to phase out of micromanaging the relationship Connor and Jolie have with their dad. They are old enough to build, or cut bonds of their own. So…

If something needs to fly, let it.
If something needs to thrive, allow it.
If standing in the way, step aside.
Aloha, Josh.

Inside Mom's Kingdom

Senior night: Connor's last high school soccer game. At halftime the announcer introduces all the senior parents and reads off some pre-written personal notes from the players. There are over a dozen of us parents on the sidelines waiting to unite with our sweaty sons. They stand at center field in an arc formation. Nine players hold a blue and white carnation to give to his mom. Of the nine couples from Connor's class, six couples have gotten divorced. Despite that status, those divorced parents walk onto the field together and proudly stand next to their varsity senior. Only my friend Natasha, Lucas's mom, and I will walk out alone as a single parent. Connor plays mid-fielder; Lucas is their stellar goalie.

Over the years, Natasha and I celebrated our sons' birthdays together. We threw one, big, raucous pool party at my house with their mutual friends. Those friends stand on this field today, but to me Lucas is special. One year Natasha had to take a job almost two hours away. Three of us gal-pals banded together. We divided the week and took care of her two sons after school. We fed them and helped them with homework. One time I called the school pretending I was Natasha to keep Lucas out of trouble. When Natasha picked-up her sons, we had dinner for her. Lucas's father, Natasha's ex-husband, recently died a tragic death. At the funeral the team players gave Lucas a soccer ball they had each signed for him. His dad was a good guy, a little broken inside. He would have been here today, side-by-side with Natasha and their son. No one at the moment has it harder than Lucas. This to say causes my bitterness to crumble.

Soccer mid-fielder number twenty-four is announced—my pumpkin! The announcer reads Connor's aspirations and favorite memory. "Connor will attend college with a full Army National Guard scholarship with interests of becoming a pilot. Connor recalls Ms. Clemente taking his pencil because he tapped it on the desk too loud. The next day Connor had 5 other pencils up his sleeve. Every time teacher Clemente took his pencil for being loud, he secretly pulled out another one. Ms. Clemente became increasingly confused that the tapping kept coming from Connor's desk as she kept taking his pencils! Thank you, Ms. Clemente, for laughing instead of kicking me out of class. Connor wishes to thank his grandparents, Uncle, Aunt, brother and sister for coming to his games. Connor especially wants to thank his mom for everything."

Connor's hair is spiked with sweat. His body has that V-shape–broad shoulders, fit core. Yet, I still see a lit-up boyish smile as I meet him on the field. He hands me a carnation mixed with fern and puffs of baby's breath. My oldest is not embarrassed to hug me extra tight. "Love you mom."

Bootcamp Graduation

Five months later I head to the stands of yet another field to see Connor graduate. This time he is graduating from bootcamp at Fort Jackson Army Base in South Carolina! It was not easy letting my son go for fourteen weeks; he had just graduated high school. A part of me feared bootcamp would make him… well…a bit cocky. Imagine my relief when Connor mentioned the results of their peer-voted "paper-plate" awards. "Mom, they gave me the 'nice guy award'," he said without an ounce of embarrassment. That is a mom win in my book!

The recruiter Connor admires, who has "shoot first" tattooed on his trigger finger, had keenly planted a seed when we visited his office. He had suggested Connor pursue officer training at college. The sergeant told him, "You'll come back here and I'd have to salute you." It was strange to watch someone see something great in my son that I couldn't, something beyond my realm. It was a humbling to see the *expression of drive* emerge on my son's face as he took in the possibilities.

The only ones able to fly out for Connor's graduation ceremony are myself, Grandmom, and Nicky now age 13 years. His sister wanted to come, but she had a marching band competition. Connor notices the difference between the number of attendees from our fractured family in comparison to his comrades'. Connor wrote in one of his last letters, "This one guy's family is renting a shuttle bus. He has 23 people coming to graduation."

Well, sorry kiddo. The three of us will be just as loud and proud as everyone else cheering for their sons and daughters after months of exchanging letters and mailing power bars, cough drops, and gum—enough for everyone in the company.

The graduation ceremony commences at a military field similar in size to a large high school. We drove around the base and filed into the stands with neither sight nor sign of any graduating soldiers. *Where are they?*

The crowd fills the sun-warmed metal bleachers to capacity. The elongated barren field of dried grass before us stretches beyond the bleachers on both sides into the massive base. Opposite the field we view a horizon of dense pine trees. Smack in front of the bleachers at the fifty-yard line, if the field had yard lines instead of caked dirt, stands a podium. To its side, a special top brass section is adorned with American flags. A decorated soldier approaches the microphone. He welcomes us to the ceremony. We stand for The Star-Spangled Banner. Veterans scattered throughout the crowd raise stiff hands to a salute. *Rockets' red glare* bursts over the loud speakers. An emotional swell about the heart and sacrifice of military service seeps through the crowd.

Throughout the mid-morning we listen to the top brass of Fort Jackson deliver motivational speeches. Still, our graduates remain no where to be found. After the inspiring words, a demonstration for the families who traveled near and far begins...

A camouflaged, lone-wolf soldier cautiously pads out to the barren landscape. Short-leafed branches cover his helmet. His body turns in all directions as he watchfully advances into enemy territory. His hands are locked on an M4 Carbine. He moves with the precision of a fanged predator. The commander explains from his microphone the basic role of the scout... gather intel...determine if it safe.

The scout on the field taps his helmet. Seven other camouflaged soldiers pad out in full stealth mode; the squad's movements scan for the unknown. Their cohesive maneuvers intensify with purpose. Suddenly, the scout puts up his fist. The squad halts in their tracks. He signals with a sharp elbow chop. His comrades shift into a V-formation, vests stocked with ammunition, weapons out. One soldier on the flank has a rocket launcher leveled over his shoulder. They advance away from the stands cautious and calculated to secure the area from possible insurgents; their own lives at risk.

The squad leader puts up his fist. Instantly the soldiers freeze. At the podium the commander no longer speaks; the squad is on their own. Raising an arm the leader points his index-finger up and circles it. Immediately the squad tugs at their vests and aggressively throw metal tubes high into the air. Among a blue sky backdrop these hand-launched tubes burst into arcs of thick, yellowish smoke. Toss after toss smoke bombs zoom across the sky. Rapidly their crisscrossing arcs expand into a dense fog. The fog thickens to create a ground-to-sky smokescreen. Right before our astonished eyes the entire squad disappears as does the dirt-caked ground. The Sulphur-yellow smokescreen grows higher and wider swallowing the entire field. We, the crowd, are locked in amazement.

Then the unexpected happens. Over the loud speakers we hear a haunting chime ring out. The chimes are accompanied by a bewildering guitar riff of four measures. Together they haunt and repeat…a single drum beat layers with the riff and the chime. It builds louder…and louder until everyone in the bleachers is hit by an intense wave of rock music. We know this song–*Hells Bells* by legendary rock band ACDC. Our soldiers are coming!

For hours they were hiding in the pine woods. But now a football field of soldiers, shoulder-to-shoulder, company beside company appear marching straight through billows of eye-stinging smoke. From camouflaged caps to their laced-up boots they march in sync. We see Alpha company first, then

Bravo, Charlie...our excitement rises like football fans at a pro-game when a favorite player runs out of the tunnel. As the smoke continues to lift, there is an end-zone to end-zone wall of camouflaged uniforms advancing at us full-force. There's Delta company (my son!), Echo, Foxtrot...we are already on our feet...stomping, cheering, hooting, waving, screaming and crying as row after row of soldiers emerge non-stop. ACDC's guttural lyrics course through our veins like heroine.

> I'm rolling thunder, I'm pouring rain
> I'm coming on like a hurricane
> My lightening's flashing across the sky
> You're only young, but you're gonna die...
> Hells Bells, gonna split the night
> Hells Bells, there's no way to fight Hells Bells

Before us stands a full US Army battalion. We are a deafening tsunami of love washing over our sons and daughters who trained and are ready to fight for the fucking United States of America!

Our country's newest soldiers hit their mark at the frontline. The battalion commander calls out, "At rest!" The army battalion responds with hands behind the back, feet apart, and full attention as the Carolina sun blazes upon their sweaty faces. Our low rumble of pride and ache to hold them again blows the last puffs of smoke off the dry dirt field. For three months families have been writing letters as we wait...waiting to see my Connor again.

The battalion commander makes his final announcements. "The military frowns upon PDA, public displays of affection. Today, however, we will make an exception." The commander faces the battalion. "Soldiers, you must remain at attention and do not move until you are touched by your family."

His chest of medals turns to face us. Bellowing into the microphone he looks directly at our excited faces and orders his final command. "Families, friends, loved ones, go get your soldier!"

It is a total *Where's Waldo* mayhem. Unleashed families pour down the bleachers and scatter onto the field every which way like a basket of hungry snakes dumped on its side. We scour the company line-up to find our son, daughter, grandchild, niece, nephew, brother, sister…some soldiers transformed by weight loss; others bulked by muscle.

One-by-one the found soldiers drop their heads and fold into the clutching embrace of loved ones. I find Connor first. His jade eyes are red from the sting of the smoke bombs.

"Connor!" I yell running towards him. The second my arms touch him–

"Mom!" His hug lifts me off the ground.

"I missed you so much."

"I missed you too."

Grandma shrieks, "Look how big you got!" She tears up as they hug.

Nicky weaves over through the crowd; side crashes into his brother. "Private Dingus," Nicky shouts.

"Scrum-num! Thanks for coming." Connor squeezes his scrawny sibling.

"Of course, bro. Wouldn't miss it."

I feel a sense of security Connor is on his way.

TWO YEARS later Jolie and I are madly completing her college application an hour before the midnight deadline. A family friend, who is a photographer, aides our plight. He uploads Jolie's portfolio to her top art school choice with five minutes to spare. Worth it—she's accepted!

Josh and I share college expenses without the need for a court order. He wants to be part of her life. She has not wanted much to do with her dad. Josh and I discuss this in brief. Truly, he wants a relationship with her. My encouragement for him was to hang in there. I told him, "A father fights for his daughter. He does not back down."

Josh gently persists. She exercises her voice. He listens. He apologizes directly for "being an asshole." Their adult relationship slowly builds. At a certain point Jolie brightens. Her brothers are glad to have her on board. Certainly, she stopped painting dead birds.

My wellness plight continued. A keto-eating lifestyle with intermittent fasting has maintained my best health, energy and appearance. No more facial-skin redness. No more hot dog arms. The loose skin tightened from my weight loss. These yoga-arms compare with my sons; their muscle definition wins, but still. My trail run pace improves from a 13-minute mile to a 9-minute pace. The runs are 2-3 miles, way further than my sofa to the fridge.

Our craftsman house remains organized. The gardens look fantastic. Many a neighborhood walker passes by commenting that I am one of their favorite houses. Some call it "the Zen house."

My finances grew solid. Instead of dating, I hustled on the weekends as a banquet server. The fast paced, thick-skinned world of the food industry thickened my character while advancing my financial stability. I maintain zero debt; used some of the extra cash to flip my mortgage. Now more of the monthly payments go towards the principle not the interest. No matter what the stock market does, paying my mortgage down years ahead of schedule guarantees savings. I call my brother with good news. Greg is in banking, head of loans.

"Guess what my credit score is?"

"770," he guesses.

"Come on."

"All right sis; 820."

"Dude, my credit score is 850!"

"What did you do, rob a bank?"

I learned to play the stock market: pot stocks, S&P, crypto. Basically, that meant I learned enough to lose more than I should. I ceased playing the stocks. Sometimes a good decision is to simply stop making a bad one. I still hold some crypto, just in case.

Back in Hawaii, Josh met someone and returned to the mainland to live with her. He is now a short plane ride away. Josh and his partner send care packages to the kids at college and to my home on holidays. One by one, the kids visit them. Trust is built. Wounds are healed at individual rates. The kids take mini-vacations at their dad's which is a stable, nurturing, and sober home. When he hosts the kids, they do lots of activities and dining.

All the court ordered back-pay Josh owed me has been paid-off. Paid-off to zero. Never thought I'd see it. The kids hit Josh up for money instead of me as they gain their adult footing. Josh consistently shows up for them. His partner's parents contribute another set of grandparents. I am happy to share my young adult kids. They deserve as much love, family and positive influence as possible.

Jolie graduates from art school. Nicky graduates from high school. I replay the same single-mom moment at Nicky's senior soccer night. This time a new feeling emerges: exhilaration. My two-decade parental tour of duty is coming to an end. Three childhoods are complete. The calendar that hangs in the kitchen will only keep track of me. I am so okay with that.

Milestone

Aviation school for Connor lasted 16-months. My son is about to graduate as a black hawk helicopter pilot. Every time I say that, it feels *cool as shit!* Unlike boot camp graduation, Lt. Connor has ten family supporters here in Alabama: myself,

Jolie, Nicolas, my mom, Josh, his partner with her aging parents, and Caleb. He is now 81 years old and flew in special.

Josh and I have not seen each other for a couple of years—since Jolie graduated art school. I am lean and fit at 119.6 per the scale. I am rocking Connor's aviation graduation with a consignment shop dress. The sleeveless, above-the-knee dress shows off my yoga arms and Pilates legs. It is a knit cream dress with black ribbon trim and a black bow at the neckline; something Audrey Hepburn might wear. Platform clogs match the dress, something Lady Gaga would wear.

"You look good mom. Work that thrifty-ass!" says Jolie standing by our rental car for the big event.

I sashay up the driveway of Connor's rental house. "Why, thank you my beautiful daughter."

"I'll drive to the base," says Nicholas holding the keys high out of anyone's reach. He has grown to be the tallest in the family. Connor had to pay up on that $50 bet. "Where we going for lunch afterwards?" Nicky asks. He is always thinking about food.

"We're going off base for barbecue ribs," answers Connor. "Dad is treating everyone."

"Are Grandmom and I included?"

Connor smiles. "Of course. He said to make sure you knew."

"That's nice of him," my mom says as Connor holds the car door for open for her. Connor's dress uniform hangs with impeccable fit over his broad shoulders. In his car he will lead our caravan to the aviation museum for the ceremony. "Make sure you keep up scrum-numb," he says pointing at Nicky. "Don't lose Dad's van behind us."

"Yes, sir, Private Dingus!" Nicholas clicks his heels and offers a sloppy middle-of-the-forehead salute.

"Dingus got promoted," blurts Jolie. She opens the rental door to ride shotgun. "He's *Private Wanker* now."

"Actually," Josh approaches the kids and I at the curb, "he's a

Lieutenant ranked wanker. Show some respect." Josh looks fit, healthy and settled. Five years of sobriety can do that. Several pairs of eyes watch us from the mini-van Josh is driving.

"I see you get to drive the geriatric shuttle," I say turning to Josh in fun. We all know it is a gift to have four individual grandparents here.

"I know. I know. Lots of talk about medical issues and prescriptions. My dad only hears every other word; that's with his hearing aide." Josh smiles at Jolie and me. He comments, "Everyone looks stupendous." He looks at me. "You never age."

"This is true."

Connor gives a strong shoulder bump to his dad. "Ouch," says Josh, "careful with your old-man. Hey, you should have seen Grandpa buttoning up his Royal Canadian Air-force jacket. It still fits him."

"It means a lot that Grandpa flew all the way out here." Connor waves his arm out toward all of us saying, "It means a lot you all made it here. It's probably the biggest day in my life besides getting married someday."

Grandma responds, "I wouldn't miss it."

"We should get going, bud," Josh says.

"See you there, Dad." Connor looks over his shoulder at Nicky and me. "Let's roll."

My mom and I sit in the back seat of the SUV rental. Nicky and Jolie are upfront. Jolie has already set the radio to play music from her phone. Techno music blares from the SUV's surround speakers.

"Is this what they listen to?" My mom asks bewildered and amused.

"It's EDM Grandma. Electronic dance music." Jolie and Nicholas start jamming out in the front seat. Their arms are poppin' and lockin'. Their heads a weaving and boppin'.

"Okay-y," Grandma responds. Oh no, the kids did not foresee this coming. Grandma imitates their jerky dance moves as if she is awkwardly throwing softballs out the windows and towards her own feet. She previously taught math, not dance. Her head turns like she's crossing the street. Grandma is slinging some real spastic toe crushers.

"Go Gram-cracker," sings out Jolie.

"I see you Grams." Nicky flicks two-fingers off his nose into the rear-view mirror. "I see you."

Grandpa is Connor's special guest for the graduation ceremony. Caleb has the distinct honor of pinning Connor's aviation wings onto his dress uniform.

The gold wings gleam as the three generations of men intertwine their arms for a special photo. Each one of these men choose to forgive his father; the fathers chose to make amends. Had they not, their lives could have gone in opposite directions.

Age Fifty

I turn the big 5-0 in a couple months. Wow, saw that coming. To embrace the milestone, I decide to do 50-days of yoga leading up to my 50th birthday with an added special feature. Each yoga session will represent a touchstone appreciation for each year of my life. I start at 49 and works backwards. An hour of Ashtanga yoga is a workout! Yoga not only gets the body feeling stretched and strong, but it calms the *monkey mind* allowing for deep reflective state. Lying still on the mat in Savasana, the final pose, I reflect on the past 49th year of my life. I raised three children into adulthood. That accomplishment is worth sinking in...not because its quite the feat (okay it is)...but that's the past. What else can I be and do if I choose? No rush; no haste; good choices one at a time. I have 48 more days to gracefully enter the roads that lie ahead.

Ninth day of yoga, age 40: I was in Ontario for an ice festival. The family slept in hotel beds while I read *Eat, Love, Pray* on the bathroom floor wondering how I will ever get divorced.

Twenty-third day of yoga, age 23; just graduated college and moved back home. Single with no responsibilities I wondered, *where will I live?* Drove across the country during the summer to decide. Three days of yoga–my first vivid memory at age three: finding a stray kitten under our trailer home. The black fuzzy guy was peeing when I picked him up. I felt bad for interrupting him. Was that my first time empathy? Finally, the last rigorous ashtanga yoga two-hour session marks my homecoming. Lying still, calm and feeling fit as fuck on the yoga mat. I am complete, appreciative, loved and worthy of peace.

Surprise

An unexpected 50th birthday package arrives at my doorstep. The sealed brown bag is about the size and weight of a small throw pillow. The mystery gift does not contain a note. With intrigue I rip open the paper bag and pull out a black T-shirt. Held up by the shoulder seams, the T-shirt unfolds before me. Across the front are words that became associated with the late Supreme Court Judge Ruth Bader-Ginsberg. Immediately, I know the gift is from Josh. In white, type-writer font it reads, *Nevertheless She Persisted.*

ACKNOWLEDGMENTS

Mom, Dad: always my brightest stars. Love you.

HL, NCK, MJ: you each fill my life, my heart and my soul.

Madre, KitKat and Nuzzle Moon, my Algonquin table: heartfelt thanks for your help and patch-work so this novel could reach its best version.

Family and friends: thank you for your support and enthusiasm, year after year, as I dreamed the same dream.

Felines Athena and Crackhead were my faithful fur-ball companions as I wrote under lofty ferns from dawn to dusk. By my side was a lit java cigar and a Tibetan singing bowl found with SK.

ABOUT THE AUTHOR

Rochelle is an occupational therapist with specialties in stroke rehab and play therapy. Her written work has been awarded by the NIEA, Writer's Digest and The Letter Review.

Rochelle has three children, each one is her favorite. When she isn't writing or gardening, find Rochelle practicing yoga on the porch of her cozy cottage in a cozy town.

Website and contact information: RochelleBooks.com. Member of ITW, International Thriller Writers.

Other Titles by Rochelle

SHOT GLASS, One woman's fight to save her kingdom ISBN 97817341614-03 paperback / ISBN 97817341614-10 E-Book. Listen where audio books are found.

www.ingramcontent.com/pod-product-compliance
Lightning Source LLC
LaVergne TN
LVHW022028310525
812539LV00008B/16